ruthless Kings

WINDSOR ACADEMY

BOOK TWO

LAURA LEE

Editing by: Ellie McLove of My Brother's Editor

Cover Design by: Lori Jackson Designs

a note
from the author

RUTHLESS KINGS is book two of three in the Windsor Academy series. You <u>must</u> read book one, WICKED LIARS, prior to this installment to follow the story properly.

This is a dark high school bully romance that may contain triggers for sensitive readers. Due to mature content, it is recommended for readers 17+ only.

This book is dedicated to medical professionals around the world. Thank you for your assiduous efforts and sacrifices during this pandemic.

chapter one

JAZZ

"Look, Jazz! Dolphins!"

I shield my eyes from the sun as I look where my sister is pointing. Sure enough, there's a pod of five dolphins playing in the ocean. We're at the top of the Pacific Place Ferris wheel, so we have an unobstructed view of them riding the waves.

My mom pulls Belle into her side. "What do you think their names are?"

The three of us play this game whenever we spot an animal. Belle insists that all animals have names, even strays or wild ones. My mom waits patiently as she pushes her long, dark hair aside. There's a light breeze up this high, so she's continually brushing it away from her face. My hair is in a messy topknot, and Belle wears hers in braids, so we don't have that problem.

"Hmm..." Belle taps her lips with her index finger, deep in thought. "Sprinkles, Tulip, Petunia, Rainbow Rose, and...Tupac!"

"Do you even know who Tupac is?" Mom's eyes twinkle in amusement.

"Sure I do," Belle insists. "Kiara says back in like, the olden days, there was this rapper named Tupac Sugar. Kiara's mommy grew up listening to his music all the time. Her mama says everyone knows the West Side is the best side!" Belle makes a peculiar hand gesture and somehow stretches that last word into three syllables.

Our mom laughs so hard, tears are welling in her eyes. "Back in the olden days, huh? How old are we talking here?"

"Oh, yeah." Belle nods her head enthusiastically. "Like, you have to be really, *really* old to listen to him."

"Hey!" I protest. "'California Love' is one of my go-to old-school jams. *I* listen to 2Pac, and I'm not old."

Belle scrunches her little nose. "Uh...yeah, you are. You're seventeen now. That's *way* old."

I raise my eyebrows. "If I'm so old, what does that make Mom?"

Belle glances up at her. "Really, really, *really* old. Like the dinosaurs."

My mom laughs again, tugging on one of Belle's braids. "Thanks a lot, kid. I can always depend on you to boost my self-esteem when it's running low."

There's an underlying sadness beneath the sarcasm, adding a ring of truth to that statement. I stare at my mom as the wheel descends, wondering how her self-esteem could ever be lacking. Mahalia Rivera is the most beautiful woman I've ever met, inside and out. And she just turned thirty-five, which isn't old at all. When the ride comes to a stop, we exit the bucket and head down the pier.

Mom loops her arm through mine. "Are you ready for your ice cream, birthday girl?"

I smile, my mom on one arm, and Belle on the other. "I'm read—"

"Eighteen-year-old female with penetrating trauma to the left lower abdomen."

I spin around, wondering where that yelling is coming from. By the time I've made a full circle, my mom and sister are gone.

What the hell?

"Mom? Belle? Where'd you go?"

I shoulder my way through the thick crowd of people, looking for them.

"Mom! Belle! *Where are you?*"

Where could they have gone? They were just here! I tell myself not to panic, maybe Belle had to pee or something. That girl has a bad habit of waiting until she's about to wet herself before notifying anyone she has to go. I can't even tell you how many times we've had to jump off the bus early to duck into a public restroom. I keep searching, and the more time goes on, the more anxious I become. I check all the bathrooms and still no luck. I'm in tears as the sun begins to set, still unable to find them.

I run from one end of the pier to the other five times, sweating and panting as I take a moment to catch my breath.

"Mom! Please answer me!"

"Multiple contusions...Lungs are clear."

Who is that?

As the sun dips below the horizon, I finally spot my mom at the opposite end and start sprinting back in that direction. When I reach her, Belle is nowhere to be found, and she has a bizarre look on her face.

"Mom, what's wrong? Where'd you go? Where's Belle?"

She smiles softly, brushing her delicate fingers against my cheek. "I love you so much, Jasmine. I'm proud of the woman you've become."

I place my hand over hers. "Uh...thanks. I love you too, Mom. Where's Belle?"

"It's not your time yet." She pulls her hand away. "You're so much stronger than I ever was. You have to go back and find the truth. Show the world what monsters they truly are."

My brows pinch together. "You're not making sense. You're the strongest person I know."

My mother shakes her head, tears streaming down her face. "I'm not. I was terrified they'd take you away from me, so I kept their secrets."

"Mom, what are you talking about? *Who's* keeping secrets? What are they hiding?"

"*Everything.*" She kisses the tips of her fingers before holding them out in my direction. "It's time to go back now. I love you, my sweet flower. Always."

"*Significant blood found on the scene.*"

I glance around again, trying to find the owner of the disembodied voice. "Do you hear that?"

My eyes widen when my mom steps onto the metal railing, climbing up to the top bar.

What is she doing?

I start running toward her, wondering how she got so far away.

"Wait!" I say as she begins to wobble. "Mom, get down from there! You're about to fall!"

"Unconscious... Treated for hypovolemic shock."

She stretches her arms out wide and glances over her shoulder. "Wake up, Jasmine. It's time to find the truth."

"Mom, don't do it!"

By the time I get to the railing, I'm too late. She disappeared. I don't even think about it; I dive in after her, down into the water below. Darkness instantly washes over me. My limbs are too heavy to move. My chest feels like there's an anvil sitting on top of it, crushing my lungs. Is this what drowning feels like?

Beep...

Beep...

Beep...

Where is that annoying sound coming from? Awareness is slowly seeping in, and the first thing that registers beyond the rhythmic beeping is the pain.

So. Much. Fucking. Pain.

My head is pounding. My throat protests as I attempt to swallow. Every muscle in my body aches as if I just went a few dozen rounds in an octagon.

I wince when warm fingers wrap around mine.

"She needs more pain meds," a deep voice barks.

Is that Kingston?

Why is someone playing the drums? I think I groan. I make a concerted effort to open my eyes and find a tall blonde wearing scrubs with pictures of little books on them. She's doing something that makes the godawful noise go away. Am I in a hospital?

"Hi, Jasmine. I'm Kristi, your nurse for the day. How are you feeling?"

"Hurts." It's difficult to speak. My tongue is sticking to the roof of my mouth.

Kristi reaches behind me, and next thing I know, a straw is pressed against my lips. "Take small sips...this should help a bit."

I startle when something squeezes my bicep.

She smiles softly. "Try to hold still. It's taking your blood pressure."

I wait for the machine to do its thing while she taps her fingers on a nearby keyboard. "On a scale of one to ten, with ten being unimaginable, how would you rate your pain?"

"Nine, maybe?" My voice is so scratchy, I hardly recognize it.

I think I doze off for a second because now the nurse is by my side, uncapping a needle and injecting something into my IV line. "It's time for another dose of morphine. This should make you feel much better in no time."

That moment can't come soon enough. I've never felt pain like this before.

"Thank you." I fade in and out as the lady finishes checking my vitals. Or at least that's what I think she's doing. "Need to...save...my mom...ocean...so tired."

"That's normal," Kristi says. "You've been through quite an ordeal. You get some more rest, and I'll be back to check on you later."

"'Kay," I mumble.

"Sleep, baby." The guy with the rumbly voice is back, pressing his lips against my forehead. "I'm not going anywhere."

"Oh, sweetheart, we like it when they run. It makes catching our prey much more satisfying."

The other one laughs, the sound of their amusement chilling me to the bones. Who are these twisted fucks? And seriously, where the hell is Kingston? I almost trip in my flip-flops, so I kick them off, running barefoot now. The sticks covering the forest floor scrape my skin, but I barely feel the pain because I'm too terrified to think of anything but escape.

"Help!" I scream. "Somebody fucking help me!"

I gasp, opening my eyes, only to slam them shut again when I'm assaulted by brightness.

"Lights," I croak.

"Turn down those fucking lights!" Softening his tone, he adds, "Take it easy, Jazz. I won't let anything happen to you."

Kingston? Where did he come from?

My eyelids flutter open, thankful the lights have been dimmed. My head shifts in the direction of the familiar voice. It *is* Kingston.

"What are you wearing?"

Kingston looks down at the green scrub top covering his torso. "Someone in the ER gave it to me. The shirt I was wearing was...stained." His expression turns grim. "I was using it to put pressure on your wound until the ambulance arrived."

"I'm in a hospital?"

Given the fluorescent lighting, the stench of antiseptic, and the obnoxious machines, the answer should be obvious, but my head is fuzzy. Nothing makes sense right now.

He nods. "Yeah, Jazz. You're in the hospital."

God, he looks like crap. His sandy hair is askew, dark circles are carved beneath his eyes, and his clothes are wrinkled.

Kingston links his pinkie finger with mine. "You scared the shit out of me."

Huh? "Why?"

His brows pinch together. "Do you remember anything?"

"I—"

"Oh, good. You're awake." A woman walks into the room with a bright smile on her face. Kingston scoots his chair back a little as she approaches the bed I'm lying in. "How are you feeling? My name is Kristi, and I'm your nurse for a few more hours."

Why do I feel like we've been through this before?

"Um...tired." I shake my head slightly, trying to clear the fog. "Weird."

"It's perfectly normal to be disoriented when you're coming out of anesthesia," she assures me. "Do you remember how you got here? Or *why* you're here?"

I think about it for a moment. I close my eyes as horrid memories flash through my brain. It's the same thing I was dreaming about just now. I can still feel that sick bastard's weight on top of me. His grubby hands touching my bare skin. The knife. Oh God, he put a knife in me! My hand moves to my stomach, just now noticing the extra weight. I open my eyes, examining the splint wrapped around my hand, going several inches up my arm.

"Your wrist is fractured," the nurse answers my unspoken question.

I ignore Kingston's penetrating gaze and focus on the woman before me.

Kristi removes her gloves and offers a smile. "I'm going to let the doctor know you're awake. He'll come in and explain everything."

When she leaves, Kingston takes my hand.

I jerk back. "Don't touch me."

He pulls away, looking perplexed as he rakes his hands through his thick hair. "What? Why not?"

Find the truth, Jasmine.

"Because..." I swallow the lump in my throat. I know it's not possible, but I swear I just heard my mom's voice. "I don't know. Just don't touch me."

I can't shake the feeling that something isn't

right. Kingston stares at me in confusion as I take a moment to piece everything together.

It takes considerable effort to level him with a glare when it finally hits me. "Where were you? Why did you have Bentley leave me all alone in that forest?"

Kingston frowns. "He was supposed to wait until I got there. I was right behind you two, but then I got held up."

"By what?"

His jaw tics. "Peyton. She was drunk and belligerent. Then she started crying, causing an even bigger scene. Reed and I were dragging her back to her house, kicking and screaming. Literally."

I fight the urge to scoff. "What convenient timing."

"What the hell does that mean?" His hazel eyes narrow.

"You tell me."

"What are you talking about?" His eyes widen. "You don't think *I* had something to do with your attack, do you?"

Do I? I honestly have no clue what the right answer is.

I sigh, already feeling worn out by this conversation. "I don't know what's true anymore."

Oh, you stupid, stupid girl. Who do you think led the lamb to the slaughter?

My attacker's words are running on repeat. I don't know who to believe. Kingston's betrayed my trust more than once in the short time I've known him. How can I say with any certainty he wasn't responsible for my attack?

Your precious boyfriend doesn't give a shit about you. Neither do his friends. Sweet talking you out of your panties was all part of the plan.

Was it all some sick joke? Part of some master plan? But why? Just to shut me up about something I overheard? Or is it more? I rub my temples when my head starts throbbing.

"Kingston, get out."

"Why would I do that? What the hell happened in that forest, Jazz?"

A soft knock precedes the nurse's return. There's a gray-haired man behind her—I'm guessing this is the doctor she was referring to earlier.

"Jasmine, I'm Dr. Yates. Are you feeling well enough to talk about your injuries?"

Kingston moves as the doc comes closer, taking a seat in the corner.

My eyes flash to Kingston. "Yes, but I don't want him here."

There's a moment of awkward silence before Dr. Yates replies. "Of course." He turns to the fuming man in the corner. "I'm going to need you to wait in the waiting room. Someone will come to get you if Miss Callahan is open to receiving visitors."

"Fuck that." Kingston shoots out of his chair. "I'm the one who found her. *I* called 911! *I'm the reason she's here!*"

Dr. Yates holds his hands up in a placating gesture. "Sir, please don't make me call security. My patient has every right to request privacy."

Kingston kicks the leg of the chair before shooting a glare in my direction. "Fine. But I'm not leaving this fucking hospital. We are *not* done with this conversation."

The doctor watches Kingston charge out of the room before speaking again. "Would you like a moment before I continue?"

I'm freakin' exhausted, but I want to get this over with. "No. Now is fine."

He clears his throat. "When you arrived, you

were suffering from a knife wound to your lower abdomen, blood loss, and contusions over several parts of your body. A CT scan revealed some internal bleeding, likely from the blunt trauma, so we needed to perform an exploratory laparotomy. Fortunately, the blade missed your intestines, and the leaking blood vessels were easily repaired.

"Your wrist suffered a distal radius fracture, which is why your arm is currently encased in a splint. I have no plans to switch that to a hard cast but won't know for sure until the swelling goes down a bit. Additionally, you have a mild concussion, which may cause temporary confusion, memory loss, or sensitivity to light or sound. We'll need to keep you under observation for about a week, considering your body is healing from several injuries at once. If all goes well, you should feel remarkably better in two to three weeks and fully recuperated in six to eight weeks."

I blow out a breath. "That's a lot to take in at once."

"It is, although I'd say you're a lucky young woman. The outcome could've been much worse if any major organs were perforated." He pauses for a moment. "Do you have any questions?"

I'm questioning *everything* right now, but I can't focus long enough on any one thing. "I'm tired."

"Understandable." Dr. Yates nods. "I'll let you get some rest. Just let the nurses know if you think of any questions, and they can page me."

My lids start to flutter as he leaves the room. "Kristi?"

My nurse comes back into view. "Yes, hun?"

"Can you please make sure no visitors come into my room? I don't want anyone in here while I sleep—especially the guy who was here before."

She lifts her eyebrows. "Is that boy hurting you, honey? Did he do this to you?"

"No," I mumble. "He definitely wasn't one of them. I just...I need to know no one will come in here while I'm asleep."

Kristi pats my arm. "Of course. I'll make sure the other nurses know as well."

I fully close my eyes, comforted by her assurance. Just because Kingston didn't physically assault me, doesn't mean he wasn't behind it. Maybe I'll feel differently once I'm clearheaded, but right now, *every* person I've met since my mom died is a suspect.

chapter two

KINGSTON

I'm livid as I make my way to the waiting room. Bentley, Reed, and my sister are all sitting in chairs, waiting for an update, but I have other matters to address first. Bentley stands when he sees me approach and braces himself, likely from my obvious rage.

I grab a fistful of his shirt and slam him back into the wall. "Why the fuck did you leave her? This would've never happened if you did what I told you to do!"

His nostrils flare. "Fuck you, man. This shit isn't my fault."

"The hell it's not!"

Reed pulls me off Bent. "Calm the hell down

before you get us all kicked out of here."

I start pacing the small room, trying to murder Bentley with my eyes.

My sister tugs on my arm. "Kingston, sit down and tell us what happened. Is she awake yet?"

I take the farthest seat away from the target of my ire. "Yes, she's awake. And she kicked me out of her room."

Ainsley's eyebrows draw together. "Why would she do that?"

"Because she thinks I had something to do with her assault. Can you believe that shit? What in the actual fuck? If it's anyone's fault, it's *that* asshole's. *He's* the one who left her vulnerable to whoever attacked her." I fling my arm in Bentley's direction.

He flips me off. "Fuck you. You told me you were right behind me. How was I supposed to know you got delayed when you didn't share that information with me?"

"I told you to stay with her until I got there! You didn't think it was odd that you didn't run into me until you were almost back to the house? It was a twenty-minute walk, you ass."

He grits his teeth. "I thought maybe you took the other path. And again, if you would've *told me* you were held up, I wouldn't have left."

"I shouldn't have *had* to. You should've never left her side."

Bentley jumps out of his chair. "Well, excuse-fucking-me for not wanting to stick around and see the hearts in her eyes when you showed up!"

Reed gets out of his chair at the same time I do and holds his arms out to both sides. "Seriously, guys, you're drawing attention. Sit the fuck down."

I'm too wired to sit, so I resume my pacing. "So, you left her alone in the woods in the middle of the night because you can't handle being second best? Are you seriously telling me your ego is the reason this happened?"

"You're the idiot who thought it'd be a good idea to drag her out there in the first place!" he counters.

"That's where the boat was docked!"

He rolls his eyes. "I still don't understand why you wanted to take it out in the middle of the night."

"I've already explained this. I wanted privacy."

"Yeah, well, you succeeded," Bentley scoffs. "My question is, why the fuck couldn't you just do the whole cake and champagne thing inside the big *empty* cabin?"

I slam my fist into the wall, hissing from the

pain. Like I haven't asked myself that question a thousand times over the last few hours.

"Kingston, stop it!" Ainsley grabs my clenched fist, examining it.

I drop back into a chair, clutching my hand. Reed sits right next to me, likely to restrain me if I try beating Bentley's face in.

"I'll go find some ice," Ainsley offers.

I take a few moments to breathe, willing the images out of my head. I don't scare easily, but finding Jazz like that...so bloody and beaten, was terrifying. I thought she was dead. I had a brief moment of relief when I felt her shallow breaths, but when I really took in her appearance, realizing she may have been raped on top of everything else, I damn near lost my shit. If I wasn't so busy trying to stop her from bleeding out, I would've raised hell.

When we first arrived at the hospital, a nurse informed me they wouldn't perform a sexual assault exam without the patient's consent because it's a fairly invasive process. So, we've been waiting until Jazz was coherent enough to tell us what happened. Not knowing what went down...whether or not someone violated her like that...it's killing me.

I hang my head, feeling dejected. "You didn't see her, man. She's black and blue with little scratches all over her body. Her arm is in a splint, her eye is half swollen shut. Even worse...when I found her...whatever sick fuck did that to her may have done even more damage that I couldn't see."

"What do you mean?" Reed asks.

I look Bentley right in the eye, knowing he'll understand how I'm feeling more than anyone. "She was practically naked when I found her. Her dress was cut up, and her underwear was missing."

Bentley blanches before falling into a chair. "Fuck."

"Yeah," I agree.

His eyes lift to mine. "Was she..."

I shake my head. "I don't know. She's only been awake a couple of times, and she was pretty out of it from the drugs they're giving her. The police are still waiting to interview her."

How did I go from having one of the best nights of my life to this? I planned on spending the evening christening my new boat, worshipping Jazz's tight little body, but instead, I'm sitting in a goddamn hospital, waiting for the chance to see her again.

Ainsley returns with a cold pack. "I got this from the nurses' station."

I place the compress on my knuckles. "Thanks."

The four of us sit silently, stewing on everything that's happened, until a throat clears, causing me to look up. Charles Callahan is standing in the doorway, taking in the scene. I'm sure we're quite the sight. We've been here for six hours now, and none of us have slept in over twenty-four hours. All of our clothes are rumpled—my jeans are muddy and stained with Jazz's blood.

"Peyton called," he explains. "Said Jasmine was taken by ambulance to a hospital. This one was the closest to the lake house, so I took an educated guess." He frowns. "They said she's not accepting visitors. They won't tell me anything about her condition since she's legally an adult now. Have any of you seen her?"

Fuck. I am not in the mood to deal with this man. I don't know if I can conceal my hatred for him right now. I sure as shit don't trust him, especially with Jazz's life. For all I know, *he* was responsible, and he's here, pretending to be a concerned father, simply to cover his ass.

"How did Peyton know?" I ask.

Charles lifts a shoulder. "You'd have to ask her."

"I was still with her when you called from the ambulance," Reed offers. "I called Bent as soon as I hung up. Peyton could've easily overheard our conversation."

Callahan nods to Reed before turning back to me. "Well, there you go. Have you seen Jasmine yet? Do you know what happened?"

I stare the prick down, not willing to give him anything. I'm sure my protectiveness over his daughter will get back to my dad, but I don't really give a shit.

Ainsley, always trying to be the peacekeeper, speaks up. "Kingston's been with her the whole time. He just came out here because she's...resting."

Charles raises an eyebrow, staring at me expectantly. "And her condition?"

Jesus. I suppose I can feed him enough information so he'll get off my back.

I clear my throat. "Jazz was beaten and stabbed, but she's stable now. They did some emergency surgical procedure and found her injuries weren't as severe as they initially thought. The doctor told me earlier she should be ready for release in a week or so. She'll be sore for a while, but she should be okay."

"That's good to hear. When you see her next, please let her know I stopped by. When she's ready to come home, just have her contact Frank, and he'll pick her up."

His tone is utterly devoid of emotion like he's not the least bit affected his daughter could've died tonight. And it doesn't go unnoticed that he has zero questions about who beat the shit out of her. The worst part is that I'm not remotely surprised by his lack of concern.

I have to forcibly unclench my jaw. "You're not staying?"

"I can't. I have to catch a flight in a few hours."

My lips thin. "Wait...weren't you just on a trip?"

Charles' jaw tics. "Not that I need to explain myself to you, but that was a quick overnight trip to meet with a client in San Diego. Madeline and I are now heading to Cabo for some R&R. Let Jasmine know we'll be gone for a few weeks. If she needs any sort of medical care when she gets back to the house, Ms. Williams can make the necessary arrangements."

Fuck bringing her back to that place. I've already decided she'll be staying with me in the pool house. At least there, I have a full security system independent from the main house. Nobody gets in or out without my knowledge.

"I'll let her know. Have a nice *vacation* while your

daughter is stuck in a hospital."

Charles' arctic eyes flash with rage before he schools his expression. Without another word, he turns on his heels and walks away.

"Damn, and I thought Dad was cold," Ainsley mutters. "I'm pretty sure he'd at least *pretend* to care if one of us got hurt."

I scoff. "No, kidding. Those two can give each other a run for their money on shittiest father of the decade."

Bentley blows out a breath. "What are you going to do if she was...if someone did attack her *in that way?*"

Two years later, and he can't even say the word. I'm sure this whole thing is dredging up some painful shit.

"I don't know." Well, besides hunting that motherfucker down and feeding him his dick. It's probably not wise to mention that in public, so I keep that thought to myself.

Ainsley grabs my non-swollen hand. "Let's hope it doesn't come to that."

I resist the urge to laugh. I can't remember the last time I ever felt hopeful about something, but I don't want to take a dump on my sister's sentiment.

"Yeah, let's hope."

chapter three

JAZZ

"Jasmine, an officer is waiting to ask you some questions. Is it okay if I let her in?"

"Um...yeah."

Marika, my assigned nurse for the day, sticks her head out the door and comes back with a brunette woman wearing a dark blue uniform.

The officer takes the seat next to my bed. "Hi, Jasmine. My name's Isa Dominguez. Is it okay if I ask you some questions?"

"Sure."

She gestures to Marika. "Would you like privacy during the interview? Or someone else to be present?"

"She can stay. No one else."

Officer Dominguez nods. "Your injuries indicate you may have been the victim of an attack. Is that accurate?"

"Yeah."

She smiles softly. "Do you remember any details?"

"It comes in flashes. There were two men. They were wearing masks—I don't know who they were."

Now that my head is clearer, I've been thinking about this nonstop. I can't stop replaying the incident over and over, trying to identify something I may have missed. I didn't recognize their voices, but something seemed familiar about the men who assaulted me, especially the main guy. I keep having these phantom pains of what it felt like when he was crushing me with his weight, pawing at me, beating me. I can still smell the alcohol on his breath as he leered down at my naked body. Feel his erection pressing against my thigh, growing bigger and bigger the more I screamed.

The officer writes notes on the pad she's carrying. "Take as much time as you need."

"Um...they came out of nowhere and started chasing me. When one of them caught up with me, he threatened me with a knife, told me he wouldn't hurt me if I'd just cooperate."

"Now listen up, you cunt. This is how it's gonna go. You're going to stop trying to maim us, and you're going to open those pretty legs of yours. If you try screaming for help again, I'll slit your fucking throat. If you take it like a good girl until we're done with you, you get to live. Understand?"

"Cooperate, how?"

I swallow the lump in my throat. "He told me to open my legs and take it like a good girl."

Officer Dominguez takes a deep breath. "And then what?"

"At one point, I got ahold of the knife, but he tried getting it back." I hold up my left arm. "That's when this got broken, I guess. Then he stabbed me during the struggle. Things get a little fuzzy after that."

More note-taking. "Can you remember any details about their physical appearance? Hair color, build, things like that?"

I think about it for a moment. "They were both tall...one guy had a thinner build, like a runner, and the one who stabbed me was pretty muscular. He was really heavy but solid. Their masks covered their whole head, so I don't know about hair color or anything."

She looks me directly in the eye. "I know this next question will be difficult, but I need to ask based on the condition you were in when you arrived. Were you sexually assaulted?"

I clear my throat, cursing the dryness. My nurse must be reading my mind because she turns on the faucet in the little sink and hands me a paper cup filled with water.

"Thank you." I take a few swallows before continuing. "Yes, but not...*fully*. He didn't put anything *inside* of me. Not for lack of trying, but when he stabbed me, they got freaked out and ran off. I think the knife was just meant to scare me."

Answering that question was hard enough when one of my nurses first asked, but I understand the officer needs to be thorough.

"Oh, shit, man! You stabbed her! You fucking stabbed her! We need to get the hell out of here!"

"Look what you did, you dumb bitch. You could've just spread your legs, and this would've never happened."

"Did either of them say anything that stands out, or do you know anyone who'd want to potentially harm you?"

"Do you see this gorgeous little pussy? She's freshly waxed and everything. It's like she was waiting for us. Our employer will understand."

"Um...I don't think so." I don't know why I

omit those facts, but my gut instinct is telling me to keep it to myself

.

"Can you think of anything else that may help locate your attackers?"

I shake my head. "Not that I can think of."

"Okay. I think I have enough for now." Officer Dominguez asks for my phone number, then removes a card from her shirt pocket and places it on the bedside table. "Here's my contact info if you remember anything else. *Anything at all.* Please don't hesitate to reach out. If I don't hear from you, I'll be in touch as soon as I have more information from the crime scene."

"Thank you."

I release a heavy sigh as she leaves the room.

"Can I get you anything?" Nurse Marika asks. "They'll be serving lunch in about an hour, but I can grab you a snack if you'd like."

I totally forgot she was here, so I jump a little when she speaks. "Uh...no, I'm okay. Thank you. I think I'd just like to nap."

I notice the surfboard print on her scrubs when she pauses in the doorway. "I'm sorry if this is overstepping, but the gentleman that was here yesterday hasn't left the hospital once. His friends have been in and out, but he's been here the whole time. He seems really worried about you—he's constantly asking if you're allowing visitors yet."

"Thanks for letting me know." I sigh. "I still don't want any visitors, though."

Marika nods. "Of course."

I stare at the ceiling as she leaves the room. Why in the hell do I feel guilty right now? So what if Kingston has been here for over forty-eight hours? I can barely walk to the bathroom that's five feet away. Under the circumstances, I think it's perfectly reasonable to not want anyone around me while I'm so defenseless. Kingston can hang around the hospital all he wants, but I'm not letting him back in my room.

"A young lady named Ainsley brought this by while you were napping." My nurse sets my cell phone on the bedside table and my overnight bag on the built-in bench. "She thought you might need them."

I pick up my phone, smiling at Ainsley's thoughtfulness. All of my things, including my phone, were back at the lake house. I was dreading trying to make arrangements to collect them. I could do without the clothes, but there's one number in my contacts that I don't have memorized and really need. Surprisingly, there's only one text notification, and of course, it's from Kingston.

I take a deep breath as I unlock my phone and read the message.

Kingston: Contact forwarded: Belle Rivera-Washington

What the heck? I open the contact card and see Belle's name with an iCloud address on it. When did she get an Apple device to have one of those?

I immediately dial Kingston's number, and he answers on the first ring.

"I see the nurse delivered your stuff."

I get straight to the point. "Why are you sending me contact information for my sister?"

He releases a deep chuckle. "I know you were frustrated having to go through Jerome, so I eliminated the middleman. Belle now has a brand new iPad so you can FaceTime as often as you'd like. It's hooked up to a cellular network, and the bill is in my name, so there's no risk of it being shut off for non-payment. Don't worry about her dad—he's been taken care of as well. He won't interfere."

"But...how? Why?"

"Ainsley and Reed dropped by your sister's house and explained why you missed our standing date last Sunday...an explanation appropriate for a seven-year-old, anyway. Belle knows you were hurt, and you're in the hospital, but that you'll be okay. She's expecting your call whenever you're feeling up to it."

Damn him. He knows my little sister, Belle, is my greatest weakness. Her father, Jerome, rarely answers the phone when I call, and half the time, he makes some excuse why Belle can't talk. I'm not sure why he's constantly keeping me away from her, but I suspect it may be a control thing. He wants to remind me who has custody of her and who's really in charge.

Kingston's assurance that Jerome won't interfere tells me he's paying him to allow it, just like he pays him for our weekly visits. I hate that Kingston did this because he's once again using Belle to get closer to me, but I can't say it doesn't make me happy having such an easy way to speak with her.

Infuriatingly confusing man.

My mother would be ashamed of me for not acknowledging the gift, so I suck it up and say, "Thank you. That was very thoughtful."

I swear I can hear him smile. "That was really hard for you to spit out, wasn't it?"

"No," I grumble.

It totally was.

Another laugh. "Are you feeling any better? Can I get you anything?"

I bite my lip, carefully crafting my response. I don't want Kingston to think I'm opening the lines of communication with us because I'm not ready for that.

"No. The nurses are taking care of me. The best thing you can do right now is give me time."

Aaaaand cue the awkward silence.

"I had *nothing* to do with this, Jazz. You have to know that."

I shake my head. "I don't know anything right now."

He growls under his breath. "When I find the motherfucker who did this to you, they *will* pay. I guaran-fucking-tee it."

"I've told you once before, I don't need a knight in shining armor, Kingston. I can take care of myself."

"Too bad. I don't want to be a knight, Jazz, but I do fully intend on doing whatever's necessary to catch this guy."

I notice he doesn't mention that *two* men attacked me. It could all be an act, though. Kingston's the most observant person I've ever met —he pays attention to details, so he would know not to make that mistake if he did, in fact, know. God, trying to detect subterfuge is exhausting.

I sigh. "Last I checked, you weren't a police officer."

"I have access to resources the police don't. They can conduct their own investigation, but I already have my own guy doing the same. If he finds anything helpful, he'll pass it on to the police."

"Why would you go through all that trouble?"

I swear I can feel his glare. "Is that a serious question? Why the fuck do you think I'd do it?"

"I'm tired, Kingston. I'm going to rest now. You should go home and do the same."

"I'm not going anywhere as long as you're here." I can just imagine him combing his hand through his hair in frustration. "You want to keep me out of your room—fine. I think it's ridiculous considering I'm one of the few people you *can* trust, but whatever. I'm not going to push you while you're laid up in a hospital bed. But know this, Jazz: Once you're out of here, I'm going to be your goddamn shadow, so you'd better get used to that idea now. I am *not* letting anyone hurt you again."

"Stalking is illegal in California." My argument is weak, but it's all I've got.

His scoff is audible through the phone line. "Yeah? Well, then it's a good thing I know some excellent attorneys."

"You're impossible."

"Persistent," he corrects. "It's why I *always* get what I want."

I know I'm probably going to regret asking this, but I do it anyway. "And what is it that you want?"

"*You*. And vengeance."

Yep. Definitely shouldn't have asked.

chapter
four

JAZZ

After seven whole days in the hospital, I finally get to go home. Kingston kept his promise of standing guard the entire time. However, my sperm donor never showed up or made any attempt to contact me as far as I know. I wondered if he even knew where I was, until the house manager, Ms. Williams, called the hospital, passing along the message that my driver, Frank, will take me home whenever I'm ready.

I can't help thinking about how differently my mom would've handled things had she been alive. She would've been fluttering about, making sure I was comfortable enough. Or baking treats for the hospital staff to show her appreciation for all their hard work. Belle would've been right by her side, coloring or reading, or snuggling in bed with me watching cartoons. I had a few bleak moments while lying in that bed, where all of my thoughts about what could've been, practically suffocated me.

"You ready to go home?" The orderly smiles, completely clueless to the fact that staying here is actually better than being at my father's McMansion.

I gingerly lower myself into the wheelchair he's offering. "Ready as I'm going to get."

Before we even roll past the waiting room, I can sense Kingston's nearness. The man always has a way of infiltrating my senses. The spiciness of his cologne, the hint of whatever soap he uses, the timbre of his voice. Most prominent is how my body stands to attention whenever he's around. I'm inexplicably drawn to him, despite my head's vehement protests. Even now, in my weakened state, my brain wars with my body. Part of me is anxiously awaiting my first glimpse of him, while the other part is telling me to run far, far away.

Kingston scrambles out of his chair when he sees us. "Wait!"

The orderly stops pushing my chair. "Do you know him?"

I sigh. "Yeah."

Kingston looks better since I last saw him—at least his clothes are clean—but he still looks exhausted. That doesn't detract from my overwhelming attraction to him, though. How someone can spend a week cooped up in a small waiting room and still be so devastatingly beautiful is beyond me.

"I'll get my car and meet you out front." Kingston turns to Ainsley, who just joined us. "You stay with Jazz."

"Kingston, no." I grab his arm before he can walk away, quickly pulling my hand back when I feel the energy crackle between us.

"What do you mean, 'no'?" His eyebrows pinch together.

Ainsley gives me a soft smile. "Hey, Jazz."

"Hey. Thanks again for bringing my bag."

She nods. "Of course."

I broke down and texted Ainsley several times over the last few days, figuring she was the safest choice. Our conversation had stayed on neutral topics, but talking with her helped curb my loneliness.

I turn back to Kingston. "Frank is waiting for me out front. I already have a ride."

Kingston's expression goes from concerned to pissed in half a second. "Fuck that. You are *not* going back to that house."

Bossy ass.

I glare at him. "Where else am I supposed to go? It's the only home I have."

"My place." The indignance in his tone is heavy as if questioning him on this is ludicrous.

Okay, I'll admit the Callahan mansion is not my first choice either, but it's my only option because I'm sure as shit not staying with Kingston. When I lived in Watts, I spent so much time watching my sister while our mom was at work, I didn't really hang out with anybody outside of school. My *friends* were more like school acquaintances. The one exception to that was my ex, Shawn, and I'm not about to ask him if I can crash at his place.

Besides, Ms. Williams told me Charles and Madeline will be in Mexico for two more weeks, so knowing I won't have to deal with them is a relief. Even if I did have money for a motel—which I don't—I don't like the thought of being completely alone. At the mansion, there's always staff on hand to help me if need be. Simple things like walking or getting dressed are still somewhat difficult to manage. I have stitches running the entire width of my pubic bone, as well as a small spot on my side, and every time I move, they're stretched, which hurts like a bitch. I never realized how often your core is engaged with the tiniest motions before now.

Not to mention the fact that half my body was clobbered. My bruises aren't nearly as dark, and my eye is no longer swollen shut, but every spot where I was punched, or kicked, or thrown to the ground, aches. I'm not going to lie; my super deluxe pillowtop mattress at Sperm Donor's house sounds like heaven after spending a week on an uncomfortable hospital bed.

I scoff. "Thanks, but no thanks."

"Why the hell not?" He's practically shouting, no concern whatsoever for the nearby people now watching the drama unfold.

Ainsley tugs on his arm. "Kingston, calm down."

"Uh...should I radio for security?" The orderly pulls my chair back a little.

"No." I shake my head. "Can we just get going?"

"Sure," he says, pushing my chair toward the elevator bay.

Of course, Kingston and Ainsley are hot on our heels. All four of us get into the elevator when the doors slide open.

"Jazz, you *cannot* go back to that house," Kingston insists. "Not until we figure out who did this to you. I don't trust them."

"Can we please discuss this later?"

"Sure."

"Really?" My eyebrows lift. I didn't expect him to agree so quickly.

Kingston smirks. "Yeah, we can talk about it later. At my house. After you get settled in."

I should've known it was too good to be true. "I'm going back to *my* house. I'm not an idiot; I know not to trust any of them. I never did. One thing I am certain of is that it's my *only* option. I can handle it."

The man behind me is probably wondering what the hell is going on. I bet he doesn't usually feel like he stepped into a soap opera when he wheels someone out of the hospital. The elevator finally reaches the first floor, so we head toward the patient pickup area. Frank is standing in front of a black town car, dutifully waiting for my arrival.

Frank opens the rear door. "Miss Jasmine, nice to see you."

I smile. "Hi, Frank. Thanks for coming to get me."

Frank lifts the overnight bag off my lap before assisting me out of the chair and into the car. "I'm happy to help." Poor guy is standing there, fidgeting awkwardly because Kingston is blocking his ability to shut the door.

I smile softly. "Give us a minute, will you?"

"Of course." He nods before rounding the vehicle and getting behind the wheel. Meanwhile, Kingston is fuming—holding the door open, no doubt calculating his odds of escape if he threw me over his shoulder and made a run for it. Ainsley's eyes widen in warning, no doubt sensing his intentions with their freaky twin brain-link.

His lips thin as I fasten my seat belt. "We'll be right behind you."

I look him straight in the eye. "No. You *won't*. I'm going straight to bed, so there's no point." I turn toward his sister. "Do *not* let him follow—there's plenty of staff at the house to watch over me. I'll text you later, okay?"

She smiles. "Okay."

Kingston grips the doorframe with both hands and leans in until he's mere inches away from my face. His eyes are forest green today with tiny gold flecks around the irises. It takes an immense amount of self-control to stay where I am and not lean into him. I can feel the heat wafting from his body as we stare at one another, and I want so badly to touch him. Have him touch me.

What is it about Kingston Davenport that entices me so much? Why can he pull me into his orbit with no effort whatsoever? This is LA—I've been around quite a few extraordinarily attractive guys in my life, but I've never had such a visceral reaction to one like I do with him.

I take a deep breath, trying to calm my racing pulse. "Kingston, please move so I can shut the door."

"This isn't over, Jazz." He straightens his spine and slams the door shut.

I watch him as we pull away from the curb, allowing his words to resonate. Of course, this isn't over. It's *far* from over. I have every intention of finding out who attacked me, who hired them, *and* whatever the hell is going on between our fathers. I just need to wait until I'm mobile enough to do anything about it.

Kingston can play the tough guy all he wants, but I'm not like the girls he's used to. I'm not afraid to get my hands dirty, and I'm definitely not afraid of the truth. Regardless of how ugly it may get, I'm *going* to get to the bottom of this. There's this darkness brewing inside of me, demanding retribution no matter the cost, and I have every intention of delivering. If I have to lose a little piece of my soul in the process...well, at least I'll still have a good chunk left.

"Jazz!"

I smile as my sister's smile lights up the screen on our FaceTime call. "Hi, sweetpea. I miss you."

Belle's round chocolate eyes squint as she takes in my appearance. I intentionally waited until I was home to contact her so I could conceal my bruises. Some strategically applied makeup and subdued lighting really did the trick. Up close, you can still see the slight discoloration lurking beneath, but over a video call, not so much.

"You don't look hurt."

I bite back a grin at Belle's accusatory tone. Her sass is one of my favorite things about her.

"That's because I feel *much* better. The doctors fixed me up almost good as new."

I hate lying, but there's no way I'm telling her

what really happened. She's too young. Even if I sugar-coated it, she's at that age where her imagination is kicking into overdrive. The last thing I'd want is for her to visualize *any* part of what happened to me.

"Kingston got me an iPad, and it's not even my birthday!" she says excitedly, ultimately moving on to the next subject. Thank God.

"I see that." I smile. "Have you thanked him yet?"

"I made a picture!" The camera is now aimed at the ceiling, so I'm guessing she set the iPad down. "See!"

I get a brief glimpse of Belle's face hovering above the screen before she shoves her drawing in front of it. She drew a picture of a tall blond boy, a shorter dark-haired girl, and an even smaller girl with braids in her hair, all holding hands. Based on Belle's color choices for the hair and skin, there's no question who each person represents: Kingston, me, and my sister.

As Belle chats on and on about her life since I last saw her, I smile and nod, occasionally chiming in with a few words. My mind is elsewhere, however. I can't stop thinking about Kingston, which is understandable, I suppose, considering he's the reason I can even FaceTime my sister right now. Belle's attachment to him after only a few outings is unsettling. But how can I blame her when he's been nothing but sweet, patient, and generous every time she sees him? I would've never believed he possessed those traits had I not seen it with my own eyes.

The man is a walking contradiction.

Most of the time, he's broody and mysterious, in a totally sexy way—like catnip for the female population. But when he's with the guys outside of school, he's laid back and even goofy sometimes. With Ainsley and me and hell, even Belle, he's super-protective, and there are these moments where he's incredibly thoughtful or kind. Regardless of which Kingston you're getting at the time, there's always this underlying rage I don't think many people pick up on. Or maybe they don't understand the extent of it.

I remember watching a video during my freshman year science class about the Mount St. Helens eruption. The landscape was breathtaking, loved by outdoor enthusiasts or simply anyone searching for a peaceful place to spend their day. The volcano sat quietly for over one hundred years, all the while, pressure was building beneath the surface. There was sufficient evidence of its impending reawakening, but the reports weren't taken seriously enough by the general public. Tourists continued flocking to the area—some even evading roadblocks and ignoring air restrictions—until the perfect combination of events caused a cataclysmic explosion. The eruption was so powerful, it literally blew the top off the mountain, killing everyone in the vicinity.

Kingston reminds me of that volcano. If you don't look beyond his surface beauty, if you ignore the warning signs, you're putting yourself at risk. He's dangerous—perhaps even deadly—and I'd be a fool to forget that.

"Are you guys gonna come get me on Sunday?"

My heart aches, seeing the hope in Belle's eyes. There's no way I'll be healed by then, and I don't want her to see me like this. Plus, until I'm sure Kingston isn't a suspect, I don't want him anywhere near my sister.

"Oh, honey, not this Sunday, but maybe the next one." If I'm well enough to see her by then, I'll have Frank drive me.

She frowns. "How come? Don't you wanna see me?"

"Of course I want to see you," I assure her.

"But...I've been in the hospital for a whole week, and I have lots and lots of homework to catch up on for school."

At least that part isn't a lie. The first thing Ms. Williams said to me when I got home was that my father expects me to keep up with schoolwork while I convalesce.

"Homework is stupid." She punctuates her statement by sticking out her lower lip.

I laugh until my stitches pull, causing sharp pain. I have to fake sneeze to cover up my yelp, but that motion makes it even worse. Damn it.

I take a moment to breathe through the pain. "It really is, but you know what's pretty awesome?"

"What?" I can see the wheels turning in her head as a little crease forms between her eyebrows.

"You can see me anytime you want before then. You just have to hit that green camera button on your iPad, and we can video chat."

"That's super-duper awesome!"

God, I love her smile.

I cover my mouth as a giant yawn sneaks up on me. Having the shit beat out of you really zaps your energy. I don't recommend it one bit.

"I think I'm going to take a nap before I get started on all that homework. I have to go now, but call me when you get home from school tomorrow, okay?"

Belle nods. "'Kay! Love you, Jazz!"

"I love you too, sweet girl."

Her face disappears as I hit the button to end the call. Carefully crawling under the covers, I rest my head on the pillow and close my eyes. I only remember taking a few deep breaths before I'm fast asleep.

chapter five

JAZZ

The persistent knocking on my door wakes me up. I carefully sit up in bed, swinging my legs to the side.

"Hold on a sec."

I slowly make my way over there, turn the lock, and open the door. Ms. Williams is standing in the hallway with her resting bitch face firmly in place.

"Miss Jasmine, you have a visitor waiting in your theater room. Would you like to meet him there, or shall I send him in here?"

I sigh. "Neither. Please tell Kingston I'll call him when I'm ready to talk. Just like I've told him every day in the week that I've been home."

"It's not Mr. Davenport."

Huh?

"Who is it, then?"

"Bentley Fitzgerald."

What is Bentley doing here? Did Kingston send him? I look down at the tank top and pajama shorts I'm wearing. It's not covering any less skin than I would show on a warm day, but I still feel exposed.

"Give me a few minutes, and you can send him here. I need to change first."

Ms. Williams nods. "Very well."

I head into my walk-in closet and shut the door. Changing entirely is going to take too much effort, so I settle for grabbing an old hoodie. I quickly peek in the full-length mirror, and I'm pleased to see that my bruises are almost entirely faded. I cringe when my eyes move up to the giant bird's nest at the top of my head. I haven't washed my hair in almost a week, and it's greasy and tangled as fuck.

Something so simple shouldn't be so challenging, but with a fucked-up wrist, it is. I can take my splint off when I shower, but I'm still not supposed to move my wrist, and trying to wash my hair with only one hand is a bitch. I may actually have to suck it up and take advantage of Madeline's in-house salon. That doesn't help me right now, though. Oh, well. It's not like I need to worry about impressing Bentley, right?

"Jazzy Jazz, you in here?"

I finish pulling up the zipper and open the door, stepping out of my closet. Bentley is standing in my doorway, his eyes shooting in my direction when I clear my throat.

"Hey. What are you doing here?"

He rushes me before I have a chance to react, pulling me into a giant bear hug, lifting me off my toes. "Thank God you're okay. I'm sorry for coming over unannounced, but I couldn't wait any longer to see you. "

I suck in a breath when he squeezes too tightly. Fuck, that hurts. "Bent...ease up."

"Shit. Sorry." He immediately releases me and looks me over. "How are you feeling?"

"Okay, all things considered." I shrug. "What are you doing here? Did Kingston send you?"

"Naw, baby. I just needed to see you were alive with my own eyes. Davenport would probably be pissed if he knew I came." Bentley clears his throat nervously. "Can we talk?"

My eyes are boring into his, searching. I decide there's no harm in hearing him out since the odds of Bentley trying something shady with my bedroom door open are slim to none.

I nod. "Yeah, we can talk. I need to sit down, though."

He lifts a dark eyebrow. "You need help?"

"No, I got it." I climb onto my bed, reclining against the padded headboard. "What do you want to talk about?"

Bentley grabs the chair from my desk and straddles it backward. "I wanted to apologize. If I had known your boy was held up, I would've never left. I swear to fucking God, Jazz, I would've never put you at risk like that."

I think about that for a moment. How am I supposed to trust this guy when leaving me alone was the perfect setup? How do I know he didn't walk away, knowing what was about to happen, so he had an alibi?

I sit up straighter when I think of a way to test his loyalty. If Bentley wants me to believe him, he needs to meet me halfway. "I have some questions."

He tilts his head to the side. "You can ask me anything."

"What really happened at Donovan's party? And no dodging the details this time. Did you guys drug me?"

"Fuck, no." He shakes his head vehemently. "I would never...*we* would *never*."

"You need to give me more than that, Bent, because my memory is *really* fuzzy from that night, which makes no sense after only two drinks."

He exhales harshly. "Baby girl, you should be asking Kingston these questions."

"I'm asking *you*, Bentley. C'mon, after what happened, I think I deserve some damn answers. How am I supposed to ever trust you if you can't answer a few measly questions? I don't even know how I got to the pool house. I remember hanging out with that guy from UCLA, and next thing I know, I'm thinking about how good you smell."

It takes him a moment to reply. "We paid Lawson—AKA, the UCLA guy—to chat you up over drinks and bring you to the pool house once you were nice and sloppy, ready to pass out."

Wow...so this Lawson guy was in on it. Yet another person to put on my watch list. I stare at Bentley for a moment, trying to read him. Well, at least he seems contrite. Or maybe he's pretending?

I frown. "Go on."

"And...you got a second wind or something, so we had to improvise." Bentley gives me a sheepish smile.

"What were you planning on doing after you got me there, all 'sloppy and ready to pass out'?"

"Definitely not what happened," he insists. "Well, before you crashed, anyway."

I cross my arms over my chest. "Explain."

Bentley sighs. "We were just after the pictures. Kingston wanted to get a few shots to make it look like we were both fucking you."

"So, you could share them with the entire student body?"

"Yeah." He cringes.

"Why?"

"Now, that *really* is a question for your boy. I can't speak for him, but he definitely had his reasons."

"Please stop calling him *my boy*. Kingston's not my *anything*."

"Aw baby, I wish that were actually true." Bentley gets a sad look on his face. "Look, if it makes a difference, our make-out sesh, or the video for that matter, was never planned. But when you slid your tongue down my neck...the way you were so responsive to a simple kiss...I've never felt such explosive chemistry before. I'm pretty sure Kingston would say the same. Just the idea of a three-way with us totally got you going. You can't deny that,

Jazz; it couldn't have been more obvious. I think Davenport and I were so stunned, our dicks kind of took over."

"It doesn't matter if I was into it. What matters is that you *fucking set me up*."

Bentley smirks. "So, you admit you wanted to take a big bite out of a Manwich?"

I pin him with a glare. "Not the time, Bentley."

He holds his palms out. "All right, all right. Lousy time for jokes. Does it help that we felt like major shit afterward? It would've never gone any farther than it did; I swear on my left nut, Jazzy. As fucked up as this sounds, we did our best to protect you. We were in complete agreement that any pics we released didn't show nudity. We made sure the house was locked up tight. Kingston even texted his sister from your phone, so she knew where you were. We wouldn't have put you in any *real* danger.

"Sure, we needed the pics to spark the gossip, but we never wanted to actually hurt you. Maybe embarrass you a little or piss you off at most. We would've *never* taken advantage of you sexually, drunk or sober. We may be pricks, but we're not fucking predators."

I scoff. "Am I supposed to thank you for supposedly *protecting me*? Yeah, I guess I'm relieved the entire school can't pick my tits out in a lineup, but the damage was done regardless. There are other ways to hurt someone beyond the physical, Bentley. Slut-shaming is *never* cool, and staging a scene to do it is even worse! That shit *hurt*."

Bentley hangs his head. "We were assholes, straight up. For the record, your tits are fan-fucking-tastic. If the entire student body *did* see 'em, they'd agree."

I growl. "Not the point, dickhead."

He scrubs a hand over his jaw. "Yeah, I know. Just sayin'. Quite frankly, we were all pretty surprised you forgave us as quickly as you did."

"I didn't forgive you," I correct. "I just didn't see the point in dwelling over it. Not to mention some pretty great things happened after that. But after homecoming night in the forest, it made me question my judgment on a lot of stuff. I don't know how I'm supposed to trust my own thoughts, let alone anyone else."

"You can trust me, Jazzy Jazz. The guys, too. I know we've done some shitty things, but those few actions aren't indicative of who we are. Of what lengths we'd go through to keep you safe. *You matter to us*; very few people fall under that umbrella."

"Why should I believe you? Why should I believe *anything* you've told me tonight?"

Bentley's gaze never wavers as he formulates his response. "Ask me about a girl named Carissa sometime. Not tonight...but soon. I promise you won't have any doubt whether or not we'd ever intentionally hurt you."

I'd be lying if I said I wasn't intrigued about this Carissa girl. "I matter, huh?"

"So fucking much, babe. It'd be a lot easier if you didn't—especially for me—but that's life, I guess."

I take a moment to really digest his words. To study his body language. Seeing him like this, regret pouring off of him in waves, I'm pretty sure Bentley is being honest. I'm still going to be cautious because I'm not stupid, but I'm willing to give him the benefit of the doubt.

"Okay."

"Okay? Okay, *what?*"

"Okay, I'll believe you. *For now.* But if I find out you lied to me about *any* of this, I *won't* give you a second chance. I'm not kidding, Bent."

Bentley exhales harshly. "I swear I won't need one. Honest Abe from here on out."

I sigh. "So, now what?"

Bentley squeezes the back of his neck. "Do you wanna talk about what happened that night?"

I briefly close my eyes, warding off the images his words conjure. I can't stop thinking about that night, and none of those thoughts are pleasant.

"Not really."

He sucks his full lower lip into his mouth. "Can I ask you one thing?"

"I reserve the right not to answer, but sure; go ahead."

"Were you...did the guy who hurt you, did he, um..."

I raise my eyebrows, waiting for him to finish the sentence. The boy looks massively uncomfortable. I'm pretty sure I know where he's going with this, but I don't want to assume.

"Did the guy who hurt me do *what*, Bentley?"

He swallows a lump in his throat. "Did he...force himself on you?"

"No." I inhale sharply. "He *tried*...but he didn't succeed."

Bentley's head drops onto his forearms, which are folded over the back of the chair. He stays that way for a moment, his back rising and falling as he takes deep breaths.

I quirk my head to the side. "You okay?"

"Just...give me a second."

Did he just sniffle?

When Bentley's head lifts, his eyes are bloodshot and filled with unshed tears. Any lingering tension in my body immediately softens at the sight.

"Bent—"

"Jazzy, I know this makes me sound like a total pussy, but can I hold you? I just need to feel you."

I nod. "Just be careful around my middle, okay? I'm still sore."

Without hesitation, Bentley stretches out beside me and wraps his arms around my upper body, tucking his face into the crook of my neck. Neither one of us says a word; we just sit there, taking comfort in each other's arms. I hug him as tightly as I can when I feel his silent tears dripping onto my skin, trickling down to my collarbone. What on earth is upsetting him so much? Who would've ever thought this guy, who's a clown more often than not, would break down like this?

I pull off his ball cap and comb my fingers through his closely cropped hair. "Bentley, what's going on in that head of yours?"

His fists clench around my hoodie. "I'm just so fucking glad you're okay. I *needed* you to be okay—I couldn't live with myself if you weren't."

I'm not sure what to say to that, so I just snuggle with him while he tries to control his sobbing. I don't know how long we lie in my bed, wrapped up in each other, before Bentley's softly snoring. I'm glad I put on an extra layer of clothing because it doesn't take long before his head is resting right over my breast, his mouth perilously close to my nipple. What is it with guys using boobs as pillows? It's not like mine are even all that cushiony.

I don't have the heart to wake him, and if I'm honest, cuddling with Bentley isn't exactly a hardship. I'm actually relieved I'm okay with being touched like this after what happened. The memory of that vile man's rough hands and lips all over my body makes my skin crawl. I was afraid I wouldn't be able to tolerate *anyone's* touch, regardless of how I felt about them. I relish in the comfort that provides, knowing I'll need to stockpile it for later. I have a feeling things are going to get a lot worse before they get better.

chapter six

JAZZ

"Well, isn't this sweet?"

My eyes flutter open and find Kingston standing in the open doorway to my bedroom, looking awfully pissed. Why am I so sweaty? A pressure on my chest causes me to look down. Oh yeah, that's right. There are over two hundred pounds of muscular man-boy lying on me. Bentley's head is still on my left breast, and his hand is cupping my right.

I nudge him. "Bentley, get up."

He squeezes my boob and mumbles, "I don't wanna. I like it here."

I don't have a chance to respond before

Kingston is pulling on the back of Bentley's shirt, hauling him off me. "Get up, asshole."

Bentley blinks rapidly, trying to clear the sleep fog. When he realizes what's happening, he glares at his friend. "Fuck you, dawg. I was comfy."

Kingston returns Bentley's glare. "Obviously. My question is, why the fuck are you here in the first place?"

Bentley stands to his full height, puffing his chest out. "I came to check on Jazzy Jazz."

Kingston lifts a brow. "And feel her up while she was sleeping?"

Bentley's eyes swing to me, panicked. "I wasn't feeling you up in your sleep. I mean...I guess I was, but I was sleeping, too. I didn't do it on purpose."

I smile softly. "I know, Bentley. It's fine."

He gives Kingston a cocky grin. "See? She likes it when I feel her up."

I shake my head at their ridiculous posturing. "That's not what I said, jackass."

If the hard set of Kingston's jaw is any indication, he doesn't find it nearly as amusing. "Get lost, Fitzgerald. I need to talk to Jazz, and your presence isn't required."

Bentley glances at me again. "Do you want me to leave you alone with this jerkoff, baby girl? Say the word, and I'll kick his ass to the curb so we can snuggle some more."

"Actually, Bent, I *would* like you to stay."

Bentley grins widely, showcasing his sexy as hell dimples. "Sure thing, babe." He approaches my bed with a little extra swagger, before taking the space beside me, folding his arms behind his head. His eyes twinkle with amusement as he taunts Kingston. "Nap time was fun. We should do it again *real soon*."

I'm pretty sure Kingston just growled before muttering, "Keep pushing it, motherfucker."

Kingston goes to shut the door, but I speak up before he gets the chance. "Leave it open."

"I'd rather not. Peyton saw me walking up the stairs, and she's definitely not happy I came to see you. Do you really want to make it easier for her to barge in here?"

I sigh. "Fine, but stay off my bed."

He scowls. "So, it's okay for Bentley, but not for me? Why's that?"

I'm not about to expose Bentley's emotional breakdown, so I shrug instead.

Kingston glowers and drops into the chair Bentley had occupied earlier. Why is it so sexy when a guy straddles a chair backward? It's not helping that Kingston's freshly showered and smells really good. Between the two of them, my whole damn room smells like hot guy.

"Why are you here, Kingston? I told you I needed time."

"We need to talk. It's been two goddamn weeks. I need to know what fucking happened in that forest from your point of view."

"The police know everything that happened. I don't really feel like rehashing it again."

"Quit being so damn stubborn. If you recall, I have access to resources the police don't."

"Like what?" I challenge.

"That part's not important." He shakes his head. "What *is* important is having as much information as possible so we can catch the guys who did this to you."

I rub my temples. "Kingston, if you want me to trust you, you've gotta give me something. You can't keep withholding information from me. I need a show of good faith."

"Jazz, like I told you before, I'm one of the few people you *can* trust. Why would I go out of my way to get you to a hospital if I wanted to hurt you?"

I know he has a point, but I'm getting so sick and tired of all this non-disclosure. This world—all these elitists—seems to be filled with nothing *but* secrets, lies, and cruelty.

"I appreciate what you did in that forest, Kingston. I really do. But I think my wariness is perfectly justified in this situation."

He studies me for a moment. "Fine, I'll give you something. I saw the police report, but I *know* you didn't tell them everything. What are you hiding, Jazz?"

I raise my brows. "How did you get a copy of the police report?"

"With those resources I mentioned earlier. Now, tell me what happened from your point of view. What *didn't* you tell the police?"

"Nuh-uh. You first. Explain that conversation we overheard." I glance in Bentley's direction. "Do you know what I'm referring to?"

He and Kingston share a loaded look before Bentley gives me a single nod in reply.

Kingston shakes his head. "That isn't something that I can just spit out, Jazz!"

"Why the hell not? Bentley knows!"

His jaw tics. "Because Bentley's been with me every step of the way! It's a lot of information that isn't easy to swallow, especially for you. Ask me something else. *Anything* else."

"Why did you have Bentley take me so far away from the house? What was so special about that spot?"

Kingston runs a hand through his hair, making it stand on end. "It was the closest dock to the house, not counting the one that leads to the boathouse. I'm not sure if you noticed, but I had a small speedboat tethered to it. I was planning to take you out on the water."

"Why not use the dock connected to the boathouse?"

He gives me a look as if I'm being dense. "Because the clearing under the dock leading up to the house is less than two feet at the deepest end. There's a slip on the front end of the house, but you can only get to it from *inside* the house. I didn't think you'd appreciate being dragged through an orgy, so I had my guy move it before anyone arrived."

"Your guy?"

"I have someone who runs errands and shit for me when I don't have time." Kingston shrugs.

"Like a gopher?"

He gives me a wry look. "Call him what you want, but I think of him more as a personal assistant."

What eighteen-year-old—who isn't in Hollywood—needs an assistant? Kingston Davenport, apparently.

"Unbelievable," I mutter. "Is this assistant one of your resources? Is he the guy you hired to look into my attack?"

He shakes his head. "I know a private investigator. He has a lot of contacts—in and out of law enforcement, hence the police report. This guy has a knack for getting information most people wouldn't have access to, including the cops."

I fold my arms over my chest. "And how exactly does he accomplish that?"

Kingston smirks. "I tend not to ask those questions. Plausible deniability and all that."

I pop an eyebrow. "In other words, this P.I. of yours obtains information through illegal means."

"I'm sure *some* of his methods are perfectly legal," Kingston argues. "Either way, it's his job to worry about how he gets the information. It's my job to pay him an obscene amount of money for that information."

"Why do you know a P.I., anyway?"

"Because information is power," he says matter-of-factly.

"Information about this thing you're keeping from me?"

"Among other things." He bites his lip, looking contemplative. "Can I say something?"

I take a deep breath and let it out. "Go ahead."

"I can't get the image of you lying on the ground, beaten and bloody out of my head. I can't stop imagining all the horrendous possibilities of what you went through. It's all I think about, day and night. It's fucking eating me alive, Jazz—all these what-ifs. *I need to know what really happened.*"

My head snaps up when he barely chokes out that last sentence. The commanding tone I've come to associate with Kingston Davenport is nowhere to be found. His voice is shaky, unsure. My chest aches when I hear the agony bleeding through his words. I know it costs him a lot to have this conversation in front of Bentley. As close as these two are, I don't get the impression they like showing vulnerability to *anyone.*

I think about Bentley asking me whether or not I was raped. How relieved he was when I refuted it. The last time I saw Bent was before my attack, so the only way he could've known it was a possibility was if Kingston had mentioned it. Is that what Kingston is so worried about? Does he think I lied to cops about it for some reason? The way he's looking at me right now—waiting on bated breath —tells me it might be.

"Tell him, baby girl," Bentley says softly. "He needs to know."

"I wasn't raped."

Kingston closes his eyes and takes a few deep breaths, muttering something under his breath. When he opens them again, he asks, "What *did* happen?"

"Everything that's on the report is what actually happened, Kingston. I didn't lie about anything if that's what you're thinking. I just didn't give them *all* the information."

Kingston frowns. "So, what—"

I hold my hand up. "It's late, and I'm fucking exhausted. I'd really like to go back to sleep now."

Bentley kisses me on the cheek and gets off the bed. "I guess that's my cue to bounce. Text if you need anything."

"Thanks, Bentley."

Bentley pauses in the doorway. "You coming, man?"

Kingston barely spares him a glance. "In a minute."

Bentley nods. "I'll wait out front. We need to talk. Bye, Jazzy Jazz."

Kingston waits until Bentley shuts the door behind him before speaking again. "Why are you hiding something from me? Withholding vital information could prevent us from catching the fuckheads who did this to you."

Because I can't ignore the doubt those men have instilled in me. If I tell you what they said, I have to face the fact that it might be true.

I try shaking off the memory, but it doesn't work.

Your precious boyfriend doesn't give a shit about you...sweet-talking you out of your panties was all part of the plan.

I suppress a shiver. "I don't think it's relevant information. I just spoke with the detective this afternoon. The police are actively working the case. I'm sure they'll figure it out."

"Oh, really? And how many leads do they have so far?"

I bite my bottom lip. "Well, none. *Yet*. But you already know that, don't you?"

"C'mon, Jazz. Deep down, you know you can trust me. You know I can *help*. You don't have to do this alone."

He seems so sincere, and I desperately want to believe this man had nothing to do with my attack, but I'm scared. I don't *ever* want to be that vulnerable again, and Kingston Davenport is probably the one person on Earth who has the power to obliterate every one of my walls.

"Kingston..." I rub at the kink in my neck. "I need more time to process my thoughts."

His Cavill-esque jaw tics as he considers that for a few moments. "How was your follow up with the doctor this morning?"

I blink rapidly from the sudden change in topic. "How did you know I had a doctor's appointment this morning?"

He gives me a wry look. "Really?"

I shake my head. "Ah, your stalker tendencies. How could I forget?"

"I'm not stalking you; I'm trying to keep you safe."

I raise my brows. "Sounds like something a stalkery stalker would say."

His eyes narrow. "Can you be serious for a minute?"

"Who says I'm not serious?"

"Christ, Jazz!" He scrubs a hand over his face. "*I'm not the goddamn enemy!* Quick picking stupid fights with me and just answer the damn question."

Is that what I'm doing? Ah, crap.

"*Fine.* The stitches came out, which was a relief because they itched like crazy. My wrist is healing well. I go back in a week, and the doctor said if all goes according to plan, he'll clear me to return to school then." I cross my arms. "Anything else you'd like to say before you G-T-F-O?"

His hazel eyes narrow. "I really don't like you staying here."

I prop a hand on my hip. "As I've already told you, I have nowhere else to go. I'm not crashing at your place, Kingston."

He releases a heavy sigh. "I'm coming back in the morning, and we *are* going to talk about this some more."

"You have classes in the morning."

He lifts an eyebrow in challenge. "I don't give a fuck."

"Haven't you missed enough school lately?"

"So have you."

I huff. "I'm not going to have your inability to graduate on my conscience."

Kingston gives me a smug look. "I have a 4.3 GPA and got a 1560 on my SATs. I think I'll be fine."

I knew he was smart, but *damn.* Kingston smirks

as he stands, and the sight of it makes my lady bits take notice. Nope, not going there.

I sigh. "Are you ready to stop hiding what you know? One hundred percent full disclosure?"

Kingston opens my bedroom door. "If that's what you need, then that's what I'll do."

"Just…give me a week. If the police don't have a suspect by then, I'll tell you everything."

Hopefully, by then, I'll have the guts to tell him.

His lips thin. "Fine. A week *max*. Then all bets are off."

I don't even get the chance to reply before he's out the door.

chapter
seven

KINGSTON

Peyton's waiting for me at the end of the hallway. Unless I want to shove her down the entire flight of stairs, I have to indulge whatever bullshit she's about to spew. As tempting as pushing her is, I don't feel like going to jail today. Or *ever*, for that matter.

"How's Jasmine?"

My eyebrows raise. "Do you really care?"

Her glossy pink lips turn up in the corners. "Not really."

"Then why'd you ask, Peyton? I don't have time for this."

"Just curious." She shrugs, trying to project indifference, but I'm not buying it. "So...my birthday is in two weeks. It falls on a Saturday this year."

"And?"

"*And* I'm having a party, remember? I mean, duh, of course, you do. It's my big one-eight. I've been planning it, like, literally *forever*."

"Get to the fucking point."

Peyton twirls a strand of long, blonde hair around her index finger. "I just wanted to make sure you knew you're still invited. What better time to put all this drama behind us and formally announce we're back together?"

This bitch is even more delusional than I thought. "Not interested." I try stepping past her, but she blocks me.

Her blue eyes narrow into slits. "Kingston, think *very carefully* about this. You have one last chance."

"One last chance for *what?*"

Her nose turns up. "To apologize for your behavior. To beg for my forgiveness. To put all this nonsense with that crack whore in the past."

My molars grind together. "*Move*, Peyton."

"You're going to regret this, Kingston."

I step forward and get right in her face. "The only thing I regret is every minute I ever spent with you. Now, fucking move before I *make you* move."

"You're an asshole!"

I scoff. "That's hardly news. Final warning, Peyton. *Move.*"

Peyton shifts her body so I can pass, but she's still close enough that her tits rub against my arm as I walk by. That stunt is no doubt, intentional on her end, and annoying as fuck on mine. I'm beginning to think she'll never get the hint. It's not like I've been subtle about the fact that I despise her.

"Just remember that whatever happens from this point, is *your* fault, Kingston. *You* asked for this! What happened to Jasmine at the lake is *nothing* compared to what *will* happen if you continue pushing me away."

I stop halfway down the stairs and turn around. "You have something to confess, Peyton?"

I'd suspected Peyton hired someone to attack Jazz from the start, but I didn't think she was stupid enough to admit it.

She folds her arms across her chest. "I suppose we'll see now, won't we?"

I laugh. "Wow...you're even dumber than I thought if you think I'll respond to one of your threats. Keep in mind, whatever you may throw at me—or anyone I care about—my retribution will *always* be ten times worse. Do your worst, Peyton.

I'd love to watch you squirm when it's time for payback."

I'm fairly certain her cheeks have paled, but she's wearing too much makeup for me to know for sure. "You don't scare me."

I continue my trek down the stairs without looking back. "We'll see about that."

Peyton releases a shrill scream as I make my way out the front door. Bentley's leaning against his car, waiting for me.

"Was that Peyton screeching like a banshee?" He jerks his chin toward the house.

"Yep. She's being especially extra today." I pull my phone out of my pocket and text my P.I., telling him to add a tail to Peyton as well. He's already watching her mom but hasn't come across anything suspicious yet. "What'd you want to talk about?"

"Do you really need to ask?"

My jaw clenches as I flip the door open on my Agera. It fucking pisses me off that Jazz can so readily trust this joker's ass but not me. "What about her?"

"She gonna be okay in that house?

I rub a hand over my jaw. "I don't like it—the Callahans are high on my list of suspects. But Jazz is a stubborn shit, so I'm paying Frank to keep an eye on her until I can convince her to stay with me. He can't be with her all the time, but it's better than nothing." I'm careful to speak low enough, so we can't be overheard.

He raises an eyebrow. "Frank? As in, the driver?"

"He used to be a bodyguard for some of Hollywood's elite, so he has the skills I need."

"No, shit?" Bentley muses. "I guess that explains why he's built like a tank. Why'd he switch careers?"

I shrug. "He became a dad a couple of years ago. The kid lives with his mom, but Frank has regular visitation. If I had to guess, I'd say he wanted a job that didn't require so much travel or carry so much risk."

"Makes sense," Bentley agrees. "How do *you* know all this?"

"How do you think?"

He rolls his eyes. "Right. Sometimes I forget about all the people you have on payroll."

"I don't have that luxury," I mutter. "You hungry? I could go for a burger."

"Bruh, you should know by now that I'll never turn down a burger."

"In-N-Out?"

Bentley opens the door to his Porsche and slides in the driver's seat. "Was that a real question?"

I laugh. "Not really. I'll meet you there."

He gives me a smartass salute before shifting into gear and pulling away. The hairs on the back of my neck stand on end, so I glance up, and sure enough, I spot Jazz leaning against her bedroom window, looking down at me. We have one of our strange silent conversations where my eyes say that I'm not giving up until she gives in. Her eyes are telling me she's going to make me work for it. I smirk as I get into my car and push the ignition button.

Bring it on, baby.

"How's Jazz?" Ainsley asks.

"Okay, all things considered."

"I can't believe you went over there after she specifically asked you not to. You're such a jerk."

"Tell me something I don't know."

Ainsley shoves a few fries into her mouth and chews them before speaking again. "Thanks for the food. Rehearsal was intense tonight. I'm starving, and I really didn't feel like waiting for delivery."

Our dad, the cheap bastard that he is, excuses the entire staff whenever he leaves town. I rarely eat in the main house, so I'm used to fending for myself, but Ainsley isn't. If our chef, Luis, has the day off, she usually orders takeout or is here, mooching off me. She's the reason I have so much damn chick food in my fridge.

"You know I'll always take care of you, baby sis." I pull her into a headlock and mess up her hair to punctuate my statement.

"Ugh! Get off me, dickface!"

I laugh as she tries—unsuccessfully, I might add—smoothing down her hair. "You love it when I fuck with you."

"No, I *don't*. Don't make me sic Reed on you."

"Don't even get me started on that nonsense."

Ainsley narrows her eyes. "*What* nonsense?"

"You and Reed," I clarify. "I don't like it."

When one of my closest friends told me he wanted to date my sister, let's say I wasn't very gracious about it. Unfortunately, my twin doesn't really give a shit what I think, and Reed is so goddamn enamored with her, he doesn't either. They're just lucky I have plenty of other things to worry about, so I'm not fighting them. But if he winds up hurting her, best friend or not, I'm going to beat his ass.

"I don't really care." Ainsley turns up her pert nose. "Besides...technically, there is no me and Reed. *Yet.*"

Well, that's news to me. You'd never know it by how often they're making fuck-me eyes at each other.

"Explain."

She shrugs. "Don't get your hopes up. There *will* be a me and Reed. We just haven't had any formal discussions or...you know, screwed each other's brains out, to make it official yet."

"Oh, Christ," I gag. "I do *not* want to hear about your sex life, Ains. Especially when Reed is involved."

Ainsley laughs. "You asked."

I point at her. "I did *not* ask. For future reference, I *never* want to hear about your sex life. *Ever.*"

My sister scoffs. "Don't be a child. We're legal adults, and it's perfectly okay to have a healthy sex life, whether you're male or female. Besides, you're the one who lost his virginity at fourteen, four *years* before me, so you have no room to judge."

"I'm not judging." I hold my hands up in a

conciliatory gesture. "But I still don't want to hear about you fucking my best friend."

Reed's sexual preferences aren't exactly vanilla. The last thing I need is to think about him doing that shit with my sister.

"Speaking of best friends..." she says. "You talk to Bentley lately? I've been worried about him since everything went down with Jazz. I'm sure he's thinking about Carissa a lot right now."

I shrug. "He seems okay so far, but I'm keeping an eye on it."

Ainsley sighs. "Bentley tries hiding it, but I know it still hurts him pretty badly."

I swallow the lump in my throat. "Yeah, I know."

"When's the last time you saw him?"

"Right before I came home, actually. Ran into him at Jazz's house, and we got burgers after."

Her eyebrows lift. "What was Bentley doing at Jazz's?"

"He was fucking *taking a nap* with her."

Ainsley's hazel eyes widen so much, they look like they're about to pop out of her skull. "Seriously?"

"Yep." I pop the P at the end of the word.

I frown as the image of Bentley and Jazz

wrapped around each other darts into my head. It drives me crazy knowing there's a mutual attraction between them, and not just in a physical sense. Granted, it's not nearly as strong as the connection Jazz and I share, but it's there nonetheless.

Frankly, it's confusing as fuck because I want my best friend to be happy. After Carissa died, Bentley blamed himself and subsequently shut down his emotions almost entirely. Hell, he *still* blames himself, even though he has no reason to. Bent drowns himself in pussy, liquor, and weed on the regular to quiet all the shit running through his brain.

I was beginning to think he'd never allow himself to get close to another girl again until Jazz came along. It's been pretty fucking obvious from day one that Bent's smitten with her. The only problem with that is I have no intention of giving her up. Bentley's like a brother to me. I'd do almost anything for him, but I'm not bending on this. I *can't*.

My sister's lips quirk like she thinks this whole fucking thing is hilarious. "How did that go? I can't imagine you were pleased."

I stretch my neck from side to side, trying to alleviate the sudden tension. "How do you think it went? Bentley was his usual wiseass self, and Jazz was being obstinate as fuck."

Now Ainsley's full-on laughing. "Dude, you've got your work cut out for you with that one."

"Tell me about it." I bite the tip of my thumb.

"God, I love her," my sister says wistfully. "It's nice having another girl in the fold again."

A smile breaks free, despite my current irritation. Ainsley has trouble forming relationships with other women since she's not superficial and catty like most chicks we know. Jazz is her first friend since Carissa, and even though I was a dick about it at first, I'm glad she has someone to talk to about girly shit. She sure as hell will never get that from our dad's wives.

"I need you to do me a favor."

Her expression sobers. "What?"

"I need you to find out what happened at the lake. Jazz won't talk to me."

Ainsley shakes her head. "Kingston, I'm not going to be your spy."

"I'm not exactly asking you to," I assure her.

"What *exactly* are you trying to find out?"

I shrug. "Jazz already put my biggest fear at ease, confirming she wasn't raped, but nothing else."

Ainsley remains silent.

My eyes widen. "Did she tell you what happened?"

She shakes her head. "Not entirely. I do know some details, though."

"And you didn't think to share them with me?" I throw my hands up. "What the hell, Ainsley?"

"I'm not going to betray her trust, Kingston. Don't you think she's been through enough? You don't need all the details to know it was pretty freakin' traumatic."

"I *do* need the fucking details, Ains. How are we supposed to catch these guys if we have nothing to go off of? The police don't have any leads."

She eyes me curiously. "How do you know that? And how did you know there were two of them?"

I've shielded my sister from a lot of shit over the last two years, but I think it's about time to clue her in on some of it. I'll only tell her enough to keep her safe, though. Some things, she's better off being in the dark about.

I take a deep breath. "I hired a private investigator to look into it. He's been working on something for me for a while now, but he's also trying to find the fuckers who attacked Jazz."

"Why did you already have a P.I. working for you? What are you not telling me?"

"Something shady is going on between Dad and Charles Callahan. Possibly Madeline, too. They're too damn good at covering their tracks, though. I couldn't dig up shit on my own, so I hired the investigator to look into it."

"Something like *what*? And what happened to make you suspect them of doing something so sketchy in the first place?"

"Ains, I don't want to drag you into it until I have more evidence. Let's just say...I'm fairly certain they have a lucrative side business that's really messed up and highly illegal. Based on some recent information I've obtained, it's been going on for almost two decades, possibly longer."

Her eyes widen. "Like drugs?"

I shake my head. "Worse."

She stares at me for a moment. "What are you planning to do when you get the evidence you're looking for?"

"Put them away for life, where they belong."

Ainsley's jaw drops. "You'd put Dad in jail? I know he's a dick, but geez, Kingston, that's harsh. He's still the person who's half responsible for giving us life."

This is precisely why I haven't told her up until this point. Our dad has treated us like we're nothing more than an inconvenience our entire lives, but she still loves him for some reason. I, however, have not had that problem in a long time. Maybe not ever.

I rub my jaw. "Ains...I need you to trust me on this. I promise I will tell you everything soon."

Some might think it's a huge risk telling her anything, but I have no doubt my sister's loyalty lies with me when all is said and done.

She hangs her head. "Fine, I won't say anything about the Dad situation. As for Jazz, the best I'll do is try convincing her to talk to you."

"Thanks. John—my P.I.—got a copy of the police report, but I don't think it's telling the whole story. Something doesn't feel right."

Ainsley tilts her head to the side. "What do you mean?"

"I don't know." I shrug. "It's just a feeling I have."

"I'm seeing her this weekend, so I'll talk to her then. Since she's still supposed to lie low, we're just gonna order pizza and watch movies."

Well, well. Looks like the guys and I have a girls' night to crash. Jazz will want to string me up by the balls if I show up at her house before a full week has passed, but she's not likely to maim me with an audience, so I'll take my chances. She's about to see firsthand why my persistence *always* pays off.

If she had any doubts about the legitimacy of that statement, they'll be erased by this weekend.

chapter
eight

JAZZ

"Hey, chica!" Ainsley bursts into my room, two reusable grocery bags hanging off her arms.

"What's in the bags?"

She smiles. "What else? Chips, popcorn, candy. You can't watch a movie without loading up on copious amounts of junk food."

I chuckle. "I thought we were ordering pizza?"

"Already did," Ainsley replies. "One large pineapple and black olive for you—which is disgusting, by the way—and one triple pepperoni for me."

"Hey, don't knock it until you try it."

"Nope." She shakes her head. "Never gonna happen."

"It's your loss." I shrug.

Ainsley looks around the room. "So, where should I set up? DoorDash says the pizza should be here in about ten minutes."

"The main theater room is in the basement, but I really don't feel like going down two flights of stairs. If you don't mind lounging on a sectional, we can use the game room down the hall."

"Sounds good to me."

"I just need to pee real quick. Meet you there?" I slide out of bed and head toward my ensuite.

"Sure thing, Jazz."

When I finally make it into the game-room-slash-mini- theater-room, Ainsley is already playing the first movie. I smile when three black Honda Civics appear on the giant screen, their drivers on a mission to hijack a semi filled with electronics.

"God, I love this movie."

"Me too," Ainsley agrees. "If we play 'em back to back, we should have time to get through the first three installments before I need to jet."

I shake my head. "Nuh-uh. As far as I'm concerned, the second and third movies don't exist. We're going straight from the first to the fourth."

"I'll give you that." Ainsley laughs. "The only good thing that came out of either of those two movies was the addition of Ludacris' character.

"Totally," I agree.

I find a comfortable position and spread a fuzzy blanket over my legs. Just as I'm reaching for the bag of popcorn Ainsley had set between us, the door bursts open.

"Somebody order pizza? The delivery guy arrived right after me. Talk about perfect timing."

My head swings around to find Bentley standing in the doorway, two boxes of pizza in his arms.

"What the heck are you doing here?" Ainsley took the words right out of my mouth.

Bentley takes a few steps forward, and right behind him are his two besties. Ainsley's grin stretches across her face as she spots Reed. I'm pretty sure I have the exact opposite expression on my face as I look at Kingston.

Bentley sets the pizza on the coffee table, flips the lid, and grabs a slice of pineapple olive. "Why else would I be here? I heard we're watching movies."

"Hey!" I shout. "That's mine."

He takes a huge bite, plops down on the middle of the couch, and makes a funny face as he chews. "That shit's nasty."

I roll my eyes. "Here's a solution: Don't eat my damn pizza."

Bentley starts picking off the olives and flicking them into the box. "Nah, this works."

While Bentley and I are arguing about the pizza, Reed sets the drinks down and takes a seat next to Ainsley. The only remaining spot on the couch is to my right, which Kingston quickly occupies, effectively wedging me between him and Bentley.

Great.

"So much for giving me time," I mutter.

Kingston's stupidly full lips tilt up in the corners. "One of these days, you'll learn patience is not my virtue."

"Oh, trust me, I'm already well aware of that."

Now he's full-on grinning. "Then what's the problem?"

I shoot daggers at him with my eyes. "*You.* You are my problem. I swear I've mentioned this before."

Bentley swings his arm over my shoulders. "Pull them claws back in, kitty. C'mon, what's the big deal? We're all just here to chill and watch some movies. Hell, I'll even order more food, so you don't have to worry about sharing your gross-ass pizza."

"My pizza is not gross," I pout.

Bentley laughs. "Whatever you say, baby girl."

"Don't patronize me, Bent."

He presses a palm to his chest and gasps. "I would *never*. I'm just sayin', if you want to make out with me during the movie, could you maybe pop a mint first?"

I give him my best stink-eye. "Don't worry, Bentley, my mouth won't be getting anywhere near yours."

"We'll see about that." He winks.

Kingston reaches over me and smacks Bentley on the back of the head. "Shut up, asshole."

Bentley rubs the back of his head. "Dick move, bro."

Kingston narrows his eyes. "Keep your hands to yourself, and we won't have a problem."

Bentley shakes his head and mutters something under his breath.

"Uh, guys," Ainsley interrupts. "Can you pause the sword fighting so we can watch the movie?"

Kingston gets off the couch and flips the overhead lights off.

"Hey! What'd you do that for?" I ask.

He falls back onto the cushion beside me. "There was a glare on the screen."

No, there wasn't, but I keep my mouth shut because I'm sick of missing the show. I do my best to focus on the fast cars and man candy on the screen, ignoring the idiots on either side of me. Sadly, I'm only doing a half-assed job because Kingston's woodsy cologne smells way too mouth-watering. I actually sniffed him at one point, but he didn't call me on it if he noticed.

Halfway into the third movie, I get fidgety because I really need to stretch out, but the sectional isn't large enough. It's supposed to seat eight, but the three giant boys and their incessant need to manspread take up a large chunk of space. After several pathetic attempts to rotate my body, I finally give up with a huff.

Kingston leans into my ear. "What's wrong?"

"I can't find a comfortable position."

"Would lying down help?"

"Probably." I shrug. "But there's not enough room to do that."

"Sure there is," he insists. "Put your head on my lap and lie down."

I snort. "I am *not* putting my head in your lap, Kingston."

"I wasn't asking you to suck me off, Jazz. I'm just trying to help." His face is illuminated enough to see the heat burning behind his eyes as if he's visualizing me doing exactly that.

Nope, not gonna go there.

"Thanks, but no thanks."

"Bent, scoot your ass over," Kingston demands. "Jazz needs to lie down."

Bentley smiles. "You can lie on me anytime, Jazzy."

Kingston pulls the throw pillow out from under his arm and chucks it at Bentley. "She can lay her head on that. *On the couch.*"

I eye the pillow longingly. "There's still not enough room."

Kingston pats his thighs. "Put your head on the damn pillow and throw your legs over my lap."

"Fine," I mutter, carefully laying on my side and stretching out. I'd hate to admit it, but this is much more comfortable.

Kingston adjusts the blanket, so it's still covering my body and rests his hands by my ankles. "This PG enough for you?"

The position is perfectly innocuous, but my hormones haven't gotten the memo.

"Yep." I turn my attention back to the screen where there's a ridiculous, implausible, yet totally awesome chase scene.

Kingston's thumb is rubbing circles right above my ankle, which is becoming increasingly more difficult to ignore. Heat is blooming beneath my skin, causing a dull ache between my thighs. I don't know if I'll ever understand this connection he and I share. Kingston's hardly touching me for fuck's sake, but I feel like I'm melting into a puddle of need. It's like there's this inherent bond between us, something that transcends logic. It's even worse now that we've had sex. Knowing what it feels like to have him moving inside of me, the sound he makes when he comes, I'm practically salivating at the thought of doing it again.

But that's not going to happen, I remind myself. Kingston's hiding something from me—*several* somethings—and until I know what that is, I can't possibly consider trusting him, let alone having any relationship with him. Those niggling doubts in my head will never go away while there are so many unknown factors. Why was he so intent on pushing me away at first? Why did he feel it was necessary to bully me, humiliate me, *take incriminating pictures* of me? God, that in itself should be an unforgivable offense, but oddly, it's the least of my worries.

I want to know what he's hiding about our parents and why he thinks I couldn't handle it. The conversation we overheard between our fathers goes against everything I know about my mom. Sure, she didn't have the best taste in men—Jerome and my father being great examples—but she wasn't promiscuous. Hell, the *only* time I saw her with a man during my childhood was her brief relationship with Jerome.

When I was fifteen, maybe sixteen, I asked my mom why she never dated, and she told me that Belle and I came first. She worked so hard to support us, she was so focused on ensuring we grew up to be strong, independent women, it left no time for anything else. It just doesn't make any sense that she would have ongoing casual sex with two considerably older men who she had nothing in common with.

I'm so lost in my head that I don't even realize the movie had ended until Ainsley got up to flip the lights back on. I blink rapidly as my eyes adjust to the brightness before carefully sitting up. Out of habit, I start cleaning up the food mess, but Bentley slaps my hand away and takes over.

"You look wiped, baby girl. The boys and I will get this before we take off."

I didn't realize it before now, but I am pretty tired. Usually, I wouldn't be so sleepy at ten o'clock, but recovering from multiple injuries isn't exactly normal for me.

"You sure?"

Bentley frames my face with his large hands and smacks a kiss on my forehead. "Positive. Go to bed, and we'll see ourselves out."

"Thanks, Bent."

I can feel Kingston waiting for my attention, but I address Ainsley first.

"Thanks for the movie night idea."

"Of course. Do you still want to hang out tomorrow?" She looks at each one of the guys pointedly. "Without these interlopers?"

"Hey!" Bentley says. "That was a little rude, don't you think?"

Reed is his usual silent and stoic self, only giving a slight smirk in response. Kingston gives his sister a middle-fingered salute.

Ainsley props a hand on her hip. "What's *rude* is interrupting our night. Which *won't* happen again. Jazz and I need to have some good old-fashioned girl talk, and we can't do that with you idiots present."

"Whatevs," Bentley pouts.

I jerk my head toward the hall as I face Kingston. "I assume you're waiting to speak with me alone?"

One side of Kingston's mouth kicks up in the corner. "Maybe I want to tuck you in."

"Not happening. But if you have something to say, walk with me." I give Ainsley, Bentley, and Reed a single wave. "'Night, guys."

"'Night," they all reply in unison.

Kingston waits until we're inside my room with the door shut before speaking. "Has Peyton given you any trouble?"

I shake my head. "I haven't seen her once since I've been home from the hospital. Why?"

He scrubs a hand over his jaw. "She said something concerning the last time I was here."

"Like what?" I head into my closet and pull some clothing out of the drawer.

"She implied she might've had something to do with your attack."

I drop my sleep shorts on the ground. "Are you shitting me?"

"She didn't outright admit anything. It could've been a baseless threat, but I'm having my P.I. keep a closer eye on her just in case. You need to tell me what happened, Jazz. If it makes you more comfortable, I can arrange for John—that's my P.I.—to be there when you do."

Kingston steps into my closet, picks up my fallen pajamas and hands them to me. He briefly looks over my shoulder and seems lost in thought. I turn my head and see nothing but a stark white wall. The same wall where I climbed him like a tree and let him finger me. Aw, hell. Now I'm thinking about it.

He smirks, obviously picking up on my train of thought. "Good memories in this closet."

I hold my hand out, shaking my head. "Nuh-uh. Don't do that."

The jackass laughs. "Do what? I didn't *do* anything."

I swirl my finger in his direction. "You're not going to charm me with your sexy smirky smirk. You owe me answers, buddy, and I refuse to wait any longer. Once I get those, I'll tell you what happened."

"So, you think I'm sexy?"

I'm pretty sure I actually growl. "Not the point, asshole."

He takes a moment, stretching his neck from side to side before he answers. "Fine. But we meet at my house. I have something I need to show you."

I narrow my eyes in suspicion. "If that *something* is in your pants, keep it to yourself."

Kingston steps forward, crowding me against

the built-in dresser in the center of the closet. "We both know you don't *really* mean that Jazz, but don't worry; I can control myself if you can."

I stare him right in the eye. "I can *definitely* control myself."

He steps back and looks me over, making no effort to disguise his thirst. "Fine, then it's settled. You feel well enough to come over tomorrow after you hang with Ains?"

"Yeah." I nod. "I can hitch a ride with her when we're done."

Kingston raps his knuckles on the doorframe. "Just text when you're on your way."

"Okay."

"One more thing. Pack a bag. It's going to take a while, so you're staying over. And before you say it, I can sleep on the couch."

I shake my head. "I never agreed to that."

"I didn't ask." He flashes a wicked smile and walks out of the room without another word.

Cocky jackass.

chapter nine

KINGSTON

"I have the equipment. When can we meet up?"

John thinks we should install a surveillance camera in my dad's corporate office because he's not getting anything useful from the bugs we placed in the home office. Since Monique, Davenport Boating's head receptionist, is freakishly vigilant, placing the camera falls on my shoulders since I'm one of the few people who can get past her desk without an invitation or appointment. I need to somehow get into Charles Callahan's office, too, but there never seems to be an opportunity. Ms. Williams lives in the Callahan house full time, and I swear the woman never leaves.

"I've got something going on tonight, but I can do it tomorrow. Same place?"

"That works," John answers. "One o'clock, okay?"

"Yep. See you then."

I hang up the call and open my GPS tracker app. Ainsley's car is only about a mile away, so I head to the front of the main house. When my sister initially said she was spending the day with Jazz, I had assumed they'd lie low since Jazz is still recovering. What I hadn't counted on was the fact that they'd go to Ainsley's ballet studio. They're right around the corner now, so I tuck my phone into my pocket and wait for them to pull up.

I originally installed the tracker on their phones for safety purposes—okay, maybe a *slightly* different reason on Jazz's—but I have to admit, it's come in handy outside of that. Even if they're perfectly safe, it eases my mind knowing where they're at considering all the shady shit up in the air. I thought for sure Jazz would throw a fit when she found out I had installed it, but since the tracker had proven useful when Peyton cornered her in the bathroom, she's logical enough to see its value. I rarely check it, but since I hadn't heard from Jazz as expected, my paranoia got the best of me.

I hear the roar of the Huracan's engine shortly before they pull into the driveway. Ainsley spots me before she makes it to the garage, so she rolls the car to a stop and shifts into park.

Rolling down her window, she says, "What are you doing?"

"Waiting for you." I bend low, so I can make eye contact with Jazz. "You were supposed to text when you were on your way."

"Why?" she sasses. "So you could clear your groupies out of the house?"

I give her a half-cocked smile. "Careful, babe. Your jealousy is showing."

Jazz's gorgeous brown eyes roll back. "I'd have to *care* to be jealous."

Ainsley rubs her temples. "Oh my God, you two. Do you ever stop? You'd think finally screwing each other would get this out of your systems." She turns her head toward Jazz, then to me. "Or maybe you need to screw *again* because that's the only way you can tolerate each other."

"I'm open to testing that theory. What do you say, Jazz?"

Jazz scoffs. "Uh, no, thanks."

I laugh. "Don't pretend you didn't love it when I—"

"Don't say it!" Ainsley shouts.

I look down at my sister. "Not so fun being on the other end of it, is it?"

The impertinent little shit gives me the finger.

I round the car and try opening the passenger door, but it's locked. "Unlock the door."

Jazz flashes a toothy grin through the window as she mouths, "No."

Ainsley throws her hands up and mutters something before hitting the button from the master control panel. The second the door is unlocked, I swing it open.

"Get out of the car, Jazz."

Jazz turns toward my sister and grumbles, "Traitor."

"Oh, for fuck's sake, Jazz, the whole reason you're here is to talk to him, so go *talk to him*."

"Yeah, Jazz, come *talk* to me."

She gets out of the car and slams the door shut. Ainsley wastes no time shifting into gear and pulling into the garage, leaving Jazz standing in front of the house with me.

"Where's your bag?" I ask.

She parks a hand on her hip. "I didn't bring one."

"Suit yourself." I shrug. "You won't hear me complaining if you want to sleep naked."

I can see her bronzed cheeks pinken under the outdoor lighting. "I won't be sleeping here *at all*. Ainsley offered to drive me home when we're done."

I slant my head to the left, ignoring her comment. We can save that argument for later. "There's a path to my place along the side of the house. Can you walk on uneven ground?"

Jazz straightens her shoulders. "I'm fine."

As we start walking, I can tell she's doing her best to hide her discomfort. This girl won't let anything hold her down, and it's hot as fuck. I rub a hand over my mouth to hide my smile because I suspect Jazz will take it the wrong way and give me even more attitude. Even though her feistiness turns me on, I need to deescalate the situation because what I'm about to tell her is likely going to birth a whole plethora of messy emotions.

Jazz looks around when we enter the pool house, making me realize she's never been here before. It's nothing special—just a standard guest house you'd find on any property around here—but every square inch is mine to do as I please, and that's important to me. Having my own security system is a nice perk, especially considering all the digging I'm doing into our fathers' activities. I moved out here right before my freshman year, and I haven't missed the luxuries of the main house one bit.

Jazz walks throughout the open space, cataloging the small kitchen and living room. I don't like a lot of clutter, so the furnishings I do have are minimal, but they're plush and built for comfort. It takes every ounce of willpower I possess not to fantasize about all the dirty things I'd like to do to her as she ventures into my bedroom. I will my dick to calm the fuck down because I'm wearing sweatpants, which would do a shit job hiding an erection.

I'm not an idiot; I know damn well that nothing physical is going to happen between us anytime soon. I may be an asshole, but I'm not going to make a move on a woman while she's recovering from a traumatic event. Sure, I give her crap and throw around all sorts of innuendo, but that's because I think Jazz needs that normalcy right now. I can't imagine all the horrible shit running through her head, and I know what I tell her tonight is only going to make that worse.

That's exactly why I was trying to delay this conversation as long as possible, but she's left me no other choice. Finding out who attacked Jazz is the most pressing issue at the moment, and if she needs me to answer some questions before she'll answer mine, so be it. Jazz heads back into the living area and lowers herself to the couch while I walk over to the kitchen and open the fridge.

I hold up a bottle of water. "You want one?"

"Sure." When I hand it to her, she adds, "Thanks."

I take a seat on the cushion next to her. I kept going back and forth on where to begin with this and finally settled on the very beginning.

"What do you know about your mom's childhood?"

Jazz frowns. "Um...basic stuff, I guess. She had kind of a crappy one, so she didn't talk about it much. She was a firm believer in the old adage, 'You can't create the future if you're all wrapped up in the past'."

I turn my body toward hers. "When you say, 'crappy', how so?"

"I'm confused as to why this matters."

"I'm getting there," I assure her. "Just go with it."

Jazz captures her lower lip between her teeth as she thinks about it. "Well, I know she bounced around the foster system. The woman who gave birth to her was really young when my mom was born—like fourteen, I think. She relinquished her parental rights before she even left the hospital. I'm not sure my mom ever knew why she was abandoned or why she was never adopted." She takes a big gulp of water. "Why are you asking me this?"

I set my water on the end table. "I'll be right back. I need to grab something out of my closet."

Jazz scrunches her brows. "Um...okay."

I grab the photo album I need and flip through it until I find the picture I was looking for. With my thumb bookmarking the page, I take a seat on the couch again.

Jazz points to the photo album. "What's that?"

"A photo album."

"Obviously. An older one, from the looks of it. You can't distract me with your cute baby pictures, Kingston."

"I'm flattered you assume I was a cute baby—which is one hundred percent accurate—but that's not why I have it."

She sighs. "Will you please get to the point?"

I take a deep breath before flipping the album open. I carefully peel back the protective layer and extract the photo of our moms.

I hand the photo to Jazz. "Look at that."

Jazz slams a hand over her mouth to cover her loud gasp. Her eyes widen, and her other hand trembles as she looks at a picture of our mothers standing next to each other with three toddlers at their feet.

After a moment, she finally speaks. "What the hell is this? Where did you get it?"

I point to the beautiful blonde on the left. "*That* is Jennifer Wilkes-Davenport. Also known as my mom."

Jazz's eyes are quickly filling with tears. "Why are *your* mom and *my* mom in a picture together?" She holds up the photo. "That little girl on the right is *me*."

"And the two on the left are Ainsley and me."

She shakes her head. "I don't understand. It has to be doctored or something."

"Jazz, there's no doubt in my mind it's an original. That album has been hidden away in my closet for the last nine *years*."

Her face softens as she traces her mom's image with her index finger. "Do you have a better explanation?"

"I do." I nod. "When I first ran into that photo, I was nine, maybe ten years old. I asked my dad who the other woman and child were, and he said it was one of my mom's old friends and her daughter. He tried taking the picture away from me—which in retrospect was really weird—but I found it on his desk a while later and stole it back."

"Our moms were friends?"

I gesture to the picture. Both women have their arms around each other in a side hug. "I'd say yes based on their smiles and body language."

"That makes no sense. How can our moms hang out with each other when we were kids when my father didn't know I existed until recently? My mom told me so herself—she left when she was pregnant without ever telling him." She studies the picture again. "Holy shit!"

"What?"

She points to the sliding glass door in the background. "That's the door leading to Charles' back yard. This photo was taken at his house."

I already knew that, so I simply nod in agreement.

Jazz pinches the bridge of her nose. "Please tell me you have an explanation because now I have even *more* questions."

I grab her hand. "Jazz, look at me." I wait until her eyes meet mine before continuing. "What do you remember from our little eavesdropping adventure?"

If she thinks about it, the conversation we overheard between our fathers proves they both knew about Mahalia's pregnancy.

Her brown eyes widen as it hits her. "Oh, my God. *They lied*—both Charles and my mom. He knew about me all along, didn't he?"

I nod my head. "Yeah, he did. I'm pretty sure Madeline knew, too. John, my P.I., dug up tax records proving your mom worked at the mansion as a live-in maid shortly before you were born until you were two or three years old. Madeline and Peyton would've moved in somewhere in the middle of that timeframe. I can't imagine she'd allow someone else's child to live in that house without good reason."

"But why would my mom hide that? She already told me he wasn't a good man, so why wouldn't she be honest about *when* she left?"

I shrug. "If I had to guess, I'd say she was trying to protect you. The less you knew, the better."

"What am I missing? There has to be more to this story."

"There is."

Here we go.

chapter ten

KINGSTON

"I don't know how to say this, other than just saying it, so..." I fill my lungs with air before releasing my breath. "I'm fairly certain our dads run some kind of sex trafficking ring and have been for a very long time."

Jazz blinks rapidly. "O-kay...that's...wow, um...that's *really* fucked up. But what does that have to do with my mom?"

My lips thin. "Because I think your mom was directly...affected by it."

I can see the wheels turning in her head. "You think she was their *victim*?"

I nod solemnly. "I do."

"Holy shit. The conversation we overheard

between them makes so much sense now." Jazz's voice is barely above a whisper.

I gulp when I see her eyes water. "Yeah, it does."

"But why would my mom stick around for so long if she was being abused? Why would they just let her go? Wouldn't they worry about her turning them in? Or did she escape somehow? God, if this is true, that means the only reason I exist is because my mom was *repeatedly raped* by that sick bastard." Jazz places a hand over her stomach. "I feel like I'm going to throw up."

I scoot closer, risking the potential vomit to wipe her tears away with my thumbs. "I have some ideas about part of it, but nothing has been confirmed."

"What kinds of ideas? Don't sex traffickers keep their victims isolated in dank places, or sell them off to the highest bidder? If she truly was their prisoner, why was she living in a multi-million dollar mansion? Why was she allowed to befriend your mom? She looks *happy* in that picture." Jazz gasps. "Oh my God, what if she wasn't a victim, but she was actually working *with* them? I can't believe she'd do something like that, though. I'm so confused."

I grab her hand. "Hey. There's *no* way she was

working *with* them, Jazz, so get that out of your head right now."

She frowns. "But how can you be so sure?"

"Because she fits the victim profile *perfectly*. Young, beautiful, no money, no family. John says your mom was listed as a runaway a few months before she turned eighteen and aged out of the system. Based on when you were born, that'd be about the same time she got pregnant, which means she already knew Charles."

"But why does she look so happy in this picture?" Jazz waves the photo around. "She looks *healthy*. Definitely not like someone who was being abused."

"That's the part I'm still working on. One thing I've learned over the last two years is that sex trafficking comes in many forms. If that is what they're doing—and like I said, I'm fairly certain it *is*—then it's a pretty sophisticated operation. They have to somehow be hiding their activities behind a legitimate business; they're too clean. John is *excellent* at what he does, and he can't find a single piece of evidence linking them to a crime. He suspects some influential people are suppressing evidence to save their own asses."

Jazz pulls back and tilts her chin up to look at

me. "You've been looking into this for two *years*? But why? What made you suspect them in the first place?"

"A lot of little things that started to add up, but a conversation with my grandfather—on my mom's side— was the catalyst."

She scoots back against the arm of the couch. "How so?"

"Ainsley and I flew to San Francisco to visit our grandfather shortly before he died, which was just over two years ago. He had colon cancer and wanted to see his only heirs before he passed. We didn't spend a lot of time with him growing up, so we weren't close, but I think Ains and I needed a chance to say goodbye because he was the only link we had to our mom beside each other." I swallow the lump in my throat. "We never got the chance to say goodbye to her."

Jazz's eyes are filled with sympathy as she listens.

"Anyway...one day, he told me we needed to talk. Man to man. He proceeded to tell me how he felt about my father; he never liked him, didn't trust him from day one. He thought my dad was only after her money. My father comes from wealth, spanning several generations back on the Davenport side. But my mom was the sole heir to one of the world's largest luxury hotel chains. Her family's money makes my dad's bank accounts look like pocket change.

"According to my grandfather, when my parents started dating, he tried putting a stop to it. He knew something wasn't right. My dad was literally old enough to be *her* father, and they seemed to have nothing in common. Unfortunately, Preston Davenport can be pretty damn charming when he wants to be, and she fell for it. Got pregnant early into their relationship. Once she found out they were having twins, she agreed to marry him.

"The honeymoon phase didn't last long, though. I was eight when she died, so it isn't too clear, but even in my earliest memories, I can easily recall how vastly different their personalities were. How often they argued. My grandfather told me she was planning to leave him right before she died. She was going to take Ainsley and me away from here and move to San Francisco, where she grew up.

"She called my grandfather one day, told him he was right all along; her husband was a liar. My mom confessed to learning something awful about my dad's business dealings. She claimed she filed a police report, detailing everything she knew, so she had to take the kids and get out as fast as possible.

When my grandfather asked her to explain, she promised she'd tell him everything once she arrived in the Bay Area." I rub the tension at the back of my neck. "She never got the chance because she died later that day."

Jazz isn't even trying to stifle her tears anymore, and it's killing me. "How did she die?"

I unclench my jaw. "The official cause of death is drowning, but a toxicology report showed she had a large amount of heroin in her system. Police concluded she shot up a little too much, went for a swim, and passed out."

Jazz stares through the windows at the illuminated pool just beyond the door. "You don't think that's what really happened?"

"Not after speaking with my grandfather." My eyes fog over as I look out the window. "The timing is too suspicious. And she was fully dressed, which is an odd choice for swimming, don't you think?"

"Do you think your dad...killed her?"

"He was somewhere in the Caribbean when she died." I exhale sharply. "But I *do* think he hired someone. Or maybe he asked *your* father to do it since he *was* in town that day. Knowing what I know now, they both would've had the same motive. They're equally guilty as far as I'm concerned, regardless of who actually did the dirty work."

"Were you and Ainsley home when it happened?"

"No. We were on a playdate a few houses down that afternoon. Looking back, I think my mom wanted to get us out of the house so she could pack our things without drawing attention. I think my dad somehow found out she was planning to run, and he put a stop to it before she could make that happen.

"I will never forget that day. It was getting late, and my mom didn't pick us up when she was supposed to. She wouldn't answer the phone when Mrs. Wallace—that's the neighbor—called. Finally, Mrs. Wallace brought us home herself, thinking maybe Mom's phone died, or she fell asleep. No one answered when we rang the bell, so we walked around the house to check the back. Ainsley tripped along the way and scraped her knee, so Mrs. Wallace stopped to take care of her.

"I kept going, though. I couldn't shake the feeling that something bad had happened. When I rounded the corner of the house, I saw her floating face down in the water. I jumped in the pool, trying to save her, but as soon as I managed to flip her over, I knew it was too late. She was heavily bloated...her skin was almost...gray. Seeing her like that will haunt me for the rest of my life."

"God, Kingston. No wonder you hate them so much."

"Yeah."

Jazz turns her head toward me. "Were you living in this house back then? Is that *the* pool?"

"Yes, on the house. Not exactly for the pool."

Her delicate eyebrows knit together. "What does that mean?"

"My dad's second wife—the one he married not even a year after my mom died—had it redone. Ainsley and I wouldn't go anywhere near it, so my dad told her about my mom's *accident*. She was freaked out by the whole thing, so she hired someone to expand and redesign the landscape of it." I grind my molars together. "That's right around the time she demanded we remove all traces of our mom from the house as if that would erase the fact that she was dead or something."

"What a bitch."

"Yeah," I agree.

"Does Ainsley know? I mean, about our fathers?"

"She knows they're involved in something shady,

but she has no idea it's this bad." I shake my head. "And I don't want that to change until I get proof that'll take them down. I have measures in place to keep her as safe as possible, but I don't want her to know the details, Jazz. Ainsley's poker face is shit, so if she knew anything specific, it'd put her at risk."

"Agreed." Jazz nods her head in understanding. "But Bentley and Reed know?"

"Yeah, they know everything. I kind of went off the rails for a while after I got back from San Francisco. I was so goddamn angry all the time. I couldn't figure out how to channel it into something productive. I was becoming reckless. I *had* to vent before I did something that couldn't be undone. They're my brothers—I trust them with my life."

Jazz takes a moment to collect herself. Swiping away the last of her tears, she asks, "What about the police report? Wasn't your dad a suspect?"

"John found no record of a report being filed."

Jazz tucks her feet beneath her. "I don't understand. How is that possible?"

My jaw tics. "I think our fathers have a lot of powerful people in their pockets."

"You think they're bribing them?"

"I think they're *blackmailing* them. I've seen some of these men at dinner parties and whatnot. Something's...off. They practically salivate whenever my sister or Peyton are nearby, even when they were barely teenagers. And the older I get, the looser their tongues get as the night wears on. They assume like father like son, I suppose. Hell, why wouldn't they? Our fathers think I'm just as misogynistic and perverted as they are."

"Why would they think that?"

"Because that's what I *want* them to believe. That's how I'm gaining their trust. Trust me, I loathe every minute I have to spend in their presence, but it's the role I have to play. And I'm going to *keep* playing it until I get what I need to nail their asses."

Jazz traps her lower lip between her teeth. "Is that why you were so awful to me at first? Because you were pretending to be like them? Or were you projecting your feelings for my sperm donor on to me?"

I think about her question for a moment. "Full honesty?"

She gives me a wry look. "I think that'd be implied at this point, but if you need me to spell it out, yes. *Full honesty.*"

"Before we met, I was indifferent more than anything. I knew your mom had just died, and that you grew up in the projects, so I assumed you'd be this meek, grieving girl, who did not want to make waves. That you'd be grateful you suddenly had a rich daddy who rescued you from the system. After a period of mourning, I thought you'd eventually fall in line with Peyton's group and just be another inconsequential rich bitch."

"And *after* we met?"

I scoff. "I realized I was so fucking wrong and so fucking screwed. The second you stepped out of that car at Windsor, with your head held high, looking fierce as hell, I knew you were trouble with a capital T. Then, when you gave me lip, my God, it made me so hard, I wanted to bend you over right there in front of everyone, showing them you were *mine*. My self-control was slipping fast, and quite frankly, it pissed me off and scared the shit out of me. I'm not a fucking Neanderthal, yet you made me feel like one. *No one* has *ever* had that kind of effect on me."

Jazz makes a time-out sign with her hands. "I beg to differ on the caveman part. Also, let's keep your boners out of this conversation."

I smile, which earns me a glare. "Why? Afraid you won't be able to stop thinking about my dick?"

"Anyway," she continues, completely ignoring

my taunt. "I still don't understand why my arrival made you feel so fucked."

I shrug. "I made that inheritance deal with Peyton so I could get closer to Charles. I had been working on it for a long-ass time, and things were finally starting to fall into place. Charles and my dad were making little comments here and there, hinting about future business *opportunities* they'd like to bring me in on. But your arrival threw an elephant-sized wrench into my plan. I felt cornered, and I didn't like that one bit."

"Why not just ignore me?"

I laugh humorlessly. "Because that's *impossible*. Christ, Jazz, you have no idea, do you?"

"No idea about what?"

"I don't think *anyone* could ignore you," I explain. "I don't know...it's like you have this X factor that draws people in. It makes them want to know you, want to *be* you, or want to fuck you. Why do you think Peyton and her minions were so aggressive with you right off the bat?"

"Uh, because they're stuck-up bitches?"

I shake my head. "It's because they're insanely jealous. They consider you a *threat*—probably more than any person they've met before. You're smart, beautiful, kind, confident, and give zero fucks what they think of you. You're *real*—what you see is what you get. That's sexy as hell, Jazz, and what's more, refreshing as fuck in our world. They could *never* be as authentic as you are, no matter how hard they tried."

"That's ridiculous."

"No, it's the *truth*." I clear my throat. "In the interest of transparency, there's uh...one more thing you need to know."

Jazz's eyes narrow in suspicion. "What?"

Fuck. This isn't going to go over well.

"About playing that role...both Charles and my dad *may* be under the impression I'm spending time with you to help get you under your father's control."

"*What?!*" she shouts. If Jazz wasn't still healing, I have no doubt she'd be launching herself at me right now. "Why would they think *that?*"

I stretch my neck from side to side. "It was before I got to know you. I can't say I wouldn't have made the same deal if I *had* known you better, but there's a good reason."

"Explain," she demands through gritted teeth.

"It was the first day we met—right before dinner at your house. I was in your dad's cigar room listening to them blather on about whatever. Then, at one point, my dad asked how things were going with you, and your dad bitched about how rough around the edges you were." I hold my hands up when her eyes flash with rage. "*His* words, not mine.

"Anyway...my dad suggested I could teach you how things worked in our world, put you in your place, so to speak. Teach you to *heel* like a woman should." Jazz eyeballs the lamp beside her like she's considering clocking me over the head with it. When she makes no move to do so, I continue. "So...I told them I'd be happy to help. Peyton was continually testing my last nerve—I saw an opportunity to get what I needed without her, and I grabbed it. Charles and my dad said if I was successful with you, they'd bring me into the fold. Reforming you would prove I was ready to take on *other* projects."

Jazz sits there for a moment, shooting daggers at me with her eyes. Finally, she takes a deep breath and speaks. "Let me get this straight. You promised our fathers you could turn me into one of their little Stepford wives?"

"Essentially, yes."

She cocks a brow. "And how, exactly, did you plan on doing that?"

"I hadn't quite figured that part out yet."

"So, after dinner, when you showed up in my room—what happened in my closet—that was because you were playing a *role?*"

"*Fuck, no.*"

Now, I'm seething right along with her. The one thing Jazz should *never* question is how much I want her.

"What *was* the purpose then?"

I shoot up from the couch and throw my hands out. "I didn't *plan* any of that! After dinner, I was *supposed* to be with our dads smoking Cubans. I don't even remember walking upstairs, now that I think about it. But when you came out of the bathroom, wearing nothing but a towel, the last thread of control I had inside of me snapped.

"I was pissed I couldn't keep myself in check around you. I was planning to say *fuck it* to the whole plan because if I couldn't control *myself*, how in the hell would I control *you*? I tried warning you to stay away, but you wouldn't fucking listen. You just *had* to keep pushing my buttons, like you always do, and I reacted."

"By putting your hands on me? By *finger fucking me* against the wall? Are you seriously trying to blame me for this shit?!"

I stare her directly in the eye. "Don't pretend

you didn't love *every fucking moment*, that night, or any other time I touched you afterward."

She stands up, fists clenching at her side. "Fuck. You."

"Gladly. Name the time and place, sweetheart."

Jazz raises her arm, but she's broadcasting her intention from a mile away.

I grab the arm mid-swing. "Nice try."

"Let. Go. Of. Me." She struggles under my grip, eyes wide.

What the fuck am I doing?

Restraining Jazz is probably giving her some kind of flashback. I immediately release my grip and take a step back. Damn it.

"I'm sorry. I didn't mean to—"

"Shut up." She balls her fist around my t-shirt. "Just shut. The. Fuck. Up."

Before I can say, "Or what?" Jazz is tugging on the cotton, pulling me down to her. She presses her full lips against mine, and the thought of challenging her dissipates into thin air. Nothing else matters after that.

Our mouths meet in a frenzy of desperation, clinging to each other for more. Jazz's soft moans shoot straight to my dick, making me go from half-mast to full sail in two seconds flat. She rubs her torso against my hard-on, but the friction isn't enough. I drop down onto the couch and pull her with me until she's straddling my lap, never breaking our kiss. I can feel the heat of her pussy through our clothes as she grinds against me. Her back arches when my lips travel down her neck. She rocks on top of me as my thumb brushes over her peaked nipple through her top.

"Fuck!"

"I know," I murmur, pressing a kiss to her collarbone. "Fuck, you feel good."

"No." Jazz presses on my chest with one hand and places the other on her abdomen. "Ouch! Fuck, as in *ouch*!"

"Shit." My eyes run the length of her upper body, trying to identify the source of the problem. "What's hurting?"

Jazz lifts the corner of her shirt. My jaw clenches when the material slides up a little more, revealing an angry, jagged red line.

"Jesus Christ. Is that from the knife?"

She nods, rolling her shirt up and tucking it beneath the band of her bra.

"Does it still hurt?"

Jazz shrugs. "The majority of the pain now is from my abdominal muscles, which are still pretty sore from being cut open during surgery. It's mainly a dull ache, like when you had an extra hard workout, but when I move a certain way, it'll trigger a really sharp pain, which is what just happened. It hurts like a bitch but only for a few seconds. Compared to how I felt in the beginning, though, it's night and day."

I lightly trace the fresh scar, causing goosebumps to scatter across her flesh. "Is this the only scar?"

Jazz shakes her head. "No. There's another one about twice as long from the surgical procedure they had to do."

My brows pinch together in confusion. I have a clear view of her entire abdomen, yet I see nothing. "Where?"

Jazz starts pulling the waistband of her leggings down, followed by her black cotton panties. Before I can ask why, another line appears, maybe five or six inches wide, about six inches below her belly button. The skin here is also red and raised slightly, creating a ridge of sorts, but it's obviously from a more precise cut. I'm so focused on the evidence of her assault, the fact that Jazz is sitting on my lap with a partially exposed pussy isn't even fazing me. Guess I do have some self-restraint after all.

My eyes travel upward, over her taut abdomen. For the most part, it's all smooth, bronzed skin. But there's one sizeable patch marring the perfection, lightly tinted in a yellowish-brown color.

My hand glides over the darkest part. "Why is there still bruising here?"

"That's where I took a boot to the stomach. It looks much better than it did. You saw my face when it first happened, right? Half my body was the same lovely shade of reddish-purple."

It was dark out, and everything happened so fast that night, I never really took the time to examine her carefully. That's probably a good thing because the damage to her face alone made me want to murder the bastards that did this to her. I'm so fucking angry, but I do my best to school my expression. My teeth grind together as I wrap my hands around her hips and place her on the cushion beside me. I'm too agitated right now to have her sitting on me.

Jazz puts her shirt back into place. "So, what now?"

"Now, you tell me what happened in that forest. After that, we work together to take all of these bastards down."

chapter eleven

JAZZ

It was much easier opening up to Kingston about my attack after everything he disclosed about our parents. My earlier concerns about Kingston's possible involvement faded entirely after seeing how passionate he is about taking our fathers down for their roles in hurting our moms. Not even the best actor in the world could fake that kind of conviction. After recapping everything those men said and did to me, along with everything I learned before that, I was exhausted, both physically and mentally. We decided to call it a night and agreed to discuss possible suspects in the morning. I agreed to stay over because it was so late, but I made it crystal clear Kingston and I would *not* be sleeping in the same room.

God, what am I going to do about him? Lying in Kingston's bed, surrounded by his sexy signature scent all night, was absolute torture. The ache between my legs that was ignited earlier in the evening intensified to an almost unbearable level. My hand slipped beneath the covers several times, intent on chasing a release before my brain kicked in. If I wasn't so tired, I probably would've kicked off the covers, marched into the other room, and begged Kingston to touch me. *Again.*

Damn it, I should've never kissed him, but we were arguing, which always gets me going for some sick reason, and he looked extra hot with his stupidly square jaw clenching half the time. Plus, he was wearing gray joggers, for fuck's sake! I'd have to be blind to miss the rather large dick print beneath that thin cotton. I shake my head, reminding myself now is not the time to think about dicks, especially Kingston's.

Fucking gray sweatpants. Total thirst traps, every damn time.

I woke up shortly before dawn and couldn't fall back asleep, so I decided to take a long, hot shower.

As I'm standing beneath the rainfall showerhead, I replay last night's conversation with Kingston in my head. He looked like he was about to kill someone when I told him what those bastards did and said to me. His fists were clenched so tightly, his knuckles were blanched, and his leg wouldn't stop bouncing. There was this crazy energy buzzing around him the whole time, but he barely said a word—just asked a clarifying question here and there. When I asked him if he was okay, he brushed it off like I imagined the whole thing.

I swear, that boy keeps such a tight leash on his emotions, he's bound to snap eventually. I thought he was about to blow last night. Oddly, when—not if—that happens, I don't believe his rage would ever be directed at me, so it's not as scary as it probably should be. I can't say the same for my assailants. Now, *they* should be terrified. I'd like to say I'd feel sorry for them if Kingston ever got a hold of them, but I can't. I *want* them to suffer, and I've no doubt he'd do the job. What that says about me, I don't know. I've never been a big proponent of violence, but recent events have me seeing things through a different scope, I suppose.

After drying off and getting dressed, I tiptoe out into the main room to grab some water. I smile when I see Kingston sprawled out on the pull-out sofa, his arm thrown over his eyes to block out the sun. It's risen just enough to slice through the windows across his face.

What the hell?

I move closer, careful not to wake him. Are my eyes playing tricks on me? Nope. Kingston definitely has a fat lip. I have to stifle a gasp when I see the nasty gash, with a little dried blood caked on it as if the cut reopened while he was asleep. What the heck happened? He was perfectly fine when I went to bed last night.

On instinct, I reach out to touch his lip but freeze when Kingston's hand locks around my wrist. His eyes fly open, relaxing slightly when he sees me.

He releases my arm and rubs his eyes. "What are you doing? Are you okay?"

"Are *you?*" I counter, swiping my thumb to the right of his mouth. "What happened to your face?" Jesus, his knuckles are swollen, too. "And your hands?"

Kingston holds his hands out, looking at the cracked skin over his knuckles. "I'm fine."

"Really? Kingston, I'm a girl. I know '*fine*' never actually means fine."

He rolls over, away from the light. "Can we do this later? I'm fucking tired."

I sit on the edge of the mattress and pull on his shoulder. "Talk to me. When I went to bed, you were about to do the same. Did you decide to punch yourself in the face a few times beforehand?"

He grabs his phone off the pillow and groans when he sees the time. "Jazz, please. I've only been asleep for an hour. I need at least a few more to function." He rolls toward me and tugs on my arm. "C'mon, just lie down with me for a bit. I'm too wiped to try anything dirty; I swear."

Why is his sleepy voice so sexy? It's all gravelly and extra deep. Against my better judgment, I slide onto the bed next to him and lie down. Kingston scoots closer until his body is molded around mine. I'd like to say I don't wiggle my butt and press into him, but I'm only human so...whatever.

Kingston nuzzles the back of my neck. "You smell like me."

"I used your shower gel," I explain.

"Mmm. I like it."

I stiffen when he grinds his massive erection between my butt cheeks. "Kingston..."

He groans. "It's morning wood; it'll go away eventually. Just ignore it."

"Easy for you to say," I mutter. "You're not the one with a dick nestled in your ass."

"Shh..." Kingston whispers. "Less talky, more sleepy."

I sigh. "You're impossible."

"Sleep, Jazz."

I close my eyes and take a deep breath. Despite my earlier hesitancy, it's hard not to relax in Kingston's embrace. It's way too comfy and the safest I've felt in a long time. Before I know it, I'm drifting off to dreamland.

A feather-light touch brushes my cheek. "Jazz, it's time to wake up."

I open my eyes, slowly blinking Kingston's face into focus. "What time is it?"

"Just after ten."

Damn. I slept for three hours.

I carefully sit up and swing my legs over the side of the mattress. "Did you just get up?"

"About twenty minutes ago. I let you sleep as long as I could, but we need to talk. I have a thing at one, so I'll need to head out shortly after noon."

I look over my shoulder as I help myself to a bottle of water from the fridge. "*What* thing?"

I notice his hair is damp, and he's wearing different clothes. His lip is still swollen, but the dried blood is gone. Kingston obviously showered in the short time he's been awake.

Kingston takes a seat at the breakfast bar directly across from me. "I'm meeting my P.I. He has some new surveillance equipment for me."

"Why do you need new surveillance equipment?"

"We're going to monitor my dad's corporate office. His home office has been bugged for months, but it's given us nothing to work with. I need to monitor your dad's office as well, but I haven't found a way in without being detected." Kingston sits up straighter. "Wait a second...I just thought of something."

"What?"

"Peyton's big birthday bash is coming up, right?"

I can feel the deep crease forming between my brows. "Yeah...and?"

"I need you to find out if Ms. Williams will be gone—if she's actually leaving the house for once. Knowing Peyton, this party is going to be a rager. I doubt that stuffy-ass woman could tolerate that, but I need to know for sure."

"So you can get into my father's office," I surmise.

"Exactly. It'd be the perfect opportunity. There should be more than enough bodies where I could sneak off unnoticed. Actually, it'd probably be better if I did it *before* making an appearance. I'll show up after the party's been going for a while, maybe around ten or so, place the camera, and *then* show my face. But I need to know that old bat is out of the house for any of it to work."

"What about Charles and Madeline?"

"I already know they'll be gone. Peyton's been planning this damn thing for over a year, so I've had the displeasure of listening to her ramble about it more than a few times."

"Fine. But I want something in return."

"Name it."

I pop an eyebrow. "Tell me what happened to you last night."

Kingston's jaw clenches. "I fight sometimes."

I'm sure I look as confused as I feel. "I'm going to need you to elaborate on that."

He blows out a breath. "Sometimes when I'm really pissed...I need to channel the aggression into something else. The only two things that seem to work are fucking and fighting. Since I don't think the former is going to happen anytime soon, I chose the latter."

"You can screw whoever you want, Kingston. Don't let me stop you."

Kingston's heated gaze travels the length of my body, and I've never felt more like a zebra in a lion's den than I do now. "I'm well aware of my options, Jazz. Just because I *can* fuck someone else, doesn't mean I *want to*." He holds up his left hand. "If you're not on the table, then this'll have to do while I imagine it's your mouth."

Nope. Not going to think about Kingston touching himself. Or you know, sucking him off.

Damn it.

He smiles when heat rises to my face. "You okay there, Jazz? You're looking a little flushed all of a sudden."

I flip him off. "Bite me."

"Name the time and place."

I wave him off. "Stick to the subject. So, how does this thing work? Do you just go out and start a brawl?"

He motions for my water bottle, so I hand it to him. After taking a big gulp, he says, "There's an underground ring in LA. A few, actually. I put some feelers out and got my name on a card."

"An underground ring," I repeat. "As in, illegal?"

Kingston shrugs. "It's certainly not sanctioned by the UFC."

I lean against the counter and cross my arms over my chest. "How often do you do this?"

He guzzles the remainder of my water. "I haven't done it in almost two years, actually."

Well, I wasn't expecting that. "So, why now?"

"I couldn't calm down after hearing your version of the events that night." Kingston rakes his hands through his thick hair. "I couldn't stop thinking about it, couldn't get the images of finding you like that out of my head. Couldn't stop feeling like the world's biggest piece of shit for putting you in that situation in the first place. When I fight, all the chaos in my head is silenced." He shrugs. "At least for a little while."

I step forward and link his fingers through mine. "Kingston, I don't blame you for what happened that night."

I didn't realize it until now, but I don't. Not anymore.

He scoffs. "Well, you *should*."

I shake my head. "If those guys were telling the truth about being hired—which at this point, I'm pretty sure they were—they would've gotten to me eventually. Maybe not that night, but soon after that."

Kingston's grip tightens. "I'm going to fucking kill those bastards when I find out who they are."

"Speaking of...where do we even begin?"

"If we can figure out who hired them, it'd be much easier to identify the henchmen. Process of elimination is a good start for that. The person behind it would've had to have been someone with the assets to pay for it."

"That doesn't exactly narrow it down now, does it?"

He thinks about that for a moment. "Yes...and no. Peyton is at the top of my suspect list—especially after she nearly claimed responsibility—but she doesn't really have the money for that to make sense."

"What do you mean? Isn't she like, a mega-billionaire?"

"Technically, not until she gets her inheritance. Not a dime can be liquidated until *all* the terms are met. The only *money* she has right now is Daddy

Callahan's credit card. It's not like she could pay for something like that with plastic."

"Well, shit."

"Yeah," he agrees. "*But*...Peyton is resourceful when she wants something. She uses everything she has at her disposal to get it."

"If she doesn't have any actual cash, what's left?"

"With Peyton...take your pick. She could blackmail someone, promise them favors. Offer her body. If she wants something—or someone—bad enough, *nothing* is off the table."

My eyebrows rise. "You sound like you're speaking from experience."

Kingston shrugs. "I am. I'm just not dumb enough to fall for it. So, the next question is, if not Peyton, who else would want to hurt you? It has to be someone who knows you. Knows *us. And* they knew we'd be at the lake."

"Wouldn't that be the entire senior class?"

"Pretty much." Kingston rubs his jaw, wincing when he gets to a discolored spot.

I reach out and brush my fingers against the slight bruising. "You okay?"

His signature, cocky smile comes into place. "You should see the other guy."

I roll my eyes. "Such a douchey thing to say."

Kingston places his hand over mine before placing a soft kiss on my knuckles. "You hungry? We can grab a bite before we have to meet John."

I smile. "Yeah, I could eat."

He nods. "Then, what are we waiting for?"

chapter twelve

JAZZ

"John Peterson, meet Jazz Rivera."

John stands up and shakes my hand. "Jazz, it's nice to finally meet you."

"You, too."

Kingston and I take a seat on the bench across from the private investigator. I thought meeting at Lake Hollywood Park was a rather odd choice for such a private matter, but now that I'm here, it makes sense. Sure, there are tons of people around, but they're all too busy taking selfies in front of the iconic sign or playing with their dogs to pay us any notice.

Everything about John is nondescript. From his

name—if that's even his real name—to his muddy brown hair, lean build, or the polo/chino combo he's rocking. He's not a bad looking guy per se—there's just nothing about him that stands out. He's completely forgettable, which I suppose comes in handy when you spy on people for a living.

John slides a small reusable grocery bag across the picnic table. "Everything we talked about is in there."

Kingston takes the bag and briefly peeks inside. "Including the additional item for Callahan's office?"

"Yep," John confirms.

"Same installation instructions?"

John nods. "The main thing you need to worry about is choosing the correct device. The Callahan house and your father's office have slightly different models. According to the intel you sent me, the equipment in that bag should be identical to the current models within each building."

"Sounds simple enough," Kingston says.

"I'm sorry, but what exactly are we talking about here?" I ask. "I feel like you're talking in code."

Kingston smiles and holds the bag open, so I

can peek inside. "Smoke detectors. They're fully functioning—these just happen to have tiny cameras in them."

"Man, it's kind of scary it's this easy to spy on someone," I muse.

John nods. "It is. That's why I never travel without a detection device. You'd be surprised how many times I've found hidden cameras in hotel rooms."

My jaw drops. "Seriously? What's the point in that?"

"Usually, it's your run-of-the-mill pervert hoping to engage in a little digital voyeurism." He shrugs.

"Gross." I make a face, suddenly glad I've never had a reason to check into a hotel room before.

John checks his watch. "I need to head out. Do either of you have any questions?"

"Nope." I shake my head.

"I'm good," Kingston says at the same time.

Kingston waits for John to walk away before inclining his head to the sizeable grass-covered area. "Feel like walking around a bit?"

"Sure." I grab the small bag and hitch it on my shoulder.

Kingston stands and offers his hand to help me

up. I start to pull away once I'm standing, but he tightens his grip and starts walking, pulling me with him. I would've never pegged Kingston Davenport as a hand holder, but he likes to do it a lot. I decide not to fight him on it as we make our way across the grounds. We don't go too far, and definitely not too fast, but the sun on my skin and the fresh air is nice after being cooped up indoors for so long.

Kingston pulls me to a stop before digging his phone out of his pocket. "Hold up a sec."

My brows pinch together. "What's wrong?"

He wraps one arm around my shoulder and uses the other to hold his phone out. Our faces appear on the screen with the Hollywood sign in the background.

"Really? You want to pretend we're tourists?"

Kingston's greenish-gold eyes sparkle with mirth. "Can you even say you're from LA without a selfie in front of the Hollywood sign?"

"I wouldn't think the great Kingston Davenport would give a shit about some old sign."

"I don't," he agrees. "But I want a picture anyway, so shut the fuck up and smile at the camera."

The camera clicks in rapid succession as I laugh.

Kingston scrolls through his photo reel and holds one out for me. "See? Perfect."

In the shot, I'm facing him with my mouth open in laughter. Kingston's eyes are directly on me, lit up with amusement but also...something else. If I didn't know better, I'd say reverence, but that can't be right.

"We're not even looking at the camera," I point out.

"I don't care." Kingston pockets his phone, his gaze never wavering.

I search his eyes. "Kingston..." He leans into me, his breath feathering against my face. "This isn't a good idea."

"Don't care about that either." His mouth presses against mine with the lightest touch, giving me a chance to pull away.

My breath stutters as indecision plagues me. My eyes drift closed when Kingston licks the seam of my lips.

"Heads up!" someone shouts.

Kingston yanks me to the side, right before a frisbee whizzes past my head.

I blink rapidly as the spell is broken. "Holy shit, that was close."

"Yeah." Kingston frowns. "A little *too* close."

A man walks up to us with a sheepish look on his face. "Sorry about that." A black Labrador runs up to him, proudly dropping a slobbery frisbee at his feet. He pats the dog on the head and says, "Good girl, Gretta."

Gretta's tongue lolls out of her mouth as her owner scratches behind her ear.

"May I?" I gesture toward his adorable companion.

"Sure," he replies. "She's super friendly."

I follow the man's lead and scratch behind her floppy ears, which she loves. Kingston kneels down and joins in, laughing when Gretta's giant tongue paints his cheek with dog drool. This moment is so ordinary—just some people playing with a cute dog in a park—but at the same time, it's surreal. Two months ago, if you would've asked me if I thought Kingston Davenport was an animal lover or was into taking cheesy selfies, I'd scream, *"Hell no."* The man is an enigma. The more I get to know him, the more complicated he becomes.

Kingston and I step back and watch the dog and her owner resume their game of fetch. Wordlessly, Kingston takes my hand as we make our way down the road to where he parked the Range Rover. I climb into the vehicle and buckle my belt as

Kingston gets behind the wheel and starts the ignition.

He releases a heavy sigh once we pull onto the road. "I really don't want to take you back to that house, Jazz. Is there anything I can say that would convince you to stay with me?"

I shake my head. "No."

"Stubborn ass woman."

I throw my head back and groan. "Kingston, please don't ruin the perfectly good morning we've had. I'll be fine. I'm scheduled to return to school on Tuesday if the doctor gives me the all-clear tomorrow, so I won't be there much anyway. Besides, if Peyton *is* a suspect, isn't it better to pretend that everything is normal to draw her out? I can't do that if I'm shacking up with you."

"I fucking hate it when you're right," he grumbles.

"Yeah, well, get used to it, buddy."

He glares at me out of the corner of his eye. "Wiseass."

I stick my tongue out because I'm mature like that. At least it gets a smile out of him.

"You're never going to stop pushing my buttons, are you?"

I shrug. "Why would I do that when you make it so fun?"

Kingston shakes his head. "Like I said, fucking trouble."

chapter thirteen

KINGSTON

"Don't you think you're being paranoid?"

I close the door to Jazz's bedroom and flip the lock. "No, I'm diligent. If you insist on staying here, I insist on doing this."

Jazz sits on the end of her bed, rolling her eyes at me. I loathe the fact that she's here right now. We may not know who did this to her, but I'm with Jazz; I do think someone hired them, and I do believe that person knows us. Nothing else makes sense, and John thinks so, too. The lake house is in a small mountain community; it's not the kind of place where you'd randomly end up or go looking for trouble. All of the locals know each other.

There's only one vacation rental, which was occupied by people at the homecoming party.

It's entirely possible Peyton, or any of the people living in this house, are innocent. At least in the case of Jazz's assault. But I'm not willing to risk Jazz's safety by slacking off or not using every possible resource at my disposal. I know she still has doubts about me, even though I'm no longer keeping secrets from her. Sure, I've given her reason to distrust me in the past, but I thought we've moved past that. Hell, I thought we moved past that the night we slept together.

I know being brutally attacked would make anyone wary, but I also know Jazz feels this connection we have. She isn't the type of girl who'd fuck someone without at least a small emotional attachment. No matter how crazy our chemistry is, she's too mindful to allow a physical attraction to rule her actions. Being with her that night was...different than it's ever been for me before. I've had some great sex in my life, but this was...*more*. I wasn't blowing smoke up Jazz's ass when I said I had no interest in fucking anyone *but* her. Since the moment we met, that woman is all I see, and I'm done pretending otherwise.

I was dead serious when I said I'd kill any motherfucker who tried taking her away from me. I know this thing started because I had an ulterior motive, but that's not the case anymore. Jasmine Rivera will be right by my side when I take down our fathers and the assholes who hurt her.

I fish the small device John gave me out of my pocket and surreptitiously scan her bedroom for bugs. Something immediately triggers the sensors, so I walk around a bit until the signal gets stronger. Jazz's eyes widen when I approach the walk-in closet, and the green light quickly turns to red, indicating there's a surveillance device nearby.

"Paranoid, my ass," I whisper, giving her an *I told you so* look.

My jaw clenches, knowing someone has been spying on Jazz. One thing's for damn sure; now, the people living in this house are *definitely* high on my suspect list. I carefully run my hand over the trim above the door until my fingertip snags on a slight dip in the wood. Sure enough, right on the upper corner of the doorframe, is a pinhole camera that could easily be mistaken for a finishing nail.

Fuck.

My eyes travel over the room as I stand beneath the camera. Depending on how wide the angle is, whoever is on the other end of that thing, can likely see the entire room. Her bed is directly in front of the closet door, so at the very least, the camera has a perfect view of that. I take deep breaths, trying to calm the rage brewing inside of me. If someone has been watching Jazz the entire time she's lived here, who knows what they've seen when she was under the illusion of privacy.

I think back to the day we overheard our fathers talking. Thank fuck I had the sense to cover our voices with loud music when we spoke about it, but there was some dry humping that occurred right on that bed afterward. My fists clench, and my nostrils flare as I figure out my next move. I don't want to tip anyone off by removing the camera until I can talk to John and see if we can trace it, but I definitely don't want this fucker watching my girl.

Sadly, if I covered it, the person on the other end would know they've been made. I finish scanning the room and move on to her attached bathroom, carefully cupping my hand over my detection device so it can't be seen. I leave the ensuite, where thankfully, there were no additional devices and approach Jazz's bed.

She eyes me carefully when I kneel onto the California King, moving closer until I'm hovering right above her. I'm careful not to put any weight on her—the last thing I want to do is cause her more discomfort. It doesn't go unnoticed she's not uttering a single word of protest. Nor does the fact that her nipples could probably cut through glass right now. Christ.

Her breath hitches when I lean into her ear and whisper, "There's a micro-camera lens embedded into the upper right corner of the doorframe to your closet. I'm guessing it has audio, too. Everything you do or say is probably being recorded or watched on a live feed. It's the only recording device my scanner detected, so your bathroom is still a safe place to talk. Blink twice if you heard me."

I pull back just enough to see Jazz blink twice. She gasps when my mouth presses against her neck, lightly sucking on the delicate skin. I'm doing this for appearances, but once my lips are on her, I can't seem to help myself.

Her back arches slightly when my tongue snakes out. "Kingston, what are you doing?"

I groan at the sound of her breathy voice. The last time I heard it, I was balls deep inside of her. "Come back to my place. I fucking miss you when you're not with me." It's a true statement, but the words are meant to be heard by anyone watching.

I nibble on her earlobe before lowering my voice again. "I need an excuse for both of us to be in the bathroom so we can talk. Just run with it, okay?"

She cups her hands on either side of my jaw and gives me a slight nod. Jazz shivers when my hand glides up her side, lightly brushing her breast.

"Didn't you say you wanted to take a shower? I could wash your back for you."

She casually looks in the direction of her closet then the bathroom door. "Oh, can you now?"

I smile. "I'm selfless like that."

Fuck, I really wish I didn't plant that visual in my brain. Now, I can't stop picturing Jazz in the shower, her naked body all wet and soapy. She smiles coyly as I take her hand and lead her into the bathroom.

Jazz takes a seat on the vanity bench while I run the water. There isn't anywhere else to sit nearby, so I lower my body to the floor directly across from her, leaning against the shower's glass door.

"Are you sure it's a camera? Someone's definitely watching me?"

"I'm positive, Jazz, but who the fuck knows how long it's been there? Maybe it's not even recording, but maybe someone's been watching you the entire time you've lived here. I need to talk to John and see if we can trace the feed somehow."

"If that's been there the entire time...that means someone has seen me naked *many* times. They've seen me..." Jazz closes her eyes briefly. "God, I feel so violated."

I remain silent, giving her time to process everything.

"I'm going to be sick." Suddenly, she darts across the room just in time to make it to the toilet.

I gather her long hair into my hands as she loses her breakfast to the porcelain gods. Fuck, after everything Jazz has been through lately, I'm surprised it took her this long to break down. It just goes to show you how strong she is.

When she has nothing left, I wet the corner of a hand towel and pass it to her. Jazz wipes her face and makes her way to the sink to rinse her mouth and brush her teeth.

Jazz takes a few deep breaths before sitting in front of the vanity again. She doesn't look green anymore, but she's fidgeting like crazy.

Her chocolate eyes widen. "Do you think my sperm donor had it installed? Do you think *he's* been watching me to see if I know anything?"

"We already know his moral code is lacking.

Charles Callahan would have no qualms about invading your privacy if he had reason to believe you knew something that could incriminate him."

Jazz props her elbows on her knees and hangs her head in her hands. "What am I supposed to do? I'm so fucking creeped out right now."

"You could stay with me," I suggest.

She raises her head. "But if I did that, I wouldn't be able to keep my eye on them to see if they do or say anything suspicious."

"Jazz, you don't need to be the martyr. You shouldn't risk your safety or put yourself in a situation that makes you so uncomfortable. There are other ways to get information."

She shakes her head. "I *need* to know what happened with my mom, Kingston. I need to know who's responsible for what happened in that forest. If that means I need to place myself in a precarious situation for a while, that's what needs to happen."

"I disagree."

Jazz straightens her spine and lifts her chin. "Well, that's not for you to decide, is it?"

I bite the inside of my cheek. "Jazz, don't be stupid. If Charles suspects you might be a threat, he's more of a danger than I originally thought. Stay with me, and we'll figure it out from there."

She shoots laser beams at me with her eyes. "Don't tell me what to do."

Jesus fuck, she's exasperating.

"If you're worried about my dad, you don't need to be. The pool house's security system is completely independent of the main house. On the rare occasion he is home, you'll still be safe as long as you're with me."

She holds her hand up. "Stop talking. I've made up my mind, and I'm staying. Obviously, I'll need to make sure I get dressed in the bathroom or closet from now on, but otherwise, if someone wants to watch me sleep or do homework, let 'em. Now that I know the camera's there, I'll be careful."

"That may not be the only camera," I point out. "There may be others across the house."

Shit, why didn't I think of that before? If someone saw us loitering outside Charles' office, we're fucked.

Jazz stands and straightens the hem of her shirt. "Then, let's take a walk and scan the rest of the house."

I stand up and shut the water off. "Nothing I say will change your mind, will it?"

"Nope." She pops the P at the end, pure sass chasing the word.

Fuck, this woman is going to be the death of me.

"So fucking stubborn." I comb my hands through my hair and tug on the ends. "You drive me crazy sometimes."

"Feeling's mutual, *babe*." She pats my cheek condescendingly. "Now, are we going to take a walk, or what?"

I narrow my eyes. "Fine. Lead the way."

chapter fourteen

JAZZ

Kingston reluctantly left after completing a scan of most of the house and back yard. The good news is we didn't find any additional surveillance devices. The bad news is that I can't deny someone is watching *me* and only me. The question is, who, and why? Despite my earlier bluster, I'm really freaked out by the whole thing. I spent the rest of the afternoon lying on a lounger by the pool and the evening watching a movie in the game room. Thankfully, this house is so huge, I didn't run into anyone other than Ms. Williams when she asked if I'd like some dinner. I didn't return to my bedroom until I absolutely had to, and when I climbed into bed, sleep didn't come easily.

"Did everything go okay with the doctor, Miss Jasmine?" Frank opens the car door for me, his giant biceps straining against his sleeves.

Geez, the man is a beast. He's typically dressed in a button-up dress shirt, so I've never really seen his muscles on display, but today, he's wearing a black polo. Frank's probably in his mid-thirties, but he's a good-looking guy, and he's super sweet. I suck in a breath when it hits me how much my mom would've liked him. Hell, I would've encouraged her to ask him out if I somehow knew him when she was still alive.

Frank quirks an eyebrow. "Miss Jasmine? Are you okay?"

"Oh yeah, totally fine." I wave my imaginary pom-poms, trying to shake off my gloomy thoughts. "The appointment went well. I got the green light to return to school tomorrow. Yay me!"

Frank laughs before closing the door and sliding into the front seat. "I'm happy to hear that."

Truthfully, as much as that stuffy academy bothers me, it's another reason to avoid my bedroom, so I'm looking forward to returning. Plus, homeschooling blows. Like, *seriously blows*. I consider myself fairly intelligent—my 4.0 GPA supports that —but statistics are not my strong suit, and I'd definitely benefit from classroom instruction. I can only hope now that I have Ainsley and Windsor's supposed *kings* in my corner, the other students will stop harassing me.

"Jasmine, it's nice to see you looking so well."

I finish descending the stairs and take a deep breath. This is the first time I've seen the sperm donor since before homecoming. Kingston told me Charles stopped by the hospital the night I was admitted, but then he left town. I had a hard enough time biting my tongue around this man before. Now that I know he's quite possibly selling human beings for profit, it's going to be even more difficult.

"Thanks." I tuck a piece of hair behind my ear, reminding myself to focus and keep my words to a minimum.

"Jasmine, you look lovely, dear." Madeline, my stepmonster, leans forward and air kisses both sides of my cheeks before taking her place beside my father, looping her arm through his. "I see you're wearing your Windsor uniform. Shall I assume you're returning to school today?"

Normal parents wouldn't have to ask that question. Then again, normal parents also wouldn't leave the country for a three-week vacation after their daughter was violently attacked and left for dead.

I lift my eyebrows. "I'd wear this any day of the week; it's so fashionable! The fact that I'm returning to school is merely a coincidence."

Madeline pretends not to pick up on my sarcasm, but her pursed lips tell me otherwise. "Well, I'm glad to hear things are going well with your recovery. You look beautiful as always."

My eyes travel from her perfectly styled bleached blonde hair down to the pearly pink nail polish on her toes. "And you look especially tan."

Madeline preens as if that was a compliment. It wasn't—the woman is practically orange. I'm pretty sure she has a spray tan on top of a regular one. "Thank you. Your father and I had a wonderful time in Cabo." She turns her head and smiles up at him. "Didn't we, dear?"

Charles looks at his wife as if she were a fly crawling over a pile of shit. "We always do."

I hitch my thumb over my shoulder toward the front door. "Well, uh, I should get going. Kingston should be here any minute to pick me up."

Madeline's features pinch together before the Stepford mask falls back in place. "You're still seeing the Davenport boy?"

"I'm not sure *seeing* him is the right word, but we're hanging out." Sort of.

She smooths imaginary wrinkles out of her white sheath dress. "I see."

I think she was about to say something else, but Charles puts his hand up to stop her. "*Enough,* Madeline. Let the girl get to school. Now that she's feeling better, we can put this whole thing behind us and move on."

Uh...no, we *can't,* asshole.

"I don't think that's possible until the people responsible are brought to justice. Anyone willing to commit such a heinous crime deserves to have the book thrown at them."

Shit. Probably shouldn't have said that.

Charles' icy blue eyes narrow in suspicion. "Yes, well, of course. *After* the perpetrators are brought to justice, we can put this whole thing behind us."

We stare each other down, reading one another's body language. His is saying that he's the king of this jungle and nobody dares to defy him. Mine's saying, *try me, old man.*

My father's face reddens as he straightens his

tie. "Have a nice day at school, Jasmine. I have business to attend to."

With that, he spins on his heels and walks toward the corridor leading to his office. Madeline is still standing right in front of me, obviously waiting for her husband to get out of earshot.

I prop a hand on my hip. "Something you'd like to say?"

For the first time since we've met, the real Madeline comes out to play. Her periwinkle eyes are burning with rage as she steps forward until her giant boobs are practically bumping against my chest. I'm five-foot-four on a good day, and Madeline's easily five-ten when she's wearing heels, so she towers over me.

"Listen up, little girl. Kingston Davenport belongs to *Peyton*. You. Can't. Have. Him. It's best to break off this fling, or whatever it is before it goes any further. They *will* marry after graduation, and there's *nothing* you can do to stop it. Trust me when I say you'll be sorry if you try."

"Did all that poison you had injected into your face go to your brain?" I scoff. "You *and* your daughter are deranged. Whether or not Kingston and I are together, he'll *never* marry Peyton."

Fuck. *Definitely* shouldn't have said that.

Madeline's orange face turns cherry red. "You little—"

"Madeline!"

Both our heads swing in the direction of the booming voice. Sperm Donor's face is rosier than his wife's, only his anger is clearly directed at her, not me. Well, that's a nice change.

Once she gets over the shock, Madeline's mask is firmly back in place. "Darling, it's not what it looks like."

Charles' jaw tics as his meaty fists clench at his sides. "I need to speak with you in my office."

"But," she sputters.

"*Now!* Do as you're told, or face the consequences!"

Madeline glances at me before averting her gaze to the marble floor, scurrying past my father like her ass is on fire. Damn, can't say I blame her. The dude's pretty scary right now.

"You!" He points a finger at me. "Go to school!"

"Consider me gone." I give a flippant wave before rushing out the door.

I lean against one of the pillars for a moment to catch my breath. Holy shit, what *was* that? Kingston's still not here, but I have no desire to wait around and risk running into either Charles or Madeline. I text Kingston as I start walking down the long driveway.

Me: ETA? I need to get the hell out of Dodge.

Kingston: I'm driving with Do Not Disturb While Driving turned on. I'll see your message when I get where I'm going.

Crap. Well, at least I know he's on his way. The Davenports live in the same gated community I do, so I know it won't be long. My phone rings by the time I make it to the end of the driveway, and Kingston's face appears on the screen. I smile when I see the picture he took of us at the park. He must've updated his contact info when I wasn't looking.

"Hey. How far away are you?"

I can hear the rumble of his engine in the background. "Look up."

Kingston's flashy black Agera RS flies down the road and rolls to a stop in front of me. I guess that engine sound was coming from down the street *and* through the phone. I hang up the call and tuck my cell into the inside pocket of my blazer. I round the car as he flips open the oddly hinged door. One time, I called it a weird-ass door, and Kingston acted like a big baby, saying they were dihedral synchro-blah-blah-something doors. The boy is *really* sensitive about his car. Although, I suppose if I spent an obscene amount of money on a vehicle, I'd be touchy about it, too.

He frowns when I get in and buckle my seat belt. "What happened?"

"Why do you think something happened?"

Kingston gives me his *Are you kidding me?* look. "Waiting at the end of the driveway was a pretty big giveaway, but you also look shaken up."

I motion toward the road. "Start driving, and I'll tell you."

He shifts the car into gear and pulls back onto the road. On the short drive to school, I recap the whole crazy interaction with Charles and Madeline. Part of me is actually worried about Madeline after seeing how pissed my father was, but the other part doesn't give a shit. To be clear, I don't think there's *ever* a valid reason for a man to hit a woman, but after that bitch threatened me, I definitely think she deserves a solid tongue-lashing. Maybe have her credit cards taken away. That would probably devastate her.

Kingston pulls into a parking spot and kills the engine. "Fuck."

"Yeah, pretty much. It was a little scary seeing him so angry, even if it wasn't directed at me for once. Even when I rile him up, he's never seemed as furious as he did back there. His voice was *loud*. Like, it echoed throughout the house. And what's up with the 'face the consequences' crap? Who talks to their spouse like that?"

His beautiful hazel eyes drill into me. "You need to get out of that house, Jazz."

"No, Kingston. I'm not having this argument with you again."

"If he's raging like that, it means he's losing control, which I'm sure enrages him even further. Charles Davenport is passionate about projecting a calm and calculated image to the world. From the sounds of it, he's dropping pretenses more and more since you've been around. I think your presence puts him on edge."

"The fact that I look almost exactly like the woman he repeatedly raped and impregnated probably has a lot to do with that," I mumble.

"All the more reason for you to get out of there."

"Again, *not happening*."

He scrubs a hand over his face. "Jesus-fucking-Christ, woman."

I tilt my chin up defiantly and pin him with a razor-edged stare. "Don't you J-F-C me! Worst-case scenario, if he flips his shit, I can defend myself just fine."

Kingston gives me a cruel smirk. "Really? Like you did at the lake?"

My mouth gapes. "You did *not* just go there!" I fling open my door and unbuckle the seat belt. "Fuck this shit. And fuck *you*." I climb out of the car and walk away as fast as I can.

"Jazz, wait!" I only make it a few feet before Kingston catches up with me, pulling on my arm.

I whip around. "Let go of me!"

"Just hold on a second, will you?" he shouts. Lowering his voice, he adds, "I'm sorry. I'm worried about you, and I was channeling it the wrong way."

A crowd has gathered around us, several people holding their phones up.

"Mind your own business, assholes!" I scream.

Snickers pass through the crowd, and of course, not a single person makes an effort to move the fuck along. I flip 'em the bird and tell myself to ignore their nosy asses.

"Can we just go somewhere and talk, please?" Kingston asks.

"I don't have time for that." I shake out of his

hold and start walking toward Lincoln Hall. "Whatever you need to say can be said after I've had time to cool off. I need to speak with my math teacher before class begins."

"Jazz—"

"Welcome back, baby girl." Bentley swoops in from out of nowhere. "You and the caveman are already starting drama, I see."

"Can it, Bentley."

"Stay out of it, Bent," Kingston says at the same time.

Bentley holds his hands up in a placating gesture. "Okay, kids, I think you two need a time-out." He hooks his arm over my shoulders. "Let me walk you to class, beautiful."

I know it's childish, but I stick my tongue out at Kingston and say, "Gladly. Get me away from this jerkface."

Ainsley and Reed join us then, sandwiching Kingston between them.

"Welcome back, Jazz," Ainsley says.

I give her a curt nod. "Thank you."

Ainsley loops her arm through her twin's. "C'mon, bro. Let's take a walk and quit giving these douchebags more fodder."

Kingston begrudgingly allows his sister to lead

him in the opposite direction. At the same time, Bentley and I head toward my statistics class. Right before Bent and I part ways, I spot Peyton, Whitney, and Imogen standing against the wall, their hate-filled stares honed in on me.

"Trouble in paradise?" Peyton asks mockingly. "Looks like things will be back to normal sooner than I thought."

Before I get a chance to tell this bitch off, Bentley does it for me.

"Get fucked, Peyton." He sneers. "And quit holding your breath for Davenport. In case you didn't get the memo, *you've been canceled*. You're washed-up pussy—nothing more." Bentley levels all three girls with a look so fierce, *I* want to cringe. "That applies to all three of you."

Goddamn, I'm so used to happy-go-lucky Bentley, I almost forgot he could be so callous. It's kind of jarring. And maybe a little hot.

Obviously, I have a problem.

As if they choreographed it ahead of time, Peyton and her sidekicks gasp dramatically, flip their hair over their shoulders, and stomp away with a huff. Man, they're freakishly in sync.

"Thanks, Bentley."

He pulls me into a hug. "Anytime, bae."

I chuckle. "Do people even say bae anymore?"

I feel him shrug before kissing the top of my head. "Don't care." He pulls back and gives me a pat on the butt. "Now, get your sexy ass to class."

I give him a mock salute. "Sir, yes, sir!"

"Smartass." Bentley jerks his head toward the room I'm supposed to be in. "Unless you wanna ditch and go make out with me, get in there and learn something."

That kicks my butt into gear. "Learning it is!"

Bentley's laughter echoes down the hall as he walks away. Right before he turns the corner, he looks back as if he can sense me watching, and winks. I shake my head as I step into the class and take a seat at my desk.

What am I going to do with that boy?

chapter fifteen

JAZZ

People have been staring and whispering behind my back all morning. I expected that knowing word would've spread about my attack, but something's off. I'm probably being paranoid, but it almost feels like a coordinated effort. Like they've *planned* this.

Both guys *and* girls have been flinging insults at me under their breath. I've been propositioned by meatheads or preppy douchebags at least a dozen times.

"Hey, Jasmine. I have a question for you," Jarod, my physics partner, whispers.

Oh, this should be good. Jarod's a jock—a baller, I think—and he's also a colossal dickhead. He's one of those dudes who thinks he's God's gift to women, so he doesn't handle blows to the ego very well. When I first came to Windsor, Jarod asked me out on a date. When I told him I wasn't interested, he acted like he was joking, and he's treated me like shit ever since.

"*What*, Jarod?"

I glance at the clock and see that we have less than two minutes before the bell rings. Thank fuck.

"I heard something interesting about you, and I wanted to know if it was true."

I arch an eyebrow. "Oh, yeah? What's that?"

He smiles lasciviously. "I heard that you weren't *really* assaulted." The asshat actually uses air quotes on the last word. "That what *really* happened was rough sex that went south. They say you're like, a total freak in bed, and you're into blood play."

I'm so shocked, I can't even form words. I just stare at him like an idiot as he continues.

"You know..." Jarod trails his finger down my forearm, and thankfully, I somehow have the where-withal to jerk away. "If that's why you turned me down, you should reconsider. I'm up for some kink if that's what you're into."

My heart beats rapidly as images from that night flash through my head. Fuck, my chest hurts. Black spots dance across my vision. I'm too busy trying to ward off a panic attack to respond to Jarod's ridiculous accusation. When the bell rings, the other students can't get out of the room fast enough, but I'm frozen.

Jarod stands up and leans into my ear, completely oblivious to my impending meltdown. "You don't have to answer me right now. Just think about it."

I take deep breaths as I watch Jarod's cocky ass saunter out of the room, making no effort to leave my table.

Fuck.

I need to get myself together. I refuse to let them own me like this. *I* control my emotions—not any of these Windsor assholes or my would-be rapists. I continue my breathing exercises.

In...and out. In...and out. In...and out.

"Miss Callahan, is everything all right?" our teacher, Mrs. Nguyen, inquires. "*Miss Callahan?*"

I blink, looking toward the front of the room where her desk sits. "What?"

She rounds her desk and sits on the edge. "I asked if you were okay. You look...pale. Do you need a pass to the health room?"

I've never been pale a day in my life, but I get the point.

I take a few more deep breaths for good measure and shake my head. "No, I'm okay. Just spaced out, I guess."

She looks skeptical. "If you're sure..."

"I'm positive. I skipped breakfast, so I'm a little out of it. Good thing lunch is next period, huh?" I stand up and sling my book bag over my shoulder. "I'll be good as new once I get some food in my stomach."

Her eyes follow my every move as I approach the front of the classroom. I offer her a smile as I walk past her desk, trying to escape without an interrogation. Right before I reach the door, she calls my name.

Damn it.

I turn around. "Yes?"

Mrs. Nguyen's lips press together. "Jasmine, I heard what happened to you after homecoming. If you ever need someone to talk to, I'd be happy to listen."

I swallow the lump in my throat, steeling my resolve. "Thanks, but, uh...I'll be fine."

"If you change your mind, it's an open-ended offer. Have a good lunch, Miss Callahan."

When I step into the hallway, Reed is waiting for me. I tried telling them I don't need a babysitter, but Ainsley or one of the guys has walked me to each of my classes so far today. Safety in numbers, or some shit like that.

"You okay?" he asks.

I sigh. "I would be if people would stop asking me that."

Reed's brows crease in confusion. "What does that mean?"

"Nothing. Forget I said anything." I wave him off. "So, how are things going with Ainsley? I hear you're spending lots of time together. You ready to nut up and make things official yet?"

His light green eyes narrow. "Nice change of subject."

"What?" I shrug. "I genuinely want to know."

"It's...complicated."

"Because of Kingston?"

He tucks his hands in his pockets. "Among other things."

"Oh, c'mon." I shake my head. "You know damn well that her happiness is what's most impor-tant to him. If you make Ainsley happy, what's the big deal?"

Reed scratches the back of his head, looking nervous. Huh. That's a new one. This boy usually exudes one hundred percent confidence or aloofness. There doesn't seem to be an in-between with him.

When he doesn't answer, I keep going. "Whatever your issues are...you'd better figure them out fast, Reed. She likes you. *A lot.* But Ainsley's not going to wait around forever."

His eyes widen in panic. "She said that?"

"Yeah, she did, actually. But the real point is that *she shouldn't have to.* It's not fair to string her along. Either you're in or you're out. Whichever path you decide to take, don't dick her around. She's good people. She doesn't deserve to be kept hanging on the line just because you don't want her to be with someone else."

Reed scrubs a hand down his face. "Fuck."

He's obviously agitated, so I take pity on him. "You want my advice?"

He gives me a curt nod.

I bump my shoulder into his arm. "Talk to her. Whatever your reservations are, *talk to her* and see if you can work through them together."

Reed considers that as we make a pit stop at my locker, so I can ditch my bag before heading to the dining room. Right before we step inside, he tugs on my elbow to pull me aside.

"Thanks, Jazz."

I grin. "Anytime, big guy. Now, let's eat. I'm fucking starving."

He laughs and ushers me through the doorway.

We stand in line to grab some food before meeting the others at the same table we sat at before my unplanned hiatus.

"What took you guys so long?" Kingston asks suspiciously. "I was about to send out a search party."

"Haha, funny guy." I take the empty seat next to him while Reed pulls out the chair next to Ainsley. "Reed and I were having a little chat, that's all."

"About what?" Ainsley and Kingston ask in unison.

I flick my finger in between them. "That was cute. Was that your freaky twin telepathy kicking in?"

Ainsley laughs while Kingston growls. Like, literally growls.

I poke him in the chest. "You don't get to be pissy with me. I'm still mad at you."

Kingston traps my finger, hooks his foot around the leg of my chair, and pulls me closer. Leaning into my ear, he whispers, "I *like it* when you're mad at me. That fiery look you get in your eyes makes me rock hard."

I tell myself not to look down, but my eyes fall to his lap anyway. Yep, Kingston's definitely sporting a semi that seems to be growing the longer I stare.

I fight a shiver as I scoot my chair back. "Asshole."

Raucous laughter sounds from across the room, stealing my attention. It's coming from the self-proclaimed royals' table—the same spot where my tablemates used to sit every day. Peyton, Imogen, and Whitney are still there, but there are four new guys and one new girl. They look familiar, but I don't know their names.

"What's going on there?" I ask. "I thought that table was reserved solely for the super-elite?"

All three guys frown while Ainsley rolls her eyes.

"Well?" I prompt. "Is anyone going to explain?"

Ainsley's the first to speak up. "During your absence, Peyton's established a new faction. She seems to think *she* can designate who the kings and queens of Windsor are, despite the fact that everyone knows that's not how it works. She's even decided to expand the court."

I turn to Kingston. "What does that mean for you guys?"

"Nothing. Peyton can spout off whatever bullshit she wants; doesn't mean the entire school will listen. There's an order that needs to be followed. It's been that way since this school was founded." Kingston's jaw clenches as he glances over there. "If we went over there and told them to get the fuck out of our seats, they'd have to obey."

I look around the room and see the other students giving the royals' table a wide berth and averting their eyes like they did when my guys sat there. From where I'm sitting, it looks like the school *is* listening.

Wait a minute...when did I start thinking of them as *my* guys?

"Who are the new people?"

"Mostly douche nuggets from the football team," Bentley replies sourly. "The guy sitting next to Pey Pey is Lucas Gale—he's been her fuckboy since Davenport here gave her the ax. He's also Windsor's star QB. Then, you have Aspen Evans— she's a cheerleader—followed by Christian Taylor, David Wright, and Barclay Baker."

"Why *don't* you tell them to leave the table?" I inquire.

Reed answers this time. "Because that would imply we *care*, and the last thing any of us wants is for Peyton to think she's getting to us."

What is Peyton hoping to accomplish by doing this?

"Is this another ploy to make you jealous?" I ask Kingston. "To make you want to be with her again?"

He finishes chewing the giant bite of pizza he just took. "Probably, which is exactly why we're not feeding into it. Just drop it, Jazz. It's no big deal."

I don't buy that for a second. She *is* getting to them. Whether they want to admit it or not, I can tell by their rigid spines and how they're discreetly watching the other table. These three are alpha males to the core, and Peyton's actions are a direct challenge.

Right before lunch is over, some girl timidly approaches our table and drops a cream-colored envelope in front of me. She's younger—couldn't be more than a sophomore—and the poor thing looks like she's about to shit herself.

"What's this?" I ask.

"It's from Peyton Devereux."

I scoff. "She couldn't give it to me herself? She lives down the hall from me. Like, literally, *right down the hall*. She could've easily slipped it under my door."

"I just do what I'm told," the girl says before scurrying away like a cockroach.

Kingston grabs the envelope and breaks the seal before I get the chance. He pulls out a square made of thick cardstock and looks it over. His nostrils flare as he angrily shoves it back in.

"What is it?" I grab it from him and pull out the card. It's an invitation to Peyton's eighteenth birthday party, only there's a big red circle over it with a backslash symbol through the middle. "What the fuck does this even mean? Is she trying to tell me I'm *not* invited to her party? As if I'd go anyway?"

"Don't react, Jazz," Kingston commands. "It's what she wants; it's why she's doing this publicly. She's trying to humiliate you."

Fuck that. Half the school has been trying to humiliate me today, and I have a sneaking suspicion she's behind it. I'm not into playing my wicked stepsister's games, but I will *not* bow down to *anyone*, especially her. I turn in my chair to find Peyton and her groupies looking in my direction, having a good ol' laugh at my expense. Or so they think. Never once breaking my stare, I grab the envelope and walk over to her table.

Peyton turns her nose up, haughtiness seeping

out of her every pore. "What do you want, whore? If you're looking for some crack, you'll need to go back to the ghetto."

"Good one, baby," the guy beside her laughs.

I completely ignore Peyton's pathetic gibe—and the idiot she's fucking—and smile, which causes her to frown. "I just wanted to let you know what I thought about your silly little birthday party, or celebrating your existence in general."

I can feel the entire room's eyes on us as I hold up the fancy invitation and rip it straight down the middle. I raise a challenging eyebrow as I tear it in half a second time. I keep going until Peyton is positively fuming, and the last piece of paper is floating in tiny little pieces down by her Louboutin-heeled feet. When I'm done, I brush my hands off and lean into her.

"You see, Peyton, the difference between you and me, is that *I* actually have the balls to fight my battles. Next time you have something to say to me, *just say it*. Grow the fuck up."

A chorus of, *damn* or *burn* or some variation thereof, echoes throughout the dining room. While Peyton's mouth is still hanging open, and that Lucas guy is glaring holes through me, I walk back to my table, sit down, and take a bite of my penne, as if none of that ever happened.

"Holy shit, Jazz," Ainsley whispers. "That was epic!"

I smile victoriously, knowing Peyton's plan back-fired. Damn, that bitch really is cuckoo if she thinks the invitation thing would bother me. I've known about the party all along—it's not like she's been keeping it to herself—but I never had *any* intention of going. Since it's being held at the mansion, Ainsley and I made plans to hang at her place that night.

Knowing Peyton though, she'll probably act like that whole confrontation never happened, which is why I'll need to take measures to reinforce my message. I chuckle under my breath as I think of the perfect solution.

Bentley pulls me into him and kisses my temple. "Jazzy Jazz, it's good to have you back."

chapter sixteen

JAZZ

"Girl, you look amazing." Ainsley coats her lips in a fresh layer of gloss. "But are you sure it's okay to take the splint off?"

I lift my arm and flex my wrist experimentally. "I'm sick of that thing; it's heavy and itchy. Besides, it doesn't exactly go with this outfit. Wearing it two-thirds of the recommended time is totally enough, don't you think?"

Ainsley shakes her head. "Um...I'm not a doctor, but I think they say six weeks for a reason. You know your body better than me, though. If you say your wrist feels okay without it, who am I to argue? Just promise me you'll be careful."

"I will."

"Peyton's going to be pissed when she sees you." Ainsley gets a Cheshire Cat grin.

I laugh. "You, too."

We both check ourselves out in the vanity mirror, pleased with our reflections. When I decided to crash Peyton's birthday party, I resigned myself to the fact that I'd have to glam myself up because that's what will annoy Peyton the most. She seems to get off on picking apart my preferred attire, and this way, she doesn't have the option. When I ducked my head out earlier and saw Peyton pre-gaming in the living room with her girls, I knew it was the right decision.

Peyton's really working the living Barbie angle tonight in a skin-tight hot pink corset and mini skirt, sky-high heels, and an actual fucking tiara. Imogen and Whitney are wearing almost identical outfits—sans the tiara—but in different colors. Since I'm totally clueless about fashion and makeup, Ainsley came over early to help me get ready.

It helps that Ainsley and I are the exact same size, so I can borrow her clothes. My walk-in closet is filled with designer pieces, but I needed something less demure and more vixen to have the most significant impact. My beautiful friend here has a freakishly vast array of club attire, which works perfectly for this evening.

"My brother's going to shit when he sees you." Ainsley laughs. "I wouldn't put it past him to take the shirt off his own body to cover you up from wandering eyes."

"Yeah, well, that's because your brother's possessiveness is misplaced."

She gives me a wry look. "You're still lying to yourself, I see."

I freshen my cherry red lip stain. "What's that supposed to mean?"

Ainsley rolls her big hazel eyes. "C'mon, Jazz. You know there's something special going on between you and Kingston. He would do anything for you. I know you have feelings for him, so why are you fighting it?"

I sigh. "Because I don't trust my feelings for him."

Her delicate eyebrows pinch together. "What do you mean?"

I hop on the counter, careful not to flash my panties in the process. Easier said than done in this dress.

"I don't understand *how* I could have feelings for him after everything he's put me through."

She gives me a sympathetic look. "But you said he explained that, right?"

I gave Ainsley the abridged version of my conversation with Kingston regarding why he was so cruel to me when we first met. I focused solely on the *he's a typical guy afraid of his feelings* type of thing, but she seems to have bought it. I hate withholding information from her, but I know Kingston's right in that respect.

"Yeah...and I want to believe him—I honestly do—but something is niggling in the back of my brain telling me to keep my guard up."

Ainsley takes a seat on the vanity bench. "Do you know what that something is?"

I wring my hands together. "It all comes back to that night at Donovan's party. Bentley swears they didn't drug me, but nothing else makes sense, Ains. I had two drinks. *Two.* You know that's not enough to fuck me up, yet I barely remember anything from that night. Only flashes here and there."

Mostly flashes of making out with Kingston and Bentley, but I keep that part to myself.

She gives me a closed-mouth smile. "What exactly did Bentley say?"

"He told me they would *never* do that to me.

Then he told me to ask him about a girl named Carissa some time, then I'd have no doubt."

Ainsley's breath stutters. "And did you? Ask him about Carissa?"

"No." I shake my head. "Honestly, it kind of slipped my mind until now. Who is she anyway?"

"She was my best friend," Ainsley whispers.

"*Was?* Did you two have a falling out or something?"

"No, Jazz." She shakes her head. "She died. Committed suicide, actually."

I suck in a harsh breath. "Oh. I'm so sorry, Ains. I know that's a shitty platitude, but it's true. I know how hard it is losing someone you love."

She sniffs, dabbing at the corners of her eyes. "I know you do, and I'm okay now. I mean, it's been almost two years. I still miss her every day, but it gets easier to not think about it so much. Bentley took it the hardest out of all of us, I think. He may joke around a lot, but that boy's holding on to a lot of grief and regret."

"What do you mean?"

"That's not my story to tell, Jazz. I think you should talk to him, though. I really do think it would alleviate your concerns." Ainsley gives me a sad smile. "I know what they did that night was awful—with the pictures, I mean—but if it's worth anything, I'm *positive* they wouldn't have drugged you. *One thousand percent positive.* And trust me, they got a mouthful from me about circulating that video and those pictures. I actually slapped my brother across the face and kneed him in the balls."

My lips twitch. "Are you serious?"

"Yep." She nods proudly. "And I would've done the same to the other two, but Reed held me back. I decided that particular revenge was a dish best served cold. With the way Reed's been behaving lately, though, his comeuppance will likely be sooner rather than later."

"He still won't tell you what's going on?"

She shakes her head. "Nope. And quite frankly, I'm done waiting."

I raise my brows. "You're giving up?"

"I don't know." Ainsley shrugs. "I don't want to, but I'm sure as shit not going to let him ruin my night. I'm going to go out there, have some drinks, maybe dance with a few hot boys, and forget about all the Reed drama for one night."

"Well, what are we waiting for? Let's get down there."

Ainsley smiles. "By the time this night is over,

the birthday bitch will know for damn sure you won't take her shit lying down."

We're both grinning like fools as we exit my bedroom and make our way down the stairs. Eminem's "Godzilla" blasts through the speakers, setting the tone perfectly for this freakin' madhouse. I still can't believe Charles and Madeline went away for the weekend just so Peyton could have a house party. Seriously, what kind of parents do that, knowing what kind of debauchery these people are capable of? Spoiler alert: shitty ones.

When we get to the main level, this shindig seems to be in full swing. Peyton's party planner certainly went all out. All of the existing furniture down here has been replaced with a large dance floor, D.J. area, and several different seating options. There's a staffed bar in the back next to a towering champagne fountain. The back patio is crammed with bodies, and the subtle lighting that was out there has been replaced with bulbs so bright, the whole area is lit up like a football field. Jesus fuck, I don't even want to know how much all this shit cost.

My jaw drops when my eyes stumble on the setup in the back corner of the living room. "*What the hell?!*"

There are actual stripper poles installed, all

three of which have half-naked drunk girls swinging around them, surrounded by two dozen or so guys.

"Wow, she really wants to make it memorable, huh?" Ainsley asks. "Just what every girl wants for her birthday: pole jockeys."

I shake my head at the ridiculousness of it all as we walk through the room. Ainsley and I are subjected to more than a few people trying to either murder us with their glares or make our clothing magically go *poof!* with their leering gazes. Funny thing is, these dresses are so short, there's not much that's not already on display. I have to keep tugging my dress down to ensure I'm not showing ass cheek.

"Let's check out the back," Ainsley suggests.

We're hit with a rush of warmth from the outdoor heaters as we step outside. Damn, I think there are more people outside than in. Although it's late-October, the pool is even packed because Madeline keeps the water heater set at a balmy 82°. Thanks to the enhanced lighting, bare tits greet me from all around, and I spot a few couples in the pool that are definitely screwing up against the tiled wall. I don't even want to know what's going on back in the small grotto.

"Remind me not to use the pool until it's fully disinfected," I mutter.

There are speakers out here, but the volume isn't nearly as high as it is on the inside. It was no doubt staged that way to avoid noise complaints. However, the massive, clearly inebriated crowd certainly isn't helping that cause.

"Holy shit, is that Peyton?" Ainsley points to the group of people playing an apparent game of chicken in the pool.

When the blonde goes down and resurfaces, we see that it is indeed Peyton. She climbs back on Lucas Gale's shoulders in her hot pink string bikini. Whitney is in the same position on that Christian guy's shoulders, only she seems to have lost her top somewhere.

"You lose, Birthday Girl!" Christian yells. "Take it off!"

I turn to Ainsley. "He can't possibly...oh, yep, that's exactly what he meant."

Peyton is making a show of untying her bikini top, swirling it in the air, and tossing it to the side.

Ainsley shakes her head when both girls start making out, groping each other's breasts, getting more into it as the catcalls get louder.

I throw my hands out. "Is this really happening right now?"

Bentley swings his arm around my shoulders.

"What's the big deal? I don't think there's a single person in our senior class who hasn't seen their tits at some point."

Where'd he come from?

I tilt my chin up. "Well, *I* hadn't seen their boobs, and I was perfectly happy keeping it that way!"

Bentley watches the two girls as they kiss. "As much as I despise those skanks, you gotta admit, they're putting on a good show."

Ainsley makes a face and verbalizes my thought. "Ew, Bent. They're acting like over-the-top porn stars."

"Exactly my point." Bentley laughs.

"God, it seems like they're *really* enjoying themselves," I observe. "I didn't realize Peyton was into girls."

"She's not," Bentley says. "My guess is they're doing this half for the attention and half because they're rolling."

My brows rise. "Molly?"

He nods. "One and the same."

"Huh." I would've never pegged Peyton as a drug user either.

Bentley seems to read my mind. "Peyton's a white-collar drug enthusiast. She thinks weed is for slackers." He rolls his eyes. "But coke, pills, or Molly is totally up to her refined standards."

"I think I need a drink." I try dislodging Bentley's arm, but he pulls me back in to him.

"Hot damn, baby girl. What are you wearing?" He scans my body head to toe, lingering on my exposed thighs and pushed-up cleavage. "And how did it take me this long to notice? You're fucked when your boy gets here, and I do mean that quite literally. He's not going to be able to keep his hands off you."

Nope. Not going to picture that. Maybe if I repeat it enough times in my head, it'll work. Gah, I definitely need a drink.

"Where is he anyway?" Ainsley asks. "Reed said they'd be here by ten."

Bent shrugs. "Don't know. Why are your hands empty? Let's get you ladies some drinks."

The three of us head inside and order drinks from the bartender. Vodka cran for me, a screwdriver for Ains, and a bottle of beer for Bentley. By the time we're nursing our third round, we're all on the edge of the temporary dance floor, swaying to the music.

When "Dark Side" by Bishop Briggs starts blasting through the speakers, Bentley grabs my red cup and sets it on the nearest surface. "C'mere, girl."

As he drags me to the center of writhing bodies, I make eye contact with Ains. She raises her drink and smiles knowingly. The last two times Bentley and I danced together, I wound up locked in a room naked with her brother. I shiver, trying to squash the memories.

Bent pulls my back to his front, wrapping his arm around my middle. We move our hips in time with the sensual beat, getting lost in the rhythm. My life doesn't revolve around dance like it does with Ainsley, but it's still one of my favorite things. Closing my eyes, zoning out on the beat, I allow the music to direct my body. It's one of the rare moments when I don't think; I just *do*.

Now, dancing with Bentley is a different story. The boy can *move*, which I can't help but relate to sex. With him, I tune *in*, rather than out. I'm aware of every little touch. Every lyric. Every breath. Most of all, I'm conscious of the dichotomy between my body and brain.

My brain knows I'm leading him on. I know Bent's developing feelings for me that veer into girl-friend territory, whereas mine end at friendship. Then, there's the part where I'm antagonizing

Kingston every time I'm tempted by his best friend. I don't want to drive a wedge between them, yet more and more each day, that seems to be the case.

The thing is, I've grown to care for Bentley. I genuinely feel he could be one of the most important people in my life, but not if we screw this up. We're at a crossroads, and we need to figure out which way to go. The problem with that is our fierce attraction to one another; it's palpable, almost as strong as the pull I feel toward Kingston. I don't know how to achieve balance, and when I'm dancing with Bentley like this, I don't want to.

I have a moment of déjà vu when Bent's erection presses against my back. I'm so tempted to reach back and touch him, and I'm sure he wouldn't object.

"You look so fucking hot in this thing, Jazz," his deep voice rumbles in my ear as his fingers flirt with the short hem of my red minidress. "I know I'm asking for trouble, but I don't fucking care right now."

My lids flutter when he grinds into me harder. More purposefully. Damn, the boy is blessed.

"Bentley..." That's all I've got. My brain seems to have short-circuited.

"You have no idea how badly I want to peel this

dress off." His fingertip brushes my inner thigh beneath the stretchy fabric. "Touch you. *Run my tongue all over your pussy.*"

He's so close to my panties—it's not a difficult task in this dress, considering there's not much material. I'm so wet, the satin is soaked through. If his finger moved up another inch, he'd discover this.

"We shouldn't." My voice is breathy, not very convincing. I doubt he can even hear me over the music.

Bentley groans before removing his hand and placing it in a more respectable place. We're crammed in the middle of so many people, it's unlikely anyone saw his hand up my skirt. Even if they did, couples are doing a lot worse on this dance floor, so I doubt they'd care.

"You don't know what you're missing if you don't try."

"He's your best friend," I argue.

Bentley runs the bridge of his nose up the side of my neck. "He is, which is exactly why he knows what a big deal this is."

I turn around to face him, but I stay close. "*What's* a big deal? That you want to screw me? You're not exactly a monk, Bent."

He gives me a soft smile. "Not even close to

what I was referring to, but that's a story for another time. Besides, I think it'd be good for him if we gave him some real competition."

I chuckle half-heartedly. "I don't think Kingston would agree."

Bentley leans down and presses his mouth against my ear. "I know you want me, Jazz. I'd bet my fucking Porsche that your panties are soaked right now. That your clit is *throbbing*, begging for attention. I'd barely have to touch you before you were coming all over my tongue." I gasp when his fingers curl under the hem of my dress, and he licks the shell of my ear. "Davenport may think he has a claim on you, but *not once* have you confirmed that. Isn't that right? You don't *belong* to anyone?"

"I belong to *myself*."

"Exactly. So, why can't we—"

I dig my nails into his forearms when I get a prickling sensation at the back of my neck. On instinct, my eyes scan the room, looking for the reason why. When I find him, he's marching toward us like a man possessed. The crowd parts, desperately trying to avoid Kingston's wrath. Bentley tenses when I turn around and shake out of his hold.

"Shit," I mutter.

When Kingston finally reaches us, his eyes slowly travel the length of my body, taking in my minuscule dress and heeled sandals. His eyes are so heated, flames lick my skin everywhere his gaze touches. After getting so worked up from dancing, and the way Kingston's looking at me right now, I know Bentley's right. If anyone touched between my thighs right now, I'd detonate in seconds.

Kingston scans me once more before drilling his gaze into the man behind me. "What the fuck's going on, Bent?"

I hold up a hand, trying to defuse the situation. "Now, hold on, you two. Why don't we——"

"Reed! What are you doing? *Stop it!*"

All three of us immediately whip our heads around when we hear Ainsley's anguished cry.

Kingston gets a lock on her first and leads the charge into action. Ainsley keeps screaming at Reed to stop, and as we get closer, I see why. He's currently beating on that Lawson guy. The music comes to a grinding halt, allowing every grunt and thud to echo throughout the cavernous room.

Kingston and Bentley both assess the situation before forming a protective barrier around Ainsley and me. A minute ago, they looked like they were ready to kill each other. Now, they're working in perfect harmony, and I don't think they even realize it.

"What the hell is going on?" Kingston asks his sister.

"I don't know!" Ainsley shouts, tears running down her face. "I was talking to Lawson, and all of a sudden, Reed is punching him in the face."

Reed and Lawson are fairly matched in both size and skill, but Reed has this feral look in his eyes that gives him an edge. I wince when Reed takes an uppercut to the jaw, but it barely affects him. When Reed's hand connects with Lawson's face, Lawson wails, cupping his cheekbone.

I throw my hands out toward the melee. "Why aren't you guys stopping this?"

"Reed wouldn't be doing this unless he had a damn good reason," Bentley explains.

"What the fuck is wrong with you, man?" Lawson yells, staggering to the side and spitting blood on the floor. "I didn't do shit to you!"

"You put something in her drink!" Reed bellows, jabbing a finger in Ainsley's direction. *Damn.* Calm and collected Reed Prescott has definitely left the building. "I fucking *saw you* do it when she turned her head away!"

Both mine and Ainsley's jaws drop at that piece

of info. Kingston and Bentley seem to realize the same thing I do because they look like they're about to jump into the fight.

Kingston points a finger at me. "Is that what you did to her? "Did you fucking *drug her*?" His tone is quiet. Deadly.

At this point, what appears to be the entire party has formed a circle around the six of us.

Lawson holds his hands out. "Now, wait just a fucking minute. I was doing you dicks a favor!"

"What?!" Bentley lunges for him, but Kingston pulls him back.

"You have two seconds to explain." Kingston's jaw and fists are clenching.

Lawson swings his arm out in Bentley's direction. "He told me to bring her to you nice and sloppy. She was barely sipping her drinks, and it was taking forever, so I sped up the process. It was a low dose; it wouldn't have done any real damage. You should be *thanking me*, assholes. You got to have your way with her, didn't you?" Lawson turns his head to leer at me. "I'm only sorry I didn't get a turn first."

A loud gasp rings through the crowd right before all hell breaks loose. Kingston releases some sort of battle cry right as he starts punching the shit out of Lawson. Bentley and Reed join in the fray, and all three of them go at him, punching, kicking, pretty much whatever they can do until Lawson is on the ground, nearly unconscious.

Bentley and Reed back off when Lawson's body goes limp, but Kingston keeps pummeling his face, over and over and over again. Lawson's head thuds against the marble floor with a resounding crack, his face is practically unrecognizable, but Kingston doesn't let up. Bentley and Reed try pulling him off, but Kingston's too enraged. He's crouched down, hulking out on this dude, and I seriously think he might kill him if he doesn't stop.

"Kingston!" I scream. "Stop it! You're going to kill him!"

Ainsley's repeating the same words, trying desperately to get through to her twin.

"Good!" he yells, punching again.

I know it's stupid, considering how scary and amped up Kingston is right now, but I charge toward him anyway. Bentley and Reed try holding me back, but I manage to squirm between them until I'm placing a hand on Kingston's shoulder. He immediately freezes and whips his head back to meet my gaze.

"He's not worth it, Kingston." I squat down next

to him, probably flashing half the room, but I don't really give a shit. I rest my forehead against his and cup my hands over his cheeks. "He's not fucking worth it. I'm okay. He didn't get to me. He didn't get to Ainsley. *We're okay*. I'm here." I kiss the corner of his mouth, tasting blood on my lips. "I'm *here*."

Kingston releases a shuddering breath before clutching my arms, hauling me off the hard floor. He crushes me to his chest, holding on for dear life as he gets his breathing under control. I turn my head to the side and see Ainsley wrapped around Reed, sobbing. He's smoothing his hand down her back, whispering something in her ear. Lawson is starting to wake up, groaning, but making no effort to peel himself off the floor. I'm half tempted to kick that fucker, but I'm pretty sure it'll only exacerbate the situation.

After a few moments, Kingston pulls back slightly and finds Bentley. "Will you take care of this?" Kingston scans the crowd and adds, "Party's over! Get the fuck out of here!"

Bentley nods. "I got it, man. Go get cleaned up."

Kingston looks down, seeing all the blood. He seems confused like he doesn't know how it got there. His grip on my hand is firm as he leads me away.

"You can't do that!" Peyton screams as her guests scurry toward the door. "Come back! You don't have to leave. It's *my* party!"

I turn back and find that she's still topless, dripping all over the floor.

I hold my hand up. "Oh my God, Peyton, put your tits away! Nobody needs to see that shit."

"Really?" she taunts. "Because I know for a fact, Kingston *loves* my tits. He's told me so many, *many* times as he was fucking them. And at the very end, he'd slide his dick into my mouth, and I'd swallow *every ounce* of his cum. He said I was the best titty fuck he'd ever had." She cups her breasts suggestively. "Isn't that right, baby?"

Snickers and *oohs* ring out through the remaining bystanders.

"Fuck off, Peyton." Kingston's grip on my hand tightens. "Let's go, Jazz. She's not worth it."

Peyton glares at both of us as Kingston repeats my words from earlier. "You'll never keep him, Jasmine. Just remember that all this bullshit will be for nothing. Everything you'll go through will be for *nothing.*"

Kingston marches toward the stairs, yanking me

behind him. As I'm trying to decode her cryptic words, Peyton yells Kingston's name, but he simply lifts his middle finger in the air. When we reach the top of the stairs, he bypasses my bedroom and pulls me into a guest room, locking the door behind us.

When I look at him questioningly, he says, "No camera."

Right. Well, at least he had enough sense to remember that.

"Come on." I incline my head toward the ensuite. "There's a first aid kit under my bathroom cabinet. Let's see if there's one in there, too."

Kingston nods, following me silently into the bathroom.

Jesus, how did everything go to shit so quickly? This seems to be a developing trend, and I really don't like the possibilities of what could happen next.

chapter seventeen

KINGSTON

I hiss when Jazz swipes a cotton ball over the torn skin on my knuckles.

She rolls her beautiful brown eyes. "Quit being such a baby."

"It fucking stings," I mutter.

"Really?" She lifts her sculpted eyebrows. "You can get punched in the face, no problem, but not handle a little antiseptic on your hand?"

My eyes narrow. "I had adrenaline working for me then."

She throws the cotton ball in the trash and steps back to assess her work. "I'm glad to see most of that blood wasn't yours. It's not nearly as bad as it looked."

I reach behind me, pulling my shirt off. I don't miss the way Jazz's eyes hone in on my upper body.

"I could really use a shower." I gesture to the smeared blood on her skin from being pressed up against me. "You too."

Jazz nods. "You're right." She grabs a bath towel from the shelf next to her. "You can take this one, and I'll go jump in mine real quick."

I hook my finger under the strap of her tiny dress. Christ, when I first saw her tonight, all I wanted to do was throw her over my shoulder and carry her to the nearest available surface. After I decked Bentley for putting his hands on her, that is.

"We could save water and take one together."

"Haha, funny guy."

"I wasn't joking."

I have to suppress a groan when Jazz wets her lips. "Kingston—"

"What? It's okay if Bentley touches you, but not me? Why is that?"

Her eyes fill with fire. "I didn't *ask* Bentley to touch me."

"You didn't *stop it* either. You know, I'm curious, what would've happened if I hadn't arrived at that very moment? Bentley looked about ready to drag you into a dark corner. Would you have let him?

Hell, would you have let him stick his hand up your dress even farther, fingering your pussy right there in the middle of a crowded room?"

"I don't know." Jazz looks away. "I'm pretty sure I wouldn't have actually slept with him."

My teeth grind together. "Not the answer I was looking for, Jazz."

She throws her hands up. "Do you want me to lie? I thought we were done hiding shit from each other."

"Okay, since we're being so honest, why don't you tell me what *this* is, then?" I flick my finger between the two of us. "Do. You. Want. Me? Do you want to *be with me?*"

"You seriously want to have the *define our relationship* talk right now?"

I cross my arms over my chest. "Why *not* now? It seems to be necessary after what I saw down there."

She mimics my pose. "For one, you just knocked a guy unconscious. Maybe even hospitalized him. Shouldn't the police be showing up any minute now to arrest you?"

I scoff. "Bentley will take care of it. Did you see all those phones trained on the fight? We have

Lawson's confession. If anyone needs to lawyer up, it'd be him."

Jazz rubs her temples. "I can't do this right now."

"It's a simple yes or no question, Jazz." I pull her hands away from her face and tilt her chin up. "I think I've already made my position clear, but just in case, let me spell it out for you. I haven't fucked anyone else since before we met. Besides a few kisses with that chick in the hot tub—which was all for show—I haven't *touched* anyone else. I don't want to. *You* are the only woman I want. In my bed, by my side, it's *all you.*"

"Kingston—"

"I'm not done." I take her face in my hands and press our foreheads together. "When I found you that night, when I thought I was going to *lose you forever*, it was like a giant wake up call. I don't want to push you away anymore, Jazz. I don't want to pretend like you're not my goddamned world—not when it's just us, Ainsley, or the guys.

"I'm sick of being surrounded by all these secrets and lies. I'm fed up with the uncertainty. I know we need to keep playing the game for the greater good, but I need something real, too, and you're the realest fucking thing I've ever known. You want the same thing, Jazz. You can't deny it. Not to me."

"This is crazy," she whispers. "We just met a couple of months ago."

"Technically speaking, we met when we were babies." Jazz's lips are so close, I can't help myself. I press my mouth against hers, tugging on her full bottom lip with my teeth.

"Kingston."

"Jasmine."

Her warm breath tickles my face as she sighs. "I don't want to keep pushing you away either. It's exhausting. But..."

I pull back a little to look her in the eyes. "But *what?*"

Jazz averts her eyes and chews on the corner of her lip. "But...I can't pretend this thing with Bentley doesn't exist. I *like* him—purely as a friend—but...not a platonic friend. We have this crazy chemistry. I don't know how to make that go away, and I don't think it's fair for me to tell you I'm all in when there's this big, unresolved issue."

Her attraction to my best friend isn't breaking news, but it still takes me a moment to formulate a reply. What I really want to do, is go apeshit on someone's face again, but instead, I say, "I can't share, Jazz. Not with you."

"I'm not asking you to. I'm not that kind of—" She shakes her head. "You and me...we're complicated enough. I have no desire to add to that." She laughs sardonically. "Besides, the thought of *you* in a poly relationship, with another guy no less, is a joke. It doesn't mesh with that whole caveman thing you've got going on."

Fuck no, it doesn't.

"Let me ask you this. Do you like being with me?"

She tilts her head to the side. "Like, *like* you, like you?"

I give her a wry look. "What are we? Twelve? *Do you have any feelings for me* that go beyond friendship or physical attraction? Could you see yourself being in a relationship with me exclusively?"

Christ, whoever thought I'd be on this end of a conversation like this?

"Yes, but—"

I press my index finger to her lips. "Then we'll figure out the rest."

Her eyebrows scrunch together. "How?"

"I don't know," I admit. "But if not having you is the alternative, I'll think of something."

Jazz combs her fingers lightly through my hair, and I swear, I almost purr like a goddamn kitten.

I gently grab her newly bared wrist and place a kiss on the pulse point. "Where's your splint?"

"Took it off." Jazz shrugs. "Thank you for what you did down there."

I lift a brow. "You're thanking me for beating the shit out of someone?"

She gives me a soft smile. "Not necessarily...but I am thanking you for defending me. For righting a wrong."

I slide Jazz's dress strap off her shoulder and place a kiss on her bare skin. "I'll keep doing it if you'll let me."

Jazz's breath hitches as I pull her into me, sliding the other strap down. "Do you think he'll be arrested? And if so, will the charges stick? I don't want someone else to get hurt."

"Don't know," I murmur against the skin below her collarbone. "But if not, I'm sure as fuck going to make sure he knows we're watching him."

Jazz moans as I push the dress down further and glide my tongue over her subtle cleavage. "Kingston, what are you doing?"

"What does it look like I'm doing? I'm helping you get out of these clothes so we can get cleaned up. Don't worry; you're not the only one getting naked." I toe my shoes off and step out of my pants to demonstrate.

She doesn't protest one bit as I slide the flimsy red material the rest of the way down. In fact, when she steps out of the dress that's pooling on the floor, she immediately unhooks the strapless bra she's wearing and flings it to the side.

"Fuck." I bite my knuckles, which hurts like a bitch since they're cut open.

This woman is temptation personified. My salvation and ruin all wrapped up in a big red bow. She has the tightest body I've ever seen. Long, lean muscles. A trim waist that tapers down to perfectly flared hips. Her tits are perky with light brown nipples just slightly darker than her skin, and her heart-shaped ass is flawless. And I really do mean fucking perfect. I could spend days worshipping it and still never get my fill.

I fall to my knees, peppering kisses over Jazz's toned abs, trailing down to her black satin G-string. When I move her panties to the side, I find she's already soaking wet, glistening with want.

I give her one long lick before pulling back.

Jesus. I almost forgot how incredible she tastes. "Is this for me? Or is it leftover from earlier with Bentley?"

Jazz's hands clamp down on the marble countertop as I continue feasting on her delicious cunt. "Probably both."

I growl against her heated flesh and punish her for that remark with my tongue. I bring her right to the edge multiple times before backing off and switching up the pattern. Jazz is a whimpering mess, begging for release. She tries taking matters into her own hands, but I shove her away and manacle her wrists with my fingers. With my other hand, I push two fingers inside of her, curving them, causing her to release a litany of curses. It's a tight fit, even more so when I add a third finger, but she's so aroused, I have no trouble pumping them in and out.

"Fuck, Kingston," she pants as I circle my thumb over her clit. "Right there. God, don't stop."

"Wasn't planning on it."

When I lean forward, adding my tongue back into the mix, she shamelessly grinds her pussy against my face, screaming for more. Telling me how good it feels. Moaning my name over and over again, begging me to never stop. After I've made her come for the third time, I stand up and turn the shower on. We really are a fucking mess and need to get cleaned up.

Jazz and I step under the spray, allowing the warm water to wash away any traces of red. After soaping up and rinsing off, and okay, getting a little handsy in between, I'm about to turn the water off and move this party to a bed, but she implores me to stay with her big brown eyes. Who am I to deny her?

Jazz guides me to sit on the built-in bench in the corner of the shower. She then lowers herself to the tiled floor, crawling in between my thighs. My head falls back as she drags her tongue on the underside of my shaft, from root to tip. She hollows her cheeks and takes me into her mouth, sliding down inch by motherfucking inch, until I'm tapping the back of her throat.

I grab a fistful of her hair and release a strangled groan. "Fuck, Jazz. You keep that up, I'm going to embarrass myself."

My dick grows impossibly harder as she smiles around my girth, working her hand in tandem with her mouth. At first, I allow her to run the show, but it's only a matter of moments before I can't hold back anymore. I gather her long hair to the side so I can watch as my hips thrust in and out of the veritable heaven that is her mouth.

Jazz takes it like a champ as I fuck her mouth, moaning and humming around me as if she's enjoying this almost as much as I am. Much faster than I'd like, I'm issuing the obligatory warning that I'm about to blow my load. Jazz increases the suction as I surge into her mouth, only releasing me after the last tremor subsides. I watch through hooded eyes as she sits back with a smile, wiping a rogue drop of cum from the corner of her mouth with an index finger. When she takes that same finger and sucks it into her mouth, moaning as she tastes me, I swear I've never seen anything hotter in my life.

"Christ, woman. What are you doing to me?"

Jazz climbs on my lap, straddling me as she wraps her hands behind my neck. "I could ask you the same thing."

I take her face in my hands. "Does this mean you're going to think about what I said earlier? *Really* consider it?"

She searches my eyes. "Yeah. I'll think about it."

"Then, that's good enough for now."

It has to be because losing this girl isn't a choice I'm willing to live with.

We dry off and quickly realize we don't have any clean clothes in here. I don't really have a choice, so I pull my soiled pants and shirt back on. I'm pretty sure I broke that fucker's nose, and unfortunately for my favorite jeans, broken noses tend to bleed a lot. Jazz's bedroom is right next door, so we make a plan to dash over there as quickly as possible so she can get to her closet. I freeze when I step out of the ensuite and find Bentley sitting on the edge of the guest bed.

I stop so suddenly, Jazz smacks into me from behind. "Ow! My nose. Why the hell did you stop?"

Hyperaware Jazz is only dressed in a towel, I try shielding her body, but she's so tiny, she squirms around me, startling when she sees Bentley.

"Bentley!" Jazz clutches the towel to her chest. "What are you doing here? Aren't you supposed to be taking care of the, uh, *problem* with Lawson?"

Bentley's eyes darken as he gets a good look at her, before lifting the paper towel he's holding against his head. Jazz winces when he reveals a nasty gash over his eyebrow.

"Reed and Ainsley took over. I didn't think it was too bad at first, but the bleeding won't stop. Fucker clocked me with a bottle before we took him down. I was hoping you had a butterfly stitch or something. Peyton disappeared after her little hissy fit, so I checked your room, but it was empty." He rolls his eyes. "Obviously. Anyway, as I was heading back downstairs, I thought I heard someone talking in here. I knocked, but no one answered, so I tried the handle, and the door swung open."

My eyes narrow. "The door was locked."

Bentley's brows draw together. "Uh, no, it wasn't, dude."

"Yes, it *was*. I locked it myself."

"Apparently not as well as you thought," he says defensively.

Jazz looks at me in confusion—because we both know damn well the door *was* locked—before addressing Bentley. "I think I saw one in the first aid kit in the bathroom. Let me, uh, put some clean clothes on, and I'll help you out."

"Thanks, Jazzy."

I wait for her to leave the room before laying into him. "What the hell, man? Were you fucking *watching us?*"

The bathroom door wasn't wide open, but it

wasn't shut either, because I *did* lock the bedroom door, despite Bentley's denial.

Bent shrugs. "What if I was?"

"That's fucked up, dude." My fists clench at my sides.

He scoffs. "Oh, screw you, Davenport. Whatever happened to, 'I don't care who she fucks, Bent. She's just a means to an end'? Also, I've seen you screwing some chick before, and vice versa. In case you've forgotten, we've fucked *the same girl at the same time*, more than once."

I shake my head. "Things are different now."

"Why's that?" His jaw clenches.

"*Because she almost died!*" I take a deep breath and lower my voice. "If I hadn't gotten there in time, she would've fucking *died*, man."

Bentley takes a deep breath. "I wasn't *watching you*. I literally just got here as the shower was cutting off. I heard you talking about getting dressed or something, so I figured I'd wait it out."

I swallow the lump in my throat as we stare each other down. "She's *mine*, Bent, so you need to back the fuck off."

"She didn't seem to think so earlier tonight," he challenges. "If anyone has the right to be pissed, it's *me*, because I'm fairly certain you just enjoyed the fruits of *my* labor, and this isn't the first time that's happened."

I take a step toward him. "Don't do this, Bentley. I'm trying to be patient with you, and give you some leeway because I know everything that's happened recently is reminding you of Carissa, but—"

Bentley shoots up from the bed and shoves me back a step. "Fuck you! Don't bring her into this. She has *nothing* to do with this!"

I rub my jaw, trying to calm down. "Whatever you say, man."

"Don't fucking patronize me, dickhead."

"Would you rather have me punch you in the face?" I suggest, flexing my fingers. "Because that can easily be arranged."

"Hey!" Jazz shouts as she reenters the room. "What's going on in here? What is the matter with you two?"

"Nothing," Bentley and I mutter at the same time.

"Uh-huh," she says skeptically. "Bentley, in the bathroom, *now*. I'll be there in a minute." She stabs her finger in my direction. "*You*, I'll talk to you tomorrow."

Bentley heads into the bathroom like a good

little boy and shuts the door behind him.

I fling my arm toward the ensuite. "I'm not leaving you alone with him."

Jazz glares at me with the force of a thousand suns. "Do *not* ruin what just happened between us by behaving like a jealous prick."

Ah, Christ, if she had said anything else, I would've kept fighting. Like, literally *anything* else.

"Fine." I take a step forward and pull Jazz's lips to mine. I infuse every bit of frustration I'm feeling into the kiss until she's clinging to me, desperate for more. "But if you want to get off again tonight, call *me*. I'll be back in a heartbeat."

Jazz smirks. "If I want to get off again tonight, my showerhead can do that for me just fine. He's not nearly as moody as you are."

I shake my head. "You're a pain in my ass."

"Likewise, cupcake." Jazz pats my cheek then follows it with a kiss on the same spot. "Go home, Kingston. You have nothing to worry about. I'll talk to you in the morning. Maybe we can grab some breakfast."

"Okay, okay, I'm going." I give her one more quick kiss and a slap on the ass. "Behave."

She sticks her tongue out at me. "Yes, master."

A genuine grin stretches across my face. "I like that. You should use it more often."

She shoves at my chest until I'm standing in the hall. I laugh when she flips me off right before slamming the door in my face.

Fuck. What am I going to do with this woman?

chapter eighteen

KINGSTON

"You wanted to see me?"

As much as I hate being summoned to my father's corporate office like this, I jumped at the chance. It's a perfect setup for me to return after he's gone to place the surveillance camera. I successfully installed the other device in Callahan's office last weekend, but I couldn't think of a way to get in here when my dad's not present until he texted me earlier, asking me to drop by.

"Yes, son. Have a seat." He motions to my face. "What happened to you?"

I shrug. "Had to put some asshole in his place."

"Ah, yes, I heard about the fight your friend started."

"Yeah? How'd you hear about that?"

He waves me off. "Doesn't matter."

I frown, not liking that answer, but I know when to cut my losses with this man. "Well, did you hear *why* we beat the shit out of him?"

"Why would I care about some fight involving a bunch of teenagers?"

Oh, no reason. Just the fact that someone tried drugging your daughter, intent on raping her.

"Right." I nod.

My dad heads over to the bar cart in the corner of his office. "Drink?"

I shake my head. "No, thanks. I have stuff to do after this."

My father smiles as he fixes himself a scotch and soda. "Do these *things* involve Jasmine Callahan?"

"Yes. Why?"

He resumes his place in the power chair behind his large mahogany desk. Swirling the amber liquid around in a crystal tumbler, he says, "It's a shame what happened to her, but Charles tells me she's recovered well. Would you agree?"

I know damn well he doesn't really care, but I'm curious enough to keep this going.

"Good as can be expected, I suppose."

The prick takes a sip of his drink. "What a perfect opportunity this has been for you to get closer to her."

A smirk forms on my lips when I imagine punching him square in the face, wiping off that smug grin.

"I couldn't agree more, Dad. Although, I will admit it's been challenging because she's a bit gun shy, with the assailants still out there somewhere and all. But don't worry; I've been showing her how committed I am to supporting her through this trying time. I was in that hospital waiting room the entire time she was there, being the perfect doting boyfriend. My plan is still falling into place nicely."

He releases a boisterous laugh. "That's great to hear, son." My dad takes another sip from his glass as he contemplates something. "You know...I can't help but wonder."

My eyebrows rise. "Can't help but wonder *what*?"

The overhead lights glint off the face of his Patek Phillipe watch as he rubs his chin. "If *you* organized the assault to knock her down a few pegs."

I'm biting my tongue so hard, blood coats my taste buds. The fact that he even mentioned that makes me wonder if *he* arranged it. Maybe he's testing me right now.

I shake my head. "Not really my style. If I wanted to '*knock her down a few pegs*', I'm perfectly capable of doing that myself."

A broad smile stretches across his face, his white veneers practically blinding me. "Please, share. You've never told me what you have planned for the girl."

I casually lean back in the chair, propping my ankle over the opposite knee. "I don't have a plan. I'm more of a *fly by the seat of my pants* type of guy, which works best with her. Jasmine's a bit of a wild card."

"Ah, but the crazy ones are always freaks in bed, right?" I have to fight a scoff when he winks.

"Yep." I nod.

My dad folds his arms behind his head and leans back. "So, Jasmine's pretty stellar in the sack, then?"

Christ, this conversation is making me nauseous. It feels wrong talking about Jazz like this, but I have to stay in character.

"Best I've ever had. Sucks cock like a pro." That part's not even a lie.

His hazel eyes light up with interest. Fuck. Definitely shouldn't have gone in that direction.

"Good for you, my boy. I'd love to experience it for myself. She's such a tiny little thing—I bet her pussy would hug my dick nice and tight. Her ass even more so. Perhaps we can tag team her one day. Or maybe a good old-fashioned spit roast." He laughs. "Think of it as a father-son bonding moment."

Over my dead body, you fucking perv.

I swear to all that is holy, I want to bash his head in with a bat. I take a deep breath, reminding myself *he's* the one who should be locked up, not me.

"Yeah, maybe," I mutter.

He laughs. "Aw, Kingston, you're not getting territorial over some pussy, are you? I know she's an exceptionally beautiful girl, but that's no reason to lose your common sense."

I do scoff this time. "Fuck no. As long as Jasmine keeps Hoovering my dick whenever I want, I don't give a rat's ass who else she fucks."

"Speaking of...I suppose I have you to thank for the flash drive I found on my desk when I returned from Miami?"

My smile is genuine this time. Getting rid of

Vanessa was an absolute pleasure and long overdue. "Of course. I couldn't let her get away with betraying you like that."

"You're a good son. I appreciate your looking out for me. That cheating slut doesn't deserve the honor of being my wife. And a delivery boy, for fuck's sake. Could she get any lower?" My father steps out from behind the desk and pats me on the shoulder. "I guess it's time to trade her in for a newer model, huh?"

Your last bride just turned twenty-two. You don't have much room to go for a younger model, fuckwad.

"Yeah." I laugh. "Definitely."

"Maybe I'll try for a brunette next time around," he muses. "Someone with some...spunk. I can't let you have all the fun, now can I?" My father holds his hands out, curling his fingers like he's cupping a pair of tits. "It's been a while since I've seen Dr. Keller. I'm sure he'd appreciate a new client."

Dr. Keller is the plastic surgeon my dad uses to inflate all of his fuck dolls' chests, though I'm pretty sure he doesn't have any of them in mind. I don't understand why my father is so interested in Jazz all of a sudden. Maybe it's genuine curiosity, or perhaps this is another test. He's studying me carefully, looking for a reaction. It's like he *wants* me to flip out on him, giving him a reason not to trust me.

I'm not taking the bait, dickhead.

I stand up and give him a firm pat on the back, maybe a little harder than I should've. "Well, good luck on your hunt, old man. If we're done here, I need to go. All this talk about pussy makes me want to sink my dick into one."

"Give it to her good, son." He thrusts his hips to punctuate his crude remark and laughs.

"Always do."

I give him a dismissive wave as I exit the office and leave Davenport Boating as fast as humanly possible without looking suspicious. If I don't get the hell out of here, I'm going to lose it.

"Kingston," Monique, my father's receptionist, says in greeting. "What are you doing here again? I'm afraid your father left early to catch his flight."

"Damn." I frown in mock disappointment. "I think I left my cell phone in his office earlier. I can't find it anywhere, and that's the last place I remember seeing it."

"Oh, that's too bad. I know how you kids are

with those smartphones. If you can't find it, it's like losing a limb." She chuckles.

I play along. "Yep, it's a curse of my generation. Hey, you don't suppose I could duck in there quickly and have a look around, do you? I'd wait for my dad, but being without it for a week would be hell."

"Of course, honey." Monique opens the top drawer of her desk and retrieves a key ring. "Take your time; I'll be here for a while." She pulls a single key off the ring and hands it to me.

I lean down and smack a kiss on her cheek. "Thanks, Monique. You're a lifesaver."

She brushes me off. "Oh, you charmer."

I feel bad using a sweet old lady like that, but sometimes, you have to utilize all the resources at your disposal for the greater good.

I make sure to lock the door behind me as I enter my father's office. Like I did with Callahan's home office, I switch on the detection device and quickly scan the room, acting like I'm searching for my phone. The last thing I need is for my dad to have video evidence of me bugging this place—there'd be no way of talking myself out of that one. Preston Davenport may be an epic douche and a criminal, but stupid he is not.

When the coast is clear, I get to work. I grab a chair to stand on and remove the existing smoke alarm. Thankfully, it's cold enough at night this time of year to justify wearing a jacket, so I could inconspicuously hide its replacement. The nice thing about this device is that it's hooked into the building's electrical, just like the original one. With this, I don't need to worry about battery life. It *has* a battery in case of a power failure, but it'll primarily feed off the grid it's attached to.

After flicking the switch to activate the camera, I twist the cover until it's secure and put the chair back in its rightful place. Before I leave, I open the monitoring app on my phone and check the feed. I smile when a crystal clear 1080 HD image of the entire room pops up. We went with this type of device not only for its ease of installation but also because of its location. Being on the ceiling, in the front corner of the room, there's no space it doesn't cover, save the ensuite. As long as my father isn't doing anything nefarious while taking a shit, I should be good.

I lock up my dad's office and head back toward reception.

"Did you find it, honey?" Monique asks.

I drop the key on her desk and hold up my cell. "Yep. Thanks again, Monique. You're the best."

She smiles. "It's my pleasure. You have a good night and say hello to that beautiful sister of yours."

I hit the call button for the elevator, which opens right away. "Will do. Have a good night."

I breathe a sigh of relief as soon as the doors are closed. I don't think that could've gone more smoothly. I was hoping the fact she's known me my whole life would work in my favor. There wasn't an inkling of doubt in her mind whether or not she should let me in. Now, I just have to wait and see if the bastard gives me anything useful.

chapter nineteen

JAZZ

"So...I've been thinking about something."

Ainsley sips on her strawberry milkshake. "What's that?"

"A few things, actually. First of all, I need to get a part-time job."

"Why?" Ainsley dips a french fry into her shake before popping the fried goodness into her mouth. It sounds gross, but it's actually pretty freakin' delicious.

"Because I need money—the little bit I had saved when I moved here is disappearing fast. I'm sure as shit not about to use the credit card my sperm donor gave me. At the very least, I'd like to be able to buy lunch once in a while." I gesture to the food on the diner's Formica table. "Or pay for things when I take Belle out. I saw a Help Wanted sign at one of the coffee shops on Calabasas Road."

"Would your dad go for that? It wouldn't look good for his reputation to have one of his daughters working in such a lowly position. Not that I think being a barista is beneath me, but *he* would. I'd never have time for it with ballet, but if I ever got a job at a coffee shop, I know my dad would *freak*."

"Charles doesn't really get a say in what I do. I'm eighteen."

"Yeah, but you live under his roof."

I shrug. "If he really wanted to fight me on it, I'll deal with it. But there's nothing to argue about until I actually get the job."

"Good point. We can swing by on the way home and grab an application."

I smile. "Thanks, Ains."

"What are the other two things? You said a *few*."

"Secondly...tomorrow's Sunday, my day with Belle. I was wondering if you'd like to come out with us?"

"I'd love to." Her face lights up. "What are we doing?"

"Last weekend, we took her to the aquarium in

Long Beach, so we thought we'd do the zoo this weekend."

Ainsley has an amused smirk on her face. "That sounds fun."

I give her a dubious look. "Why are you making that face?"

"*What* face?"

I twirl my finger in her direction. "You look entertained by something I said, but I can't think of anything that would warrant your current expression."

She chuckles. "Oh, nothing. I was just imagining you and my brother taking a little girl to the aquarium. And the zoo. And an amusement park. Kingston's always been protective, but I never thought I'd see him playing Daddy anytime soon. I think it's adorable you've formed your own little blended family."

I scoff. "That's not true. He just drives us around."

And pays for everything. And is super sweet to Belle, giving her piggybacks all the time. And goes out of his way to ensure every Sunday is my favorite day of the week.

Damn that sneaky bastard.

"Okay, what's next?" Ainsley asks.

I smile, glad to switch to a less confusing topic. "Well, I never got the chance to do something to celebrate turning eighteen because...well, you know. I've wanted to get a tattoo for a while now, and I always said I'd do it right after my birthday. I happen to know a pretty fantastic artist who's offered to do it for free. I'd love it if you came with me."

Ainsley rubs her hands together. "Ooh, now this I can get behind. When and where?"

"Um...does today work for you?"

She laughs. "Really? You can just walk in for something like that?"

I shake my head. "Technically, yes, but the really good artists are booked up from what I understand, especially on weekends. But the other day, I texted Kai, the tattooist, to see if his offer still stands. He said he had a cancelation today if I wanted to drop by at five."

"I'm totally in." She looks at the time on her phone. "Where is it? How long of a drive do you think it'd be?"

Now, here's the part I'm not sure she'd be so chill with. "It's in my old neck of the woods, which takes about an hour or so, depending on traffic. The shop is right in between Watts and Compton."

"Okay. So, if we left by three-thirty, we'd for sure get there on time?"

I blink a few times, honestly surprised she agreed so fast. "Uh...yeah. That should be good."

Ainsley pops another fry into her mouth. "It's a date."

"Here we are, Atlas Ink." Ainsley shifts her car into park and kills the ignition. She looks around the strip mall parking lot, taking in the surroundings. "Wow. A yellow Lamborghini kind of sticks out like a sore thumb around here, huh?"

I feel like an idiot for not thinking about the culture shock Ainsley must be going through. I'd imagine it's similar to what I felt moving to Kardashian Land, only in reverse. I love how she didn't even hesitate when I asked her to come with me, though. Someone like Peyton would probably laugh her ass off and make a bad joke about not wanting to get shot. Yeah, there's a lot of crime in this area, but most people who live here are hard-working and honest. They have a strong sense of community, and they take care of their own. Growing up in Watts made me who I am, and regardless of my zip code, I'll always be a proud South Central girl at heart.

"It'll be fine. The shop is small enough to where we'll be able to see it the whole time. If anyone starts creepin' around, Kai will take care of them."

Ainsley smiles, seemingly satisfied. "How did you know about this place again?"

I nod to the hot as hell man leaning against the building, watching us. "Malakai is my ex's older brother."

Ainsley drinks him in. "Damn, girl. Does his brother look anything like him? If so, why in the hell did you two break up?"

"They're three years apart, but they get mistaken for twins all the time."

Her eyebrows lift. "I'll ask again. *Why in the hell did you two break up? He looks like a young, badass version of Idris Elba, for shit's sake!*"

I laugh. "Right? I used to tell them that all the time."

"Seriously, though, what happened? Why'd you break up?"

I bite the tip of my thumbnail. "When my mom died, I just couldn't deal with it, ya know? I was put into the system, my sister was ripped away from me, and I had no idea what would happen next. I told him I needed space to get my head together, and he didn't argue. Didn't even text. I heard he was already hooking up with another girl a week later."

Ainsley gives me a sympathetic smile. "I'm sorry."

"It's no biggie, honestly. I wasn't in love with him or anything. I mean, I cared for him a lot, but he was always more of a friend than a boyfriend. He's a few years older than me, but we were next-door neighbors growing up, so we've known each other forever. He treated me well, he looked like *that*, and he was *there* so..."

"So...you two fornicated like bunnies whenever the mood struck?"

I shrug. "Pretty much. When my mom died, Shawn—that's his name—didn't make any effort to console me. Maybe he just didn't know what to say, but the fact he didn't even *try* was a big eye-opener for me. It's one of the reasons I never bothered reaching out to him after I moved to Hidden Hills. He's not a bad guy—he's actually really sweet and fun to hang out with—just emotionally stunted with relationships, I guess."

"You know what I think? I think we should stop talking about stupid boys and get you some ink."

Ainsley's a dependable shoulder to cry on when

you need one, but she's equally reliable for focusing on the brighter side. It's one of my favorite things about her. I need all the lightness I can get in my life right now.

I grin. "Sounds good to me."

Malakai offers me a big smile when we approach the shop and motions to come in for a hug. "Girl, you look fly as fuck. No cap."

I give him a good squeeze before pulling back. "You too, Kai."

Kai gives Ainsley an appreciative once over. "And who's this lovely lady?"

I gesture to Malakai. "Ainsley, this is Kai Cooper." I jerk my head to Ains. "Kai, this is Ainsley Davenport. She's gotta man, so don't get any ideas."

He holds his hands up in surrender. "A'ight, say no more. Nice to meet you, Ainsley Davenport. Your ride is dope."

Ainsley's cheeks pinken under his perusal. I totally feel her; he's made me blush on more than one occasion. The man can charm practically anyone out of their panties.

"It's nice to meet you, too," she says shyly. "And thank you."

"Ladies, step into my humble abode." Kai steps aside so we can enter the tattoo parlor.

I nod my head to the beat of Nipsey Hussle's "The Life" as it bumps through the overhead speakers. God, this place brings back memories. Shawn and I spent a lot of time here just chillin' when Belle was on a playdate or if my mom had a day off. I see that nothing's changed, which is comforting considering how much change I've had in my life lately. A small reception desk still sits in the corner, and framed photos still cover the walls, showcasing various designs. A workstation is set up in the middle of the floor where Kai sees most of his clients, but I know from previous visits, there's also a room in the back for people who get tattoos in areas that shouldn't be exposed to the general public.

Malakai's always kept the place in pristine condition—I could probably eat off these floors. If you ask me, that's a huge selling point when selecting a tattoo parlor. Kai's a true artist, and he takes pride in that, but he's also an astute businessman. He bought into the shop when it was struggling, and it's done really well ever since he made some minor changes to their operations. It's given him purpose, too, which keeps him out of trouble.

There was a point in time where he could've easily gone in the other direction.

A burly guy with a scruffy beard steps out of the back. He looks like a big, scary biker, but in reality, he's a teddy bear.

The man smiles, showing off a set of white, perfectly straight teeth. "Well, I'll be damned. It's been a minute since I've seen your beautiful face. Look at you, girl."

I laugh when he swoops me into a hug. "Hey, Ty."

Tyson is Malakai's business partner and fellow artist. He's also the uncle I mentioned earlier.

Ty pulls back, holding on to my upper arms. "What brings you to the neighborhood, Jazz?"

"I turned eighteen recently, so I wanted to get my first tat. Rumor has it, Kai's the best in town."

"Damn straight," Malakai boasts.

Ty laughs. "Baby, that boy don't need an ego boost. His damn head barely fits through the door already."

Kai flips off his uncle in response.

Ainsley tries to stifle her laughter, but she's not very successful.

I tilt my head in her direction. "Tyson, this is my friend, Ainsley."

Ty's large hand swallows hers as they shake. "Nice to meet you, pretty lady." He turns back to me. "I heard you moved up to a big house in the hills. Why'd you come back? I'm sure they have plenty of fancy artists up there by the rich folk." He winks at Ainsley. "No offense, beautiful."

She smiles. "None taken."

I cross my arms over my chest and narrow my eyes once Ty's attention is back on me. "Because this is my home. This is where my roots are, and that will *never* change. You got a problem with that?"

His lips curve. "Naw, girl. I'm just makin' sure you're still the same old Jazz we know and love. And from the fireballs you're shootin' at me with those pretty brown eyes, I'd say there's no doubt."

My lips twitch. "Well, as long as we're clear."

"A'ight, enough small talk, Ty. Some of us have work to do." Malakai swings his arm over my shoulder and leads me to the client's chair. "Make yourself comfortable while I get set up." He pulls a chair from the waiting area and scoots it closer. "Ainsley, you wanna watch?"

Ainsley's eyes widen. "Really? I wouldn't get in the way?"

Kai shakes his head. "Nah. It's cool."

Tyson wanders toward the back of the shop while Ainsley takes a seat beside me.

Kai starts digging through his trolley, setting everything he needs up top. "Same spot we talked about?"

"Yeah," I confirm.

"So, are you going to tell me what you're getting now?" Ainsley asks. "And where?"

She's asked the same question no less than a dozen times on the drive over. I wanted her to see the design first, and explain its significance, so she wouldn't think it was a narcissistic choice on my end.

I smile. "You'll see."

Malakai raises his eyebrows—probably wondering about the secrecy—but says nothing as he readies his tattoo gun. About a year ago, Kai had some downtime between clients, so I told him what I was looking for. In less than five minutes, he sketched out exactly what I saw in my mind. The boy is insanely talented in bringing ideas to life. The design I'm going with is delicate and simple in appearance but heavy on substance.

Kai twists in his chair to face me. "You ready?"

"I am." I nod.

He lifts my arm and props it on a padded stool

covered in plastic wrap. After swiping some rubbing alcohol over my skin, he picks up a disposable razor and runs it along the same spot.

"What's the razor for?" Ainsley asks. "She doesn't exactly have hairy arms."

"Almost every*one* has body hair almost every*where*, regardless of how visible it is. This ensures a clean work surface," Kai explains.

"Huh," Ainsley muses. "The more you know."

He takes a stick of clear deodorant and runs it over the place we agreed on before grabbing the transfer paper and holding it against my arm for a few seconds. Kai inspects his work after peeling back the paper before turning my arm so I can see it.

"That look okay to you?" he asks.

I take in the small flower running about two inches down the side of my forearm, starting right below my wrist. "It's perfect."

Ainsley stretches her neck so she can see. "A flower? That's really pretty."

"Not just a flower," I correct. "It's a jasmine flower."

Ainsley giggles. "In case you get drunk and forget your name?"

I give her a head shake. "No, smartass. It was

my mom's favorite. She used to call me her sweet flower all the time. Plus, it's the Philippines' official flower, so it's in homage to our heritage."

She gives me a closed-mouth smile. "I love it, Jazz. It's perfect."

"Thank you."

Malakai grabs his gun and sets my arm back on the stool. "You ready? It's going to pinch at first—especially near the wrist since that's one of the more sensitive spots."

"Sure, now you tell me," I grumble.

He laughs. "Regardless, I need you to remain as still as possible unless you want me to fuck this up."

I take a deep breath and let it out. "Let's do this."

Kai nods and gets to work. He's right; the needles do pinch at first, but I adjust pretty quickly as he outlines the flower. The pain isn't nearly as bad as I was expecting. Maybe my threshold went up after recent...events.

"Smile!" Ainsley holds her phone out to take a selfie of us.

I comply and wait for her to take the shot before speaking. "What's that for?"

"Girl, we're making memories here." Ainsley turns her phone to face me, showing me her Instagram page. "I *had* to post it on Insta. I figured Malakai wouldn't mind me tagging the shop, right?"

"Free publicity is always good publicity, baby," Kai agrees. "Even better if two beautiful ladies such as yourselves are promoting the shop."

I roll my eyes. "You do remember she's taken, right? And don't you think you're a little old?"

Kai laughs. "First of all, I'm *twenty-four*. That's not old. Secondly, who says Ainsley's the one I'm trying to charm?"

"Well, it sure as hell isn't me."

He raises his eyebrows. "Why not?"

"Uh, because I dated your brother."

"So?" He shrugs. "I have eyes, and you're no longer jailbait. What's the problem? Are you taken, too?"

I pull my lower lip between my teeth. "Um...it's complicated."

Ainsley's phone pings with a text alert, and she laughs. "Speaking of the *complication*...his ears must've been burning. Or, more likely, he just saw my post." She runs her thumbs over the screen, presumably replying to her brother's message. "Ooh, somebody's cranky."

Kai's full lips quirk as he works on shading in

the leaves. "Damn, that sounds like a story I need to hear."

"Maybe another ti—"

The bell over the front door rings, causing the three of us to look up.

Shit.

"Whose sweet ride is that out front?" the man asks.

Ainsley's eyes widen, obviously knowing who the newcomer is based on his resemblance to his brother. It takes him a moment, but as soon as Shawn's eyes land on me, his jaw drops.

"Jazz. What are you doing here?"

I gesture to my arm. "What people come here to do."

Shawn eats up the distance between us in a few strides and checks out my ink in progress. "Nice. It suits you."

"Thanks," I mumble.

"Isn't that the same design Kai sketched out a while back?"

I nod. "Yeah, it is."

Neither one of us says a word for a good minute. Jesus, this is awkward. What's the protocol here? This is the guy I lost my virginity to. Is this what it always feels like when you run into an ex?

Am I supposed to pretend like the boy's never been inside me? Oddly, I can't even recall what sex with Shawn felt like, which helps, but I can't deny that it happened. Many times.

He makes eye contact with Ainsley. "I'm Shawn. You a friend of Jazz's?"

"The bestest," she replies. "And you're the ex."

Shawn gets a shit-eating grin on his face. "She's mentioned me, huh? All good things, I'm sure."

Ainsley lifts her eyebrows. "Something like that."

"What are you doing here?" Kai asks his brother.

"I just got off work," Shawn replies. "Came to see if you wanted to grab a bite."

"As you can see, I'm with a client."

Shawn pulls up a chair and takes a seat next to Malakai. "It's all good. I don't mind waiting." His eyes roam my face and venture south, lingering on my chest. "Can't beat the view. Damn, Jazz, you're a sight for sore eyes. I almost forgot how fine you are."

"Thanks. I think."

"How've you been, baby?"

I glare. "I'm *not* your baby."

Shawn holds his hands up, his whiskey eyes

twinkling in amusement. "So, it's like that, huh? It's nice to see you still got that sexy attitude. You know it just gets me hot when you're like this."

"A slight breeze would get you hot," I counter.

"Why you gotta be like that, baby? *You* broke up with *me*, remember? And from what I recall, it didn't take much to get you going either." He emphasizes his statement with a wink.

"Okay, man, you've made your point," Malakai says. "Quit making the woman uncomfortable, or take your ass outside."

Shawn ducks his head to meet my eyes. "C'mon, Jasmine. You know I'm playin'. Look, I'm sorry, a'ight? Is that what you want to hear? We were friends once, you know. No reason we can't be that way again." He sticks out his lower lip in an exaggerated pout. I try not to smile because he looks so ridiculous, but I fail. "C'mon, baby. Will you *please* be my friend? When you're done here, we can grab some of those quesadillas you love from Keith's food truck. My treat—think of it as a peace offering."

Damn him. He knows I can't resist a quesadilla from Keith's. And as much as I hate to admit it, he's right. We *were* friends for a long time before we started sleeping together. Shawn knew me better than almost anyone. It was always so easy to be around him. I guess I don't see the harm in hanging out for a little while, especially with Ainsley and Kai tagging along.

I look to Ainsley, and she nods in approval. "Fine. But I want a quesadilla *and* some tacos."

Shawn's smile stretches from ear to ear. "Deal."

chapter twenty

KINGSTON

It's driving me crazy Jazz and Ainsley are in Southern LA right now. I was tempted to drive down there, but knowing Jazz, she'd have my balls, and it'd do more harm than good. She's just starting to let me back in, and I can't fuck that up. I have to keep reminding myself Jazz knows that area better than I can ever hope to, and she'd never put my sister in danger.

But still, why did they go all the way down there for a tattoo? And when did Jazz even decide to get one in the first place? I can't say the thought of her with some ink isn't hot, but I don't like being caught off guard like this. Not with everything so up in the air.

Also, who the fuck are those guys? I know one of them is the artist because he held a tattoo gun in the first picture Ainsley posted. But why are all four of them hanging out at a fucking taco truck together? I don't like the way the second guy looks at Jazz. His eyes are glued to her in every single shot like he can't possibly force himself to look away. I pull up Ainsley's latest post, and sure enough, the fuck nugget is still undressing Jazz with his eyes. Aw, hell. I know that look. That dick *knows* what's under her clothing, no doubt. My sister actually tagged both guys in this one, so I do the only thing someone in my situation would do: I stalk that fucker's page.

Two seconds into scanning Shawn Cooper's photos, I really wish I hadn't. He's been posting his own pics tonight, but his shots only include him and Jazz. The first caption said, "Eating my favorite tacos with my favorite girl." As if that wasn't bad enough, Jazz is snuggled into his side with a huge smile on her face. I don't have to go too far into this asshole's feed to find *a lot* more pictures of the two of them from several months back. In well over half of them, that motherfucker has his lips on Jazz, or his limbs are wrapped around her like a goddamn octopus. It's obvious these two have history, and I don't like it one bit. Even though she's not big on social media, I check Jazz's page while I'm at it, but there haven't been any recent posts.

I knew Jazz wasn't a virgin before we met, but knowing she fucked someone else and *seeing* who she fucked are two entirely different things. Yes, I'm hypocritical considering Jazz has to live with a girl I screwed countless times and said girl likes to rub it in, but that fact does fuck-all for my rage right now. I'm clenching my phone so tightly, I'm honestly surprised it hasn't cracked in half. It's bad enough I have to deal with the Bentley situation, but now I have to worry about an overly friendly ex?

This jealousy crap is all so new to me, I don't know what to do with it. I swear to Christ, my sister chronicled their entire night on her Instagram page just to fuck with me. She knows damn well I'd be driving myself crazy.

I fist my hair as I pace back and forth. "Fuck!"

My phone starts buzzing, so I look down and see my P.I. is calling.

"What?"

"Did I catch you at a bad time?"

I shake my head even though he can't see me. "No. What's up, John?"

"Following Madeline Callahan has finally produced something," he says.

I take a seat on the couch, adjusting the phone against my ear. "What'd you get?"

"She's been to the same location in the financial district several times over the last few weeks, but it's a condo building, so I had no way of knowing who she was visiting. On average, she stays for one or two hours before leaving and driving straight home."

"Okay...and?"

"And...I managed to slip past the doorman the other day, and Madeline and I happened to share an elevator up to the twentieth floor. She went left while I went right, but I hung back long enough to see which door she ducked into. Take a guess who's on the deed for unit twenty-ten."

"I have no fucking clue, John. Just tell me."

I can practically hear his smile over the phone line. "It's owned by none other than Davenport Boating Incorporated."

"Is this building on Wilshire?"

"It sure is," he confirms.

"That's my dad's corporate apartment. It's supposed to serve as a place to stay for any big dollar clients or vendors that come into town, but

I'm pretty sure my dad uses it as his own personal fuck pad."

"I would say your assumptions are correct based on what I just saw while reviewing the feed. I would also say it's fair to assume he's screwing Mrs. Callahan regularly."

Holy fuck.

"Wait a sec...*what* feed?"

"Luckily, I had a small camera on me when I followed her into the building. Never leave home without one, right? Anyway, I placed it on a light fixture on the opposite wall, aiming it at twenty-ten's door. I reviewed the feed just now and saw Madeline Callahan leaving the apartment, but not before giving your father a *very friendly* goodbye kiss. And when I say *friendly*, I mean they were shoving their tongues down each other's throats, and he was palming her ass."

Gross. I could've gone my whole life without that visual.

I shake the thought out of my head. "Sadly, I can't say I'm surprised, but this could be a good thing."

"How so?"

"Charles Callahan and my father have the same antiquated ideal on how a wife should behave.

According to them, two of the biggest offenses a wife can commit is not spreading her legs when her husband wants to bust a nut or adultery. They're both grounds for some serious consequences. Hell, my dad is currently filing for divorce from his fourth wife because Vanessa decided that if he can cheat on her, she can do the same to him. If Madeline is fucking my father, I can guarantee Charles doesn't know about it. And when he finds out, shit's going to hit the fan."

"So, what do you want to do?"

I think about it for a moment. "Let's hang back and watch for a while. It's in our best interest to keep Charles in the dark for now, but compile any footage of them in compromising positions for when the time is right. I can't have any dissension between them if I have any chance of getting into the fold. I'm too close."

"You got it."

"What about Peyton?" I ask. "Anything on her yet?"

"Nothing that stands out. Basic rich teenage girl routine—the four S's: school, shopping, spas, or socializing. She's been spending more time at the Gale residence lately, but you already know the reason behind that."

"Right." I nod. "Keep an eye on her. Any news from your contact in the police department?"

John clears his throat. "This isn't official yet, but they're stopping the investigation unless somebody comes forward with new information. They claim they've hit a dead end."

"How can that be?" I comb a hand through my hair. "I know it's a small town department, but how could they still have found *nothing*? It's been five weeks."

"According to my source, the report will state they've exhausted all their resources and have insufficient evidence. They're saying the elements likely didn't help. With the leaves falling and the heavy showers that rolled up on the mountain, anything useful was likely washed away. Since Jazz never told the cops the perpetrators mentioned having an employer, they've nowhere else to look."

"Fuck." I take a few deep breaths, trying to calm myself. "Where do we go from here? Do you think she should tell them about the employer thing?"

"No, I don't. I think she should let them close it."

"Why the fuck would she do that?"

John sighs audibly. "Because they're covering

something up. My source was personally present when they combed the scene. They found two sets of fresh footprints heading away from the scene, both of which appeared to be male, based on the size and shape of their shoes. Photos and soil evidence *were* collected. Somewhere along the way, they magically disappeared."

"You've got to be kidding me," I mutter.

"Afraid not. When my source questioned it, her supervisor feigned complete ignorance—said she must have been mistaken. The only prints or DNA evidence they have on record belong to you and Jasmine." John clears his throat. "Somebody with money *and* influence is definitely involved, Kingston. Who do you know that fits that description?"

"Fuck." I scrub my hand down my face. "You think my father or Callahan hired those men?"

"It's possible. At the very least, I think one of them knows who did, and they're helping cover it up."

"So, what the hell do we do?"

"The best thing you can do right now is continue acting normal. The same goes for Jasmine. Go to school, go to parties, and whatever else you did before she was assaulted. Don't raise suspicion, but keep your eyes and ears open. If these people think they got away with it, they'll get cocky, which causes people to get sloppy. In my professional opinion, it's your best shot."

"Why would my father or Callahan want Jazz dead? That part makes no sense to me. If they didn't want her around, why file the paternity affidavit after almost eighteen years? Jazz would've never known either of them existed."

"But Callahan or your father had no way of knowing that for sure. As far as they're concerned, Jasmine's a loose end—her mother could have told her *everything*, which would explain the camera in Jasmine's bedroom. Maybe Callahan installed it to keep an eye on her. Determine what she knows, if anything."

"Jazz thought the same thing, and as fucked up as this is, I'd rather have that be true instead of someone perving on her."

"I don't think they want her dead—at least not unless they confirm she's a threat. But I do think Jasmine was right about the stabbing being an accident. I think someone was trying to scare her, not necessarily cause bodily harm. The attempted rape may or may not have been a hired gun going rogue."

"My dad said something to me the other day that raised some flags. The prick actually asked if *I* organized the assault to knock her down a few pegs. Maybe that was a test, trying to determine where my loyalty lies before he admits anything. A few times now, he's asked probing questions about her. Has made his interest in fucking her blatantly obvious. The prick actually suggested we tag team her. It felt like he was intentionally goading me.

"As far as I know, the one and only time he's seen Jazz in person was at a dinner party over two months ago. You and I both know Preston Davenport is one sick fuck, and he likes 'em young, but something about this doesn't sit right. Peyton is beautiful—and blonde, which seems to be his preference—yet he never made a suggestive comment about her the entire time she and I were together. I'm playing it off, but my dad definitely suspects I have feelings for Jazz. Maybe this is all one big test."

"Maybe," John agrees. "Or maybe Peyton hired those men because she's jealous and Callahan or even his wife are covering for her. Or maybe we're grasping at straws, and it's none of the above. We need more information, Kingston. The last thing we'd want to do is throw around accusations without absolute certainty. Hopefully, the new bugs will give us something."

"Fuck. There are so many balls in the air, and it only seems to be getting worse by the day."

John is silent for so long, I have to check my phone to make sure the call is still connected.

"John? You still there?"

"Yes, I'm here. Just thinking." He clears his throat. "Jasmine bears a striking resemblance to her late mother, correct?"

"Freakishly so."

"When I was looking into Mahalia's past, I was primarily focusing on her connection to Charles. I think I need to dig deeper."

"If it helps any, Jasmine's mom may have been friends with my mom," I offer. "There's this picture I found in an old album."

"Can you scan that and send it to me?"

I nod, then remember he can't see me, so I say, "I'll do it as soon as we hang up."

"Good. I'll see what I can come up with."

I start walking toward my closet to retrieve the photo album. "Are you looking for something specific?"

"I don't quite know yet," he says. "But I think there may be another angle we haven't explored.

And if that's the case, Jasmine may be in even more danger."

"Fuck."

"We'll figure this out, Kingston," he assures me. "Send me that picture, and I'll get back to you ASAP."

I hang up the call, forward the photo to John, and delete the text thread. I can't just sit on my ass, waiting for him to get back to me, so I grab my keys and head out for a drive.

chapter twenty-one

JAZZ

"What are you doing here?" I frown. "Please don't kill my vibe right now. I actually had a fantastic day, which rarely happens unless I'm with my sister."

Kingston was waiting in my driveway as Ainsley dropped me off. She drove off, mouthing, "Good luck" before I had a chance to stop her. I swear to God that if Kingston tries reaming me for going to South Central with Ains, I'm going to punch him in the throat.

"I'm so glad you and *Shawn* had such a fantastic time."

I roll my eyes. "Seriously? You're pulling the jealous boyfriend shit right now? Newsflash,

Kingston: You're *not* my boyfriend. I said I'd think about it."

Ugh, I knew this was going to happen when Ainsley kept posting on Insta. She denied it, but I'm pretty sure she was trying to piss her brother off.

"Who is he?"

I look Kingston dead in the eye. "A friend."

His nostrils flare. "A friend you've fucked."

My eyes narrow. "Why does it matter?"

"Because it fucking *does*," he growls.

"I am *not* having this conversation in my driveway."

Kingston flips open the passenger door of his car. "Get in."

I scoff. "You've got to be kidding me."

His eyes slide to the passenger seat, then back up to me.

"Yeah, not gonna happen." I fold my arms over my chest.

Kingston's eyes flash with rage doused in a side of lust. "Jazz, get in the car before I fucking throw you in the car."

"I'd like to see you try." I'm pretty sure my expression matches his.

My toes curl from the sheer alphaness on

display, but Kingston should know by now I don't appreciate being bossed around.

I squeal when Kingston's arms band around me, and he effortlessly lifts me off the ground. "Put me down, you ass!"

He tries setting me in the car, but I give him a good fight. I know damn well we're making enough of a ruckus to be heard inside the house, but I wouldn't be surprised if Charles was looking out the window, enjoying the fact that I'm being manhandled.

Kingston's teeth clamp down on the fleshy part of my shoulder, giving him the element of surprise he needs to get me in the car. The locks immediately engage as I sit there in shock, holding the sore spot.

I lay into him the second he gets behind the wheel. "Did you just *bite me?*"

This bastard actually has the nerve to smirk. "You were trying to knee me in the balls. What was I supposed to do? Think of it as self-defense."

My head slams back into the seat. "So, what? You're going to abduct me now?"

He starts the ignition and shifts into gear. "Buckle up, babe."

I'd like to keep my head attached to my body if

we got into an accident, so I begrudgingly comply. "You're wasting your time. I'll just have Ainsley take me home, or I'll walk."

He glances at me as he turns left out of my driveway, the opposite direction of his house.

"That's why we're not going to my house." He winks.

"Oh, for fuck's sake!"

Kingston belts out a laugh as I release a string of curses.

"I'm glad I can be so amusing." I flip him the bird. "Are you at least going to tell me where we're going?"

He pulls through the gates that seal off this housing community from the main road and hooks a right. "Bentley's. Reed's there, too. Bent's parents are on safari in Namibia or some shit like that, so we have the place to ourselves."

"And why do I need to crash your little bromance party?"

Kingston waggles his eyebrows suggestively. "You'll see."

Crap, why did my mind automatically go to dirty places?

"Kingston, will you be serious?"

"We need to talk." Kingston's tongue sneaks out

to wet his lips, which I'm *totally* unaffected by. Yeah, right. I can't even convince myself.

"About what?"

"It's a lot easier if we're all together, so I don't have to repeat myself."

"Oh, c'mon, you can't leave me hanging like that."

His lips turn up in the corner. "Patience, Jazz. We're almost there."

I drill holes into the side of his stupidly sexy jaw. "You're the last person who should be lecturing someone on patience."

Kingston pulls up to the gate of another community and punches in a code. I'm sure the residents aren't supposed to openly share their access codes, but the fact that Kingston has one doesn't surprise me.

I've never been to Bentley's house before, so my eyes wander as we drive through his neighborhood. It's dark, and most of the homes are set further back from the road, so I mostly see shrubbery or expansive lawns, which is similar to the area Kingston and I live in. Kingston's car ambles down a long driveway before parking in front of a giant Spanish-style mansion. Kingston opens the heavy wooden doors like he owns the place, so I follow him until we stop in what appears to be the living room.

I shake my head as I look around, wondering if I'll ever get used to the fact that my friends live in houses like this. Hell, or the fact that *I* live in a house like this. I'm not even touching the fact that the front door was left unlocked. I don't care how safe your neighborhood supposedly is; that shit's just stupid.

"Bent!" Kingston shouts. "Where're you at?"

"Game room!" Bentley shouts back.

Kingston inclines his head toward the staircase to our right, so I take the hint and walk in that direction. Once we get to the second level, he directs me down a hallway until we reach an open door. I peek inside and see Bentley and Reed playing some special ops game in front of the largest television I've ever seen.

Bentley smiles when he sees me. "Jazzy Jazz!" He tosses the Xbox controller on the table in front of him, walks toward me, and pulls me into a hug. "You look good in my house, baby girl. You should come over more often, but next time, ditch the caveman."

I chuckle, trying not to be too obvious that I'm sniffing his yummy cologne. "Hi, Bent."

"Very funny, asshole," Kingston mutters as he pulls me out of Bentley's grasp.

Bentley gives Kingston a *whatever* look and busies himself at the corner minibar. "What's your poison, Jazz? I have vodka, whiskey, tequila, beer, ganja—"

I hold my hand up to stop his ramble. "Just water is fine."

"Bor-ing," Bentley singsongs as he tosses a bottle of water in my direction. "Davenport?"

"Macallan." Kingston's eyes meet mine. "You sure you don't want something stronger?"

"I'm positive," I deadpan. Drinking alcohol around these boys always seems to lead to trouble.

Kingston accepts the drink from Bentley and downs it in one go. He holds the glass out for a refill and does it again. Meanwhile, Bentley is gulping down at least three fingers of scotch from his own glass. Yikes, it's tense in here. It looks like it's up to me to inject some levity into the situation.

"Whoa there, boys." I poke Kingston's shoulder. "Looking to get wasted so you can have your wicked way with each other?"

Bentley laughs. "Princess, if Davenport here wants to suck my cock, no need for the liquor. He just needs to tell me I'm pretty, and I'll happily whip it out for him."

Kingston scoffs. "Fuck you, Fitzgerald. If anyone is going to have a dick in their mouth in this situation, it'd be you."

Bentley blows him a kiss, which earns him a middle finger salute.

I'm laughing as I notice Reed shaking his head, muttering, "Idiots."

Kingston steps forward and gently grabs my arm. "Let me see it."

It takes me a moment to figure out what he's talking about. "It's all covered up." I nod to the plastic that's taped over my new tattoo like some weird band-aid.

"So, take it off." With the way Kingston is looking at me right now, I'm not so sure he's talking about plastic wrap.

"I'm supposed to wash it and put some ointment on when I take the plastic off." Geez, could I sound any lamer? Like he gives a flying fuck about my aftercare instructions.

"We'll be right back," Kingston says to the guys as he leads me across the hall to a bathroom.

Rather than embarrass myself again, I busy myself unwrapping the bandage and washing the tattoo with soap and water. Kingston comes up behind me as I'm pulling the sample tube of A&D out of my pocket, and I can see his smirk in the mirror when I shiver from the proximity. God, I hate it that I have no game around him. He turns me into this mindless bitch in heat by merely existing. I can't stop thinking about what happened after Peyton's party and how badly I want to do it again.

Kingston watches over my shoulder as I pat my arm dry and start spreading the ointment over my fresh ink. As soon as I'm done, he takes my hand and lifts my arm to get a closer look. His finger lightly traces around the design, careful not to touch the tattoo.

"That's jasmine, isn't it?"

"It is." Not gonna lie; I'm impressed he knew that. "They were my mom's favorite. She used to call me her sweet flower."

My eyes get watery like they usually do whenever I recall a happy memory involving my mom. I hope one day I can think of her and smile, but right now, all those memories do is remind me I'll never have those experiences again. I'll never again hear my mom say a single word, let alone use her favorite term of endearment. God, I miss her so much, I physically ache. I briefly squeeze my eyes shut to force the tears back.

Kingston's still trailing his finger down my arm, leaving goosebumps in its wake. "It's perfect."

My lips curve in a soft smile. "That's *exactly* what Ainsley said."

I never bought into the theory that twins' brains are linked together until I met Kingston and Ainsley. As different as their personalities are, they have this uncanny ability to know what the other one is thinking. Ainsley once told me she can even sense when her brother is hurt or really upset. Their bond isn't something that can be explained by science, but they've made me a firm believer.

Kingston returns my grin in the mirror. "That's because she's smart. Obviously, my intelligence rubbed off on her in the womb."

"How do you know it's not the other way around?"

"Uh, because I'm older and bigger. I even have a picture somewhere that proves it. My umbilical cord was twice as thick as hers, which means I got more nutrients in utero."

I chuckle. "Why am I not surprised you sucked at sharing, even back then?"

The amusement fades from Kingston's greenish-gold eyes as his fingers curl over my shoulders. "That's a recent development. Never really cared about anything enough to feel possessive before."

My eyes search his. "Why do I get the feeling we're not talking about toys?"

"Because we're *not*," he says matter-of-factly.

He steps back slightly so I can turn around. "Kingston—"

"Jazz."

My breath hitches when his hands bracket my hips, and he lowers his head. "Don't you...didn't you say you had to talk to me about something?"

Kingston nods. "I did."

"So..." His hands flex, the tips of his fingers kneading into the globes of my ass. "Shouldn't we, uh, do that? Talk, I mean?"

I can smell the whiskey on his breath as Kingston's lips hover above mine. God, it'd be so easy to close the gap. "Yeah, we should."

"If you're about to bitch me out for something, you can save it." Crap, why did that sound so breathy when I was going for stern?

"I'm not going to bitch you out, Jazz."

Well, that's a surprise.

"Really?" I'm sure the skepticism shows on my face. "You're not going to read me the riot act for going to such a *dangerous* place at night with your sister in tow?"

Kingston's head slowly slices to the left and then the right. "You know what you're doing down there, and I trust that you wouldn't put Ainsley in a compromising position."

"Huh." I blink a few times, not quite sure what to say. "So, are you gonna tell me what's going on then, or stand there staring at me all night?

Kingston's eyes meet mine. "Staring at you all night doesn't sound like a bad way to pass the time, but I do have some new information to share. You know, in the interest of full disclosure."

I pop an eyebrow. "Didn't you say you wanted the guys to hear, too?"

"I did. But I need to do something else first."

I bite my lip. "Okay, wha—"

My thoughts scramble when Kingston presses his lips to mine. The kiss is gentle at first, nothing like our usual frantic pairing. He takes his time, exploring my lips before demanding entry. Kingston groans as I slide my tongue into his mouth, grabbing the back of his neck and pulling him closer.

Why is kissing this man such a full-body experience? All of my senses are on high alert. My panties are embarrassingly wet already. My heart beats wildly as Kingston's mouth moves along the column of my neck. He stretches the cotton of my t-shirt, nibbling and biting a path to my newly bared shoulder. I don't utter a single complaint as Kingston lifts my shirt over my head, tossing it to the floor.

He drops his head to my shoulder, groaning as I rub his erection through his pants. "Fuck, Jazz. I'm trying not to be a selfish prick, but I need you so fucking bad. I need to feel something good in the middle of all this fucked up shit."

I know the feeling. Sex with Kingston is the only thing that gives me relief from the deafening noise running rampant through my head, at least temporarily. Instead of verbalizing that, I decide actions are louder than words. I pop the button on his jeans and slide the zipper down. My hand slips beneath his boxer briefs, wrapping around his cock and pumping up and down a few times. Kingston subconsciously juts his hips forward as my thumb swipes through the precum leaking from the tip.

I gasp when his thumbs brush over my nipples through my lacy bra. I moan as his tongue swirls around the pointed tips. I brace my hands on the counter and lean back, allowing Kingston better access as his mouth ventures south.

"Kiss me," I pant.

He sucks on the skin right below my belly button, making my pussy throb. "I *am* kissing you."

"Fuck." I throw my head back as he undoes my jeans and licks right above my panties' top seam.

"I'm about two seconds away from pulling my dick out and joining the party."

I scream at the sound of Bentley's deep voice. "*Holyshitballfuck!*"

Kingston instantly shields me with his body, so I have to peek over his shoulder to see Bentley. "What the fuck, man? Ever hear of a thing called privacy?"

Bentley scoffs. "First of all, you left the goddamn door open. *Again.* And we could easily hear you because you're *right across the hall.* Secondly, I'm beginning to think one or both of you has some kind of freaky bathroom fetish. Third, *it's my fucking house.*" He meets my eyes and shoots me a cheeky wink. "Hot bra, Jazz. I especially like the see-through feature."

I blush as Kingston growls under his breath. A muscle jumps in Kingston's jaw as he and Bentley stare each other down. There's too much damn testosterone in this small space. It's giving me all sorts of ideas I have no business thinking. Like, you know, inviting Bentley in and telling him to lock the door behind him.

"Leave, Bent," Kingston grits out. "We'll be there in a minute."

Bentley's eyes travel back to mine. "Is that what *you* want, Jazz?"

"Uh..." My face is probably twice as red now. Why is it so damn hot all of a sudden?

Bentley grins. "I don't know, man, it seems like our girl here might want me to stick around." He's talking to Kingston, but his gaze is still locked on me.

Kingston steps forward and slams his hand into Bentley's chest, shoving him backward. "Fuck off, Fitzgerald."

"Ditto, asshole," Bentley spits out.

Jesus, this needs to stop. I hate knowing I'm the cause of this rift between them.

I bend down to pick up my shirt and quickly pull it over my head. "Look, no need to hang out in here anymore."

Bentley spins around and stomps into the game room.

Kingston's nostrils flare as he scowls. "You're not fucking helping the situation, you know. What am I supposed to do when you act like you wanted him to stay?"

I yank the zipper up and button my jeans. "Who said I was acting?"

Damn it. Did I really say that out loud?

His lips thin as he scans my face for something. "Just fucking forget it. Let's get this over with."

Kingston leaves the bathroom with me trailing behind. When we return to the game room, it's as if the air got sucked out of the room. There's so much tension between Kingston and Bentley, it's putting *me* on edge.

Bentley grabs the glass pipe in front of him and lights up the bowl. After taking a huge hit, he says, "Let's fucking get this over with. Shall we? I'm sure Kingston is anxious to get his dick wet."

I cringe as Kingston drops onto the opposite end of the couch, leveling his friend with a vicious glare. I purposely take the seat next to Reed, which happens to be across the room from the other two. I don't know what Kingston has to share with us, but one thing's for sure, this conversation is going to be super awesome.

Not.

chapter twenty-two

JAZZ

The scotch Kingston and Bentley had consumed earlier kicked in shortly after the bathroom incident, plus they smoked a little weed, so thankfully, the testosterone has been taken down several notches. Both men are so large that they still fully have their wits about them—unlike someone with a much smaller stature—but they've chilled out quite a bit. Reed's the only one who is completely sober, but he looks ready to fall on his face.

"Welp, I'm out," Reed says. "You guys have fun."

"Later, man," Kingston and Bentley say in unison.

"See ya," I mutter as Reed's halfway out the door.

I head to the bar and mix myself another vodka cran. I know I said I wouldn't drink tonight, but after learning all that shit about the police corruption, on top of all the other fucked up shit going on with Preston and Charles, all I want to do is drown my sorrows. I've only had two drinks, so I'm barely buzzed, but I need more to quell this panic rising inside of me. I'm trying hard not to flip the fuck out, but my brain won't shut up.

"Hey." Kingston grabs the glass out of my hand and sets it to the side. Fuck, I'm so inside my head, I didn't even see his approach. "What's going on?"

"Nothing," I lie. "I'm fine."

"Really?" His eyebrows lift. "Aren't you the one who told me you know 'fine' doesn't *really* mean fine?"

"That rule doesn't apply when I'm the one saying it."

Kingston takes my hand and leads me back to the couch. "Sit down with me for a sec."

Bentley grabs his pipe and refills the bowl before passing it to me. "Relax, baby girl. You're making *me* anxious, and that's a damn near impossible feat with all the THC I have floating in my system."

He flicks the lighter while I press my lips to the mouthpiece and inhale. I take a little too much and wind up in a coughing fit, making both guys laugh.

I flip 'em the bird. "Fuck off. Like it's never happened to you."

I pass the pipe to Kingston, but he declines, setting it on the coffee table. "What's going on in that head of yours? No bullshit this time."

I shrug. "I can't turn my brain off. The police stopping their investigation, the missing evidence, the proof that once again, money talks, or black-mail, or what-the-fuck-ever these assholes are using to cover their tracks. I can't stop wondering how many other victims are out there, suffering the same fate because some evil bastard had the right connections. How many unavenged assault cases are sitting in a file collecting dust? All the while, the victims are living in this constant state of terror. How does someone continue with their life, trying to find some semblance of normalcy when they're continually expecting their own personal boogie man to jump out of the shadows?"

Kingston's hand lands on my bouncing thigh. "Hey. That's *not* going to happen. *I'm* not giving up. *John's* not giving up. We will do everything in our power to figure this out. You're not alone in this, Jazz."

Bentley bumps his arm against mine. "It's true, Jazzy. We're here for you one hundo percent, girl."

"You guys can't be with me every second of every day."

"The fuck we can't," Kingston scoffs. "If that's what it takes to ease your mind, that's what we'll do."

I shake my head. "You can't slay every goddamn dragon out there that looks at me funny. *And I don't want you to*. Don't you get it? I have to do this for myself. I have to show them I'm stronger than they think. I refuse to let those fuckers win. I will *not* give them that power over me!"

He cups my face in his hands. "Hey, you won't. I promise we'll fix this."

I brush his hands away. "Did you know that everywhere I go, everything I do, I'm waiting for the assholes who attacked me to show up? Wondering if they're watching me. Sometimes, I swear I hear his voice—the fuckwit who beat the crap out of me—in the hallways at school. And then I ask myself, *could it be someone from Windsor?* Do we share any classes? Do they see me every weekday, laughing amongst themselves about how clueless I am that they're right in front of my face? Don't even get me started on the fact that every suspect we have may not be a suspect after all." I fist my hair and scream in frustration. "All these unknowns are driving me fucking crazy."

Is this what my mom lived with for however many years? Was she always looking over her shoulder? I don't know how she survived with her sanity intact, let alone being such an incredible mother of two.

I blink through a thick layer of tears. "And then there's the camera in my bedroom. I know I said I was fine with it, but *I'm not fucking fine with it, Kingston.*"

"Wait...*what* camera?" Bentley asks.

"Oh, he didn't tell you?" I tuck my legs under me, turning toward Bent. There's a manic edge to my voice, but I couldn't give a single fuck right now. "There's a hidden spy camera in my bedroom. And *only* my bedroom. My pervy dad, or his pervy dad" —I hitch my thumb over my shoulder— "or Madeline, or Peyton, or whichever other psycho in my life wants to watch me is *watching me.* They've seen me naked. They've seen me thrash about when I'm having nightmares. They've seen me do *other* things! God, the thought of what they're doing with that particular footage makes my skin crawl."

Bentley's jaw clenches as he looks over my shoulder. "Why is it still there? Can you figure out who's on the other end?"

Kingston grips each side of my waist and pulls me back into him. I know he's trying to ground me, to ward off my hysteria, but it's not helping. "Not without tipping them off. John thinks Callahan may have installed it to monitor Jazz to see if her mom told her anything incriminating about them, but we don't know for sure."

Bentley's dark chocolate eyes drill into me. "You have to get out of that house, Jazz."

"I've told her the same fucking thing," Kingston adds.

I roll my eyes. "Not this again."

Bentley throws his hands up. "What the hell does that mean? Why would you stay there? You know we'll take care of you. It's not like you'd be on the streets."

I fly off the couch and point an accusing finger at Kingston. "For the same reason he's still living at his house even though he can afford to buy a two million dollar car! I don't want them to know that I'm on to them. I need to be close enough to get information if they slip up. I need to know the truth about my mom! I need to ensure that what she went through wasn't in vain. I need to know if they...if she was...if they..."

I'm losing my train of thought. I can't fucking think. It's too much. Everything is *too goddamn much*. I angrily swipe at my tears as I sob uncontrollably. How is this my life? This isn't a life; it's a fucking living nightmare. I just want to wake up in my old shitty apartment, see my sister in the bed across from me, holding her stuffed panda. My mom would still be alive. Charles Callahan wouldn't exist. *None of this would fucking exist.*

"Jazz, breathe." Kingston is standing in front of me, lips moving, but I can't hear him over the noise in my head.

My throat is constricting. Spots flicker before my eyes. There's this charged tension in the air, dancing around me, making me dizzy. I'm weightless. Floating. I feel like a specter, witnessing someone else's meltdown.

"Kingston, fucking do something!" I think that was Bentley. He's standing now, too, running his hand along my back, looking at me like I've lost my mind. Hell, maybe I have.

Kingston's face is so close, some of the spots

fade away. "Jazz, look at me." He grabs my shoulders and shakes me so hard, my teeth rattle. "Fucking look at me! Breathe, goddammit!"

I can see the fear in his greenish-gold eyes. He wants to make the pain stop, but doesn't he know he *can't* make it stop? I'm flayed open, raw, nerve endings exposed. I don't know if *anything* can make it stop. I can't pretend to be okay anymore. I just *can't.*

Kingston's fingertips are bruising as he grips my jaw, but I welcome the pain. "Fuck. Baby, you have to breathe. You're scaring the shit out of me."

Whatever Kingston sees in my eyes has him launching into action. My body jerks in shock as his lips press against mine. It's like I've been hit with a bolt of lightning as he pries my mouth open, sliding his tongue against mine. Kingston pulls back after a moment, and I gasp, greedily gulping in precious air. He opens his mouth to say something, but I don't give him a chance. I grip the back of his neck and pull him into me. Now, *I'm* the one kissing *him,* but it doesn't take long for him to reciprocate.

Blissful silence surrounds me as our kiss deepens, and our hands roam, but the panic resurfaces at the sudden absence of heat. I open my eyes to find Bentley trying to slip away.

Without thinking, I rip my mouth away from Kingston's and cry, "Don't."

Bentley freezes in place, instantly bathing me in relief.

Kingston looks at me questioningly. His eyes bounce back and forth between Bentley and me, searching for answers I don't know how to provide. I don't know exactly *what* I'm asking for. Words are inadequate. All I know right now is *need*. I *need* to feel safe. I *need* to feel loved. I need to feel *whole*. A giant piece of my heart has been missing since my mom's beautiful soul left this earth. I'm tired of feeling sad. I'm tired of feeling broken. I'm tired of feeling numb.

I'm just so. Fucking. Tired.

Kingston's eyes lock on Bentley's before giving his friend an almost imperceptible nod. If I wasn't watching him so carefully, I would've missed it.

Kingston takes my arms and raises them straight above my head. His fingers curl under the hem of my shirt, briefly clenching the material in his fists before lifting it over my head. He pops the button on my pants next, waiting for permission to continue. I slide the zipper down and push them over my hips, wordlessly giving him the green light. Bentley groans as Kingston crouches down, first removing my shoes one by one, then my socks, then finally, my pants. I'm left standing in my bra and panties, while both men are still fully dressed.

Kingston gently wipes my remaining tears away before leaning down to whisper in my ear. "If this is what you need right now, we'll take care of you, but you have to be sure Jazz. You can't take it back. I don't want you to regret this."

I honestly don't know if I'm going to regret this come morning. Or what exactly is about to happen. But what I *do* know is that life is unpredictable. Life is short. I'm unsure of many things, but I've never felt safer than in their arms. And the one thing I'm most certain of? Kingston and Bentley will give me what I so desperately need right now: They'll make me feel *alive*.

I give Kingston a single nod. "I'm sure."

A low rumble sounds in Kingston's chest before he pulls back slightly. Our eyes meet, and we have one of those strange, wordless conversations we're so good at. I'm telling Kingston it's time for him to take charge because I don't want to think; I only want to feel. He tells me he knows where my boundaries lie better than I do, and he promises not to let anyone cross them, least of all me.

Bentley is watching us on bated breath, waiting

to see his role in all of this. The bulge in his pants reflects his excitement, but his mocha eyes are filled with curiosity. Astonishment.

Kingston takes a deep breath and briefly closes his eyes. When he opens them, they're filled with determination as he reaches one arm behind his neck and removes his t-shirt. Then, he grabs my face and kisses the shit out of me until I'm breathless and aching. At some point, Kingston beckons Bentley closer, and I sigh against Kingston's mouth as Bentley's bare chest warms my back. I have no idea when he took his shirt off, but the feeling of being sandwiched between these two men, skin to skin, is indescribable. Bentley's fingertips trail down my sides, eliciting a full-body shiver. When he reaches the curve of my ass, a groan is ripped from his throat as he palms my cheeks with both hands.

"Fuck, Jazz." Bentley's tone is adoring. Reverent.

I break my kiss with Kingston and turn to face Bentley. With slow deliberation, I slide my hands up the firm muscles of his arms until my fingers are linked behind his neck. "Hi."

Bent's sexy as fuck dimples pop out when a grin stretches across his face. "Hey, Jazzy."

Bentley cups my face with both hands, slowly

pulling me closer, giving me plenty of chances to back out. When I rise up on my toes to close the remaining gap, Bentley breathes out a curse as our lips meet. I moan when he slides his tongue into my mouth, deepening the kiss. Bentley's lips are soft, yet demanding. Firm yet pliable. I can taste the liquor on his tongue, the faint notes of spiced plums hitting my taste buds.

Kingston's belt buckle clangs as it hits the ground. He releases the clasp of my bra and pushes down the straps, freeing my breasts. I whimper into Bentley's mouth as Kingston's hands find my boobs, rolling my nipples between his thumbs and forefingers, with the perfect balance between pleasure and pain.

I keep one hand on the back of Bentley's neck and hook the other behind Kingston's neck. When I break away from Bentley, I immediately step into Kingston and claim his mouth again. He lifts me off my toes as he kisses me with even more ferocity than before. I'm sure he can taste Bentley on my lips, and now his inner caveman is trying to assert its claim.

I hear the telltale signs of Bentley removing his own pants, and a quick peek proves me right. Both he and Kingston are seriously testing the limits of their boxer briefs, making a thrill race through me. There's entirely too much sexy in this room. Both men have strong legs and thick biceps. Ridiculously rippled abs and a deeply carved V framing their thin treasure trails. Their bodies are works of art, plain and simple, and they both damn well know it.

I gasp as Bentley's fingers brush the underside of my breasts. "Fuck, Jazz. You have no idea how badly I want this. How badly I want *you*. We're going to make you feel so good, baby."

I turn back to Bent and run my finger over the small tattoo on his chest. The words, "Sleep well, Tiny Dancer" are written in a delicate script right above his heart.

I brush my fingers over the cryptic phrase. "What's this mean?"

Bentley frowns and shakes his head. "Not here. Not now. I swear I'll explain later."

Kingston drops back to the couch and extends his hand. "Come here."

I sit next to him, but Kingston's not having any part of that. He effortlessly lifts me up and places me on his lap. Instinctively, I grind into the hardness beneath me, causing us both to suck in a harsh breath.

"Lie back," Kingston commands, guiding my

upper body against his. My spine bows as Kingston's hands skate down my torso, dipping below the waistband of my flimsy panties. "Bent, you wanna help me out here?"

Bentley's muttering something under his breath, but I can't quite make out the words. I'm pretty sure "Praise Jesus" was in there somewhere. He kneels in front of me, slowly running his hands up my legs. When Bentley replaces his hands with open-mouthed kisses, I swear I can feel my pulse in my clit.

While Bentley works his way up my legs, Kingston kisses my neck and rolls my nipples. God, I'm on sensation overload. Bentley's skin is marginally darker than mine, and Kingston's slightly lighter. Seeing both sets of hands on me, the contrast between all three of us, I don't think I've ever beheld something so stunning.

Every brush of their fingers, or their lips, causes a rush of heat to soar through my body. I'm needy, and restless, and desperate for more. Bent kisses his way to my upper thighs, exploring, teasing, not quite venturing where I need him most. I moan as Bentley's index finger glides over my panties, right down the middle. Kingston's lips leave my neck, and we both watch as Bentley curls his fingers around the strings on my hips.

Bentley searches my eyes for permission.

"It's okay," I assure him.

Kingston's hands are still covering my boobs, so I can feel his fingers flex as Bentley slides my underwear down my legs, now leaving me completely bare. Bentley's eyes lift to Kingston, and they seem to have some sort of silent exchange. Bentley's hands wrap around my ankles, lifting my legs slightly and placing them over Kingston's knees, spreading me wide. I'm completely exposed—I'm sure Bentley can see exactly how excited I am right now.

"Fuck, Jazz," Bentley whispers as he gazes between my thighs. "That's the most beautiful thing I've ever seen."

Kingston's hand moves down the flat expanse of my stomach. His fingers slide through my wetness, before making small, slow, tortuous circles around my clit. Bentley's fingers join in the exploration, teasing my opening before inserting one long finger inside of me.

"Shit," I pant.

Bentley groans. "God, you're so wet."

"You like that, baby?" Kingston asks. "You want us to keep going?"

"Yes," I practically scream. "Fuck, don't stop."

Shudders ripple through me as Kingston works my clit while Bentley pumps his finger in and out. When Bent adds a second finger and increases his tempo, my toes curl. I should probably be embarrassed by the wet sucking sounds coming out of my body, but I can't find the will to care. This is filthy, and some might even say depraved, but it feels so fucking good. At this moment, I'm serving my body, succumbing to its desires, and there's not an ounce of shame to go around.

Kingston brings his fingers to my lips. "Suck. Taste how much you want this."

"Jesus, that's so fucking hot," Bentley mutters as I take Kingston's fingers into my mouth, sucking and licking them clean. His eyes drop to my pussy, and the intensity of his gaze makes me squirm with need. "I need to know how you taste, Jazz. Can I please fucking taste you?"

I moan. "God, yes."

Bentley pulls me closer, hooking my legs over his shoulders, my ass partially suspended in the air between Kingston's thighs. At the first swipe of Bentley's tongue, I scream, releasing a string of curses. I raise my arms, clasping my hands behind Kingston's neck. I'm afraid I'll float away if I don't have something to anchor myself to. Kingston leans down whispering words of encouragement in my ear and playing with my nipples as his best friend eats my pussy like it's his fucking job.

"Watch, Jazz," Kingston commands. "You love how he's eating that pretty little cunt of yours, don't you?"

"So much." I gasp as Bentley points his tongue, adding the perfect amount of pressure.

I shamelessly ride Bentley's face as he licks me harder and faster, my arched spine and rolling hips only seem to spur him on.

"I can't wait to be inside of you," Kingston whispers as he presses his erection into my back. "To prove that no matter how good you feel right now, *I'm* the only man who owns that pussy. *My* dick is the only one you want. But you already know that, don't you?"

I whimper as he pinches my nipples. Hard. "Fuck."

I can feel Kingston's smile against my cheek. "That's what I thought." He lifts his head and watches as Bentley's tongue swirls around my clit. "How's she taste, Bent?"

Bentley gives me one long lick from bottom to top. "Like fucking heaven. No pussy has ever tasted this good." I squeal when he curls his fingers inside of me.

"Mmm," Kingston murmurs. "That she does. C'mon, Jazz, get there. Show Bentley how gorgeous you are when you come."

"Oh, God," I pant.

I feel like I'm burning up from the inside, yet shivers are coursing throughout my body. I've never known pleasure like this before. Two sets of hands working in tandem, Kingston's filthy words whispered in my ear, watching as Bentley's dark head move between my thighs, it's too much. I can't hold back anymore. A ragged scream tears from my lips as my orgasm finally peaks. When I come down, I'm so blissed out, I feel like I'm floating in a completely different dimension.

Bentley removes his fingers and places a soft kiss right over the scar above my pubic bone. "You're absolutely stunning, Jazz."

"She'd look even better riding my cock." Kingston grabs my chin, yanking my neck to the side so I can look at him. "Do you want to show him?"

"Do *you?*"

Kingston places a soft kiss on my lips. "Yeah, I really fucking do."

I turn to Bentley. He seems to read my mind because he answers my question before I can even ask. "Yeah, pretty girl. I'm in. Show me what you've got."

chapter twenty-three

KINGSTON

Is this really happening? One minute, my best friend and I are squaring off, ready to battle for this girl. In the next, we're working together, doing whatever we can to bring her more pleasure than she's ever known.

"Remember, if you want to stop at any time, just say the word." I place a chaste kiss on Jazz's temple.

"Not gonna happen." Her voice is breathy, needy. Her body is pliant. Not a trace of anxiety remains, which is precisely what I was aiming for.

My hand slides down her taut abdomen until it lands on her bare mound. I go lower, dipping a finger inside to collect her moisture. My beautiful girl's pussy clenches at the intrusion, making my cock jump in anticipation. Jazz's back arches on a gasp while I pump my finger in and out a few times.

Bentley groans from his place on the floor in front of us, watching my finger disappear inside her tight little cunt. There's no doubt Jazz is more than ready, so I remove my finger and give her pussy a little tap. "Turn around, baby."

I fumble with my underwear, sliding it down just enough to free my dick as her lithe body faces me, bourbon eyes shining with desire. Christ, I don't think she's ever looked better. I thread my fingers through her thick hair, pulling her mouth to mine. Jazz glides her pussy over my shaft as we kiss, trying to get friction. I don't think she realizes she's doing it, but the natural lube all over my dick doesn't lie.

The couch dips as Bentley sits beside us to get a better view. He's stripped down as well, stroking his cock as he watches us. Jazz turns her attention to him, her eyes fixated on how he moves his hand up and down. I pinch her chin between my fingers, diverting her attention back to me while I nudge the head of my dick against her swollen clit.

"You on the pill?" I ask.

She nods. "Yeah."

I line myself up with her entrance. "You trust me?"

She nods again, more fervently this time.

"Then fucking ride me, baby."

Jazz gives me a saucy smile and sinks down on my cock, inch by inch until her ass is in my lap.

Ho-ly fuck.

I groan, firmly grabbing her hips. "Hold up a sec."

Jazz whimpers. "Kingston, I can't. I need to move."

"Just give me a second," I choke out.

This is even better than I imagined, and I've imagined it a helluva lot with Jazz. I've *never* fucked without a condom before—never trusted a chick enough not to pull the oops baby thing with me.

"How does it feel, man?"

Shit, I almost forgot he was here. Bentley's eyes are rooted to the spot where Jazz and I are joined.

I guide Jazz slowly up my shaft and back down again, testing my resolve. "*So* much tighter. Hotter. Wetter. So fucking *good*."

Jazz doesn't waste any time as soon as I loosen my hold. She braces one hand on my shoulder, the other behind her on my thigh. Her tits are pointed to the ceiling as she rolls her hips, riding me like it's her sole fucking purpose on this earth.

"God," she pants. "I almost forgot how full you make me feel."

I lean forward and lave each of her nipples with my tongue as she bounces on my dick.

Bentley throws his head back, closing his eyes, listening to the sounds of our skin slapping against each other. Jazz watches as he strokes himself, grunting as he likely imagines her on top of *him* instead of me. Her curious eyes flicker to mine, and I immediately know what she wants.

We're both well aware I can't *really* tell her what to do, but I appreciate the fact she's seeking permission to touch another guy's cock while mine is inside her. There's no way in hell I'm watching her put his dick in her mouth—I don't think I could ever get that image out of my head—but I'm okay if she uses her hand to get him off. It is proper foreplay etiquette to return the favor and all.

I incline my head, giving her the green light.

Bentley's eyes fly open when Jazz reaches out and cups his balls. "Oh, fuck!"

He watches in awe, mouth open in shock as she wraps her hand around his. "Bent, I wanna touch you."

He seeks me out, doing almost the exact same thing Jazz did a minute ago. That move right there tells me he's accepted what he wasn't willing to admit before now. Jazz is *mine*, and he's never going to have a real shot with her. He knows I would never consider going bareback otherwise. I give him a slight nod, silently granting approval.

When Jazz spits on her palm and fists Bentley's dick, I take over, thrusting into her from below. He groans every time she twists her hand a little as she reaches the flared head, before gliding back down. I've reached my limit of watching them, so I hook my hand behind her neck and pull her into another kiss. This one's not even a little bit gentle. It's hard. It's fast. It's claiming. She may be jerking Fitzgerald off right now, but that doesn't make her any less mine.

When I rip my mouth away, we're both panting. I'm sure my eyes are as wild as hers. I can tell she's close, and I'm not going to last much longer, so I thumb her clit, giving her that extra boost she needs to fall over the edge. When Jasmine comes, she strangles my dick so tightly, I'm actually worried I might lose circulation for a moment. The second she stops spasming around me, I give a few more hard thrusts before I'm spilling inside her.

My head falls to her chest, and out of the corner of my eye, I see thick ropes of Bentley's cum shooting out of him. My jaw clenches as the sticky substance coats Jazz's hand while she strokes him through the aftershocks. I'm well aware of what's happening, and that *her* hand just made it happen, but that doesn't mean I have to like his mark on her. In fact, I fucking hate it, but I will myself to calm down for Jazz's sake. I knew what I was getting myself into when we started this, and I'm sure as shit not going to do anything that will make her feel guilty.

Jazz rests her head on top of mine, and we all take a minute to catch our breath. Bentley reaches down and grabs the shirt he was wearing, using it to clean Jazz's hand. She sits up, observing him removing any trace of him from each one of her fingers. When Bent's done, he offers her a bashful smile.

She leans to the side as he cups his hands around her face and presses a quick kiss against her lips. "Thank you, baby girl."

She releases a surprised laugh, making me choke back a groan since I'm still inside her. "What are you thanking me for? I'm the one who came twice."

Bentley grins. "Naw, girl. That was hot as fuck, and believe me when I say the pleasure was *all mine.*" His expression takes a serious turn. "I was thanking you for trusting me enough to do that." He flicks his finger between the three of us. "To do *this.* You have my word that what happened here tonight will *never* leave this room."

Jazz's cheeks flush as she gives him a soft smile. "Thanks, Bent."

Bentley stands and pulls his pants back on. Putting one hand on my shoulder, he says, "I'm going to shower and hit the hay. You know where the guest room is."

"Yep," I confirm.

After he leaves the room, Jazz presses her lips to the corner of my mouth. "So, what now?"

She yelps when I stand abruptly, wrapping her ankles behind my back. "*Now,* we go take our own shower."

Her musical laughter rings down the hall as I carry her to the guest bedroom. I decide at that moment that I'm going to do everything in my power to hear that sound as often as possible.

"Mmm. Good morning." Jazz draws lazy circles on my chest as she snuggles into me.

"Yes. Yes, it is. Although, I think my dick may be broken."

Jazz laughs, sliding her hand beneath the stark white sheet. "Hmm...doesn't feel broken."

I was already hard before she touched me, but as she pumps her hand up and down, I swell. Jesus, we've fucked five times in the last nine hours, and when I say fucked, I do mean thoroughly. I honestly don't know how my dick is still working.

I still can't believe last night started out the way it did. I've never felt more helpless than I did when Jazz had that panic attack. Her eyes, which are typically so expressive, were completely vacant. Haunted. I wasn't getting through to her with words, so I did the only thing I could think of and kissed her.

While the kiss helped pull Jazz out of the headspace she was trapped in, it also brought out the most primitive version of her. I meant every word when I told her I wouldn't share. And I still feel that way now, but apparently, I can't say no to this girl. When Jazz called out to Bentley, asking him to stay, putting a stop to it never crossed my mind.

Every instinct inside of me wanted to push Fitzgerald away and beat his ass. I won't lie and say watching him devour her pussy didn't turn me on.

It was live porn, for fuck's sake. But it was more about her getting off than the act itself.

If I'm honest with myself, the rational part of my brain knew what happened last night was inevitable. Well, minus the panic attack. Jazz had to resolve the tension between them, and Bentley needed to learn that Jazz isn't going to replace Carissa. I know he thinks he might love Jazz, but I know my brother, and I know that's not true. Bentley may love Jazz, but he's not *in love* with her. He's just confused because she's the first girl to come along since Carissa died that he actually cares about.

Regardless of his misguided affection, Bent's acquiescence couldn't have been any more apparent. After last night, I'd say he's crystal clear that Jazz could never be his because she was made for *me*. I've no doubt there will never be another woman who gets me the way she does. This girl sees straight down into the darkest depths of my soul. She knows there's a monster lurking inside of me, but there's a similar darkness in her, waiting to be unleashed.

Jazz needs someone who understands the pull. Her meltdown last night proves there's a fucking hurricane of diverging emotions that she doesn't understand, doesn't know how to control. Lucky for her, I've become quite familiar with my demons over the last couple of years. I've learned when to chain them and when to set them free, and I can share that knowledge with her when she's ready.

I tilt Jazz's chin up so she can look me in the eye. "You okay?"

She sucks her lower lip into her mouth. "Yeah. I mean, I'll probably be walking funny for a week, but I feel pretty damn great."

"Well, then my job here is done." We both laugh. "I was talking about up here, though." I tap her temple.

Jazz's full lips turn down. "Um...yeah, I guess. I don't feel like I'm losing my mind, so that's a plus. I'm sorry you had to witness that."

"Nuh-uh." I shake my head. "Don't do that. Everyone's allowed to lose it every now and again. We wouldn't be human if we didn't. Considering what a rock you've been, after everything you've gone through lately, I'd say it was long overdue."

"Maybe." Jazz climbs on top of me and straddles my hips.

Her tits are bare, so I can't help myself. I yank her into me and suck her peaked nipple into my mouth.

"God, I fucking love your tits," I mumble against her skin.

Her body immediately tenses, and I internally curse myself for using those words. I know she's thinking about what Peyton said at her goddamn birthday party.

Jazz tries scooting off of me, but I grab her hips to stop the movement. "Hey, look at me."

Jazz normally exudes confidence, but I see the insecurity trying to force its way in as she pulls the sheet around her to cover her chest.

Fucking Peyton.

My grip on her tightens. "Don't let Peyton get inside your head. She's a bitter, jealous bitch. Being with you is a world away from any other chick I've slept with. There's no comparison, Jazz. Nobody else matters. And I love *every goddamn inch* of your body."

"But you *did* say those words to her. *Many, many times*, as you were fucking her tits. And I'm guessing Peyton's not the only one who's heard those exact same words while you were doing that exact same thing."

I take a deep breath and let it out. "I don't know what the right thing to say here is, Jazz. I don't want to lie to you."

She sighs. "If that's what you're really into...if that's something you need, I can't give that to you, Kingston. A boob job will never be in my future. I don't *want* giant tits."

I maneuver our bodies, so Jazz is beneath me. "That's not something I will ever *need*. If you really want to know, anything I've done in my past was likely because it was offered. Plain and simple. There was never a request on my end or something I felt was missing.

"Yeah, sometimes, nothing was off-limits because those chicks thought sex was their golden ticket to my wallet, but here's the thing: I never cared if they got off. *Not once.* I've never had a sleepover before you or cuddled with someone afterward. Because *I never wanted to.* I'll be the first to admit I was a selfish prick. All I cared about with any of them—including Peyton—was getting off and getting out as fast as possible."

Jazz takes a moment to digest everything. "And how many of 'those chicks' are we talking about here?"

I look her straight in the eye, so she sees the truth in my words. "Eight."

"Eight." Her brows rise. "How is that possible?

Are you not counting all the random blowies in the janitor's closet?"

I flop to the side. "First of all, I've never had a random blow job in the janitor's closet—that's Bentley's thing. But if that's a dirty fantasy of yours, just tell me when and where, and I'd be happy to *make it my thing.*" I smile when Jazz smacks me playfully on the chest. "Contrary to popular belief, I've been very selective with my dick, and I wasn't opposed to repeats with the same girl. Plus, I was with Peyton for almost two years, and I didn't assume we had an open relationship like she did."

"God, I still can't believe she did that to you." She tilts her head to the side. "On second thought, yeah, I can. I don't know if Peyton's capable of loyalty in any respect."

"I'd agree with you on that." I tuck a strand of hair behind her ear. "Since we're apparently doing the number thing, I think it's only fair you tell me yours."

"Besides you, one."

"Taco Truck Shawn?" I can't help it; I think about the pictures on Insta and frown. "He's seriously the only dude you've fucked?"

"First of all, it's *just* Shawn, no taco trucks involved. And yes, he's the only other person I've had sex with, or even fooled around with, for that matter." Jazz bites her lip. "Well, I guess after last night, there's two if Bentley counts."

I groan. "I think we need to set a rule that Bentley does *not* count. In fact, let's forget Bentley ever happened."

Jazz's eyes are filled with unease. "Kingston, why did—"

I lightly pinch her lips together. "I don't regret it, Jazz. It needed to happen for multiple reasons, and I'd be lying if I said it wasn't hot. But you have to know it was a one-time thing. It took a shit ton of self-control to prevent myself from knocking Bentley's teeth out while he was touching you. Every instinct inside of me was screaming to make it stop. I don't think I could control myself if it happened again."

"I don't *want* it to happen again," she assures me.

"No?"

"No. But I'm glad it *did* happen. What you did for me last night, what you *both* did for me, I could never forget. You *saved* me. I've had a few moments of heightened anxiety since the attack, but nothing close to what happened last night. Losing control of my own body, being consumed by panic like that, was terrifying. I was trapped in this really dark place, and I had no idea how to make it stop, which only exacerbated the situation."

"You don't have to be strong twenty-four-seven, Jazz."

She shakes her head. "That's just it. I *do*. Or I thought so, anyway. The way I grew up, you *had* to be vigilant at all times. If you lacked awareness or showed any weakness, you were painting a target on your back. For the most part, I kept to myself, but if it ever came down to fight or flight, I'd almost always choose fight because there was always someone looking to prey on the vulnerable. That's why jumping into a gang is so alluring for some people. You have instant protection. Instant family. They're not always just a bunch of criminals. Sometimes, it's good people trying to make the best out of shitty circumstances.

"But last night taught me that it's *okay* to be vulnerable sometimes. That I don't *have to* shoulder everything by myself. That I *can* fully trust someone else to take control of a situation. And it also taught me that it's okay to be self-indulgent every once in a while. I can't remember the last time I did something for myself for the pure joy of it, Kingston. I loved *every moment* of what happened between the three of us, but I'll never want to do that again." Jazz scoots a little closer and traces my eyebrow with her finger. "I know how hard that was for you, and I am so grateful for it. The fact that you could be so selfless only reaffirms my decision."

I run my fingers down Jazz's spine. "What decision is that?"

"I want a relationship with *you* and only you. I don't want to fight it anymore, either."

"Yeah?"

"Yeah." Jazz reaches out and fists my dick, forcing a groan past my lips as her thumb brushes the ridge right beneath the head. "And I think we should celebrate."

A smile tugs at the corners of my lips. "Again?"

She nods. "Again."

"But we have to hit the road soon to pick up your sister."

Jazz climbs back on top of me. "We'll make it fast. We can do slow later."

"Well, in that case, get up here and sit on my face." I tap my lips.

She laughs and gives me a cheeky wink. "Well, if you insist."

I'm smiling so hard, my cheeks hurt. "Oh, baby, I abso-fucking-lutely insist."

chapter twenty-four

JAZZ

"Is this going to be weird? Did he ever reply to your text?"

Kingston takes my bag for me as we walk to my locker. "Yeah. He said he smoked a little too much last night and slept through his alarm. Didn't get here until right before third period. He seemed okay. Nothing out of the ordinary."

Kingston and I haven't seen Bentley since our little party of three the other night. He must've been sleeping when we left yesterday morning, and we spent most of the day at the zoo with my sister and Ainsley. I expected to run into Bent in the parking lot this morning before school like we usually do, but he was suspiciously absent. Now, we're heading to lunch, where Bentley should be.

"Has this happened before? The sleeping in

late? I know he smokes a lot of weed—more so lately—but it doesn't seem like it gets in the way of everyday life. He seems pretty responsible."

"He is." Kingston glances at me out of the corner of his eye. "This *has* happened before, but it's been a long time, and his head wasn't in a good place. Back then, it was several times a week. I don't think we need to worry about him sleeping in one time."

"Do you think he's avoiding us?" I chew on the tip of my thumb. "Do you think he regrets what happened? Do you think it's—"

Kingston presses me into a locker and slams his mouth down on mine. My lips part in surprise, and when his tongue dives inside, I forget what I was saying. I'm instantly on fire, reaching up on my toes, chasing his retreating lips.

"What was that for?"

His lips kick up in the corners. "It shut you up, didn't it?"

I shoot him a glare then fist his hair with both hands, pulling him back to me until our teeth clash. Kingston growls into my mouth as our tongues tangle and twist. We're desperate for one another, almost violently so. He moves his body, so one of his muscular thighs is wedged between mine. I shamelessly grind my core into his leg, trying to relieve the ache building inside of me.

Kingston's hand wraps around my throat, putting slight pressure on it. It's not painful, more like possessive. Claiming. So are the fingers on his other hand as they duck beneath my plaid skirt, feathering over my inner thighs. I widen my legs, silently begging him to go higher, to—

"Whoa there, kiddos. This is crazy hot and all, but you're about to corrupt all these impressionable youths."

Kingston rips his mouth away from mine at the sound of Bentley's voice. Bent's standing next to us, with a devious grin on his face. He takes a step back, gesturing to the dozen or so students gathered in the hall, watching us, shock and amusement evident on their faces. Kingston and I instantly break apart, fixing our skewed uniforms.

Bentley swings one arm around each of us and starts leading us into the dining room. "How goes it, boys and girls? What are you in the mood to eat? I'm starving, so everything sounds fucking fantastic."

Bentley's arms drop from our shoulders when he reaches for a tray in the food line. That's when I get my first good look at him. His eyes aren't bloodshot, but they *are* droopy, and he's sporting a perma smirk. The boy is definitely rocking a decent high, and I'd bet every last penny I have, he has a vial of Visine in his pocket.

Bentley grabs a slice of pizza and an artisan cheeseburger with fries before looking back at me. "What's up, Jazzy Jazz? How's your day going so far?"

"Uh...fine, I guess."

"After what I just witnessed, it seems *a lot* better than fine. You know, before you came around, Davenport had a pretty strict anti-PDA policy. Nowadays...not so much."

"Watch it, asshole," Kingston mutters.

Bentley elbows Kingston playfully. "It's all good, dawg. I'm just fuckin' with you. I can't blame you; if Jazz were my girl, I'd definitely have trouble keeping my hands off her. You're a lucky fucker, fo' sho'."

Kingston and I share a quick look behind Bentley's back as we walk toward our table. He's acting like the same old Bentley—a little antagonistic, a lot flirty, but at the same time, there's something different, like he's drawn a clear line in the sand.

"Fo' sho'?" I repeat. "When did you become Snoop D-O-double G?"

"Ha! I wish. If I could be that successful while smoking weed by the truckload, I'd be one happy camper." Bentley winks.

Kingston laughs and bumps fists with his bestie. The awkwardness I've been worried about all morning is nonexistent. In fact, the animosity that's been building between these two men seems to be missing entirely. I'm sure it helps that Bentley's definitely not behaving like someone who ate me out in front of my boyfriend two days ago.

Wait a second...

I lean over to whisper into Kingston's ear. "Are you my boyfriend?"

Kingston's eyes—more amber than emerald today—twinkle in amusement. "You're shitting me, right?"

I shrug. "I dunno. I mean, I know we talked about having a relationship, but we kinda skipped over the label part."

We set our trays on the table, but before I can take a seat, Kingston fists the hair at the nape of my neck and plants another searing kiss on my lips.

He's full-on smiling when he pulls away, catching a glimpse of my likely dazed expression. "You're *mine*, Jazz, and vice versa. I don't give a fuck what label you use, it's not going to change what *this* is."

My face heats as I sink into my chair. I'm sure if I turned around right now, every set of eyes would be trained in our direction.

"O-kay then."

I take a bite of my turkey club. I'm sure it's delicious because all the food here is, but my brain isn't communicating with my taste buds. It's too busy trying to convince my vag that I can't mount the man next to me in front of all these people.

A piercing scream echoes from behind us. We all turn around just in time to see Peyton shaking out of her fuckboy's hold and stomping away. Not before she levels me with a withering glare, though. As Lucas Gale follows her like a lost puppy, he sends me an even harsher expression.

"Damn. What'd I do to get his panties in such a bunch?"

Bentley laughs. "*That*, baby girl, was jealousy rearing its ugly head."

My brows scrunch in confusion. "Why would Lucas Gale be jealous of *me?*"

"Not you, per se," Bentley says. "Your boy, and *then* you by association. That fucker has had a hard-on for the kings for as long as I can remember. He wants the power, and he knows he can't have it. No matter how far he crawls up Peyton's ass, the only way he'll ever be a king is if one of us steps down. His grandfather and father were kings. He should've been one, too, but there are only three from each graduating class. There's *never* been an exception, which is why Peyton's attempt to expand the court is such a joke."

"Why did you guys make the cut when Lucas didn't?"

"Because our grandfathers were the three *founding* fathers," Reed explains. "That trumps everything."

I shake my head. "I still don't get what the big deal is. You guys don't seem to wield *that* much power."

All three guys smirk. Even Ainsley joins in.

"What am I missing?" I ask Ainsley.

"You don't see it, Jazz, because you've never given them the power over you from day one. You'd have to buy into the order for them to successfully reign. But here's the thing: *You* may think it's a bunch of bullshit, but everyone else at Windsor believes it's the law. They've all been conditioned since their freshman orientation, maybe even before then.

"Even Headmaster Davis won't reprimand them unless they break the no violence policy. Even then, as long as there aren't too many witnesses, he'd turn his head. Same with the teachers. You don't fuck with the royals, *especially* the kings. As sexist and antiquated as it is, if the court is ever divided, the ones with the dicks will always have the final word."

"Well, that's a bunch of crap," I mutter.

"It is," Ainsley agrees. "But, in this case, it might be a good thing. If someone *didn't* have that power over Peyton, that girl would be even worse than she is. If you ask me, the boys are being too kind by ignoring her bullshit."

"You know what, Ains," Kingston says. "I think you're right. I think they need a reminder of who's really in charge, especially after the shit Peyton pulled with Jazz at the party." He looks to Reed. "Headmaster Douche is out of the office for that boosters' luncheon, right?"

Bentley grins. "I like where you're going with this."

"What are you going to do?" I ask Kingston.

Kingston smacks a quick kiss on my lips and stands. "Watch, baby."

Reed and Bentley follow him as they walk

toward the royals' table. Peyton and Lucas are still missing, but the remaining six look terrified as the guys approach. I slam a hand over my mouth as Kingston sweeps his arm out, knocking three trays onto the floor at once.

Ainsley laughs. "Oh, shit. He's really going for a dramatic flair, isn't he?"

The entire room is frozen. Silent. You could legit hear a pin drop right now.

"What is he doing?" I whisper.

Kingston's eyes flash to that Christian guy. "Clean that shit up."

"Excuse me?" the guy balks.

Bentley belts out this creepy evil laugh as he yanks the guy out of his chair and throws him to the floor. "Are you hard of hearing, or just a dumb-ass? He said, *clean that shit up*."

Christian's jaw tics. "What am I supposed to use? Do you see a mop and broom anywhere?"

Reed's eyes scan the room until they land on a teacher. I think that guy teaches history, but I'm not in any of his classes. "You! Find this asshole a mop and broom."

What the hell? He can't talk to a teacher like that! My jaw drops as history guy scurries off, presumably to raid the utility closet.

"Holy shit."

Reed looks down on Christian. "Use your blazer until he gets back."

"*What are you doing?!*" Peyton practically sprints back into the room, Lucas hot on her tail. "Kingston, what do you think you're doing?"

"Ooh, this is gonna be good." Ainsley channels her inner Mr. Burns, tapping her fingertips together.

I'm just as enthralled by this shit show as the rest of the room.

Kingston ignores Peyton and addresses Lucas instead. "Help him. *Now!*"

Lucas looks down on his friend, who's now splattered in marinara. "Fuck you. *You* clean it up."

My eyes widen. "Oh, snap."

Kingston's eyes fill with rage. Before any of us know what's happening, Kingston has Lucas by the back of the neck, his face pinned to the table. Half the room winces in sympathy, the other half laughs.

"Kingston! Stop it!" Peyton screams. "Tell me what to do to make this stop!"

"*Now* you get to do it in your underwear, and use your uniform to mop it up," Kingston grits out, still talking to our star QB. When Lucas stubbornly refuses to acknowledge him, Kingston turns to

Peyton. "You wanna help me out here, Peyton? For old time's sake? Either this fucker strips down and helps clean up the mess, or *you* strip down and do it for him. What's it gonna be?"

"Lucas, you heard him. Strip down to your fucking underwear and clean up this mess!" Peyton looks like she's on the verge of tears. I'd feel sorry for her, you know, if she wasn't a colossal cunt. "Your king and queen have spoken."

Kingston steps back, allowing Lucas to stand. Lucas glares at Peyton the entire time he's undressing until he's left in nothing but a pair of tighty whities.

"What am I supposed to wear after this?" Lucas whines.

Kingston brushes imaginary lint off his sleeve. "Not my problem."

"Cute undies, bro," Bentley remarks, holding up a pinky. "Although they don't do much to conceal your *little* problem."

From what I can see, Bentley's not wrong. Lucas is a *big* guy. He's tall and has a great body with stacked muscles, but the obvious dick print beneath the white cotton is less than impressive. Laughter and micro dick jokes are all around as Lucas gets on his hands and knees, attempting to mop up the spilled red sauce using his stark white shirt.

"Maybe he's a grower." Ainsley giggles.

I chuckle. "I certainly hope so for Peyton's sake."

"Listen up," Kingston's voice booms across the room, but he's staring Peyton down. "Starting tomorrow, the queens and their little lackeys will be sitting at that table." He points to the back corner of the room. "That nice one right next to the kitchen."

Peyton gasps. "Kingston, no. Please, don't do this."

His eyes turn away from her to address the room. "The kings are reclaiming their rightful place in this dining hall, and any person we see fit to join us is at our discretion, and our discretion only."

Peyton tugs on Kingston's hand. "Please, I'll do anything."

Kingston pulls his arm back like it's been burned. "Don't fucking touch me. For *any* reason. The only woman's hands I want on me is sitting right across from my sister. Starting tomorrow..." He pats the chair Peyton usually occupies. "Jazz will sit here, right next to me. Any questions?"

Peyton's face is doing its best impression of a tomato. "No."

Kingston cups his hand over his ear, acting like he didn't hear her. "I'm sorry; I didn't catch that. What'd you say?"

Peyton's fists are clenched so hard, I wouldn't be surprised if her palms have little bloody crescent marks on them. "I said, *no!* I have *no* questions."

A huge smile stretches across Ainsley's face. "Do you believe they have some power now?"

I'm still staring in awe as Kingston prowls in my direction, his gaze never leaving mine. When he reaches the table, he extends his hand, helping me up from the chair.

Kingston gets a wicked smile on his face and leans into my ear. "Remember that thing we were talking about doing in the janitor's closet? We should go do that *now*."

If my panties weren't already soaked from Kingston's ruthless display of authority earlier, they would be with that visual.

I start walking backward out of the room, tugging him with me. "Whatever you say, your highness."

Now Kingston's pulling on *my* hand, and I have to run to keep up with him, laughing the entire way.

chapter
twenty-five

JAZZ

The last three weeks have been freakishly uneventful as we've all fallen into a routine of sorts. At school, not a single person has messed with me, verbally or otherwise, which I have to admit, is as odd as it is refreshing. After Kingston's showdown in the dining hall, Peyton and her groupies haven't stepped into that room. I don't know where they're eating lunch, but then again, I don't really care. I'm guessing Peyton and Lucas figured it was their best way of saving face without incurring Kingston's wrath.

After school, the boys and I have been reviewing surveillance footage while Ainsley's at ballet, but neither Kingston's father or mine have given us anything we didn't already know. It probably doesn't help that they've been out of town even more than usual. Given how rarely they were around before, that's saying a lot. After Ainsley's done with rehearsal, the five of us usually get dinner together and hang out. On Sundays, Ainsley has become a regular addition to Belle's outings, which my sister has loved. I think Kingston may be getting a little salty because Belle seems to adore his twin more than she does him.

Speaking of Kingston...things between us have been incredible. Not only is the sex mind-blowing every single time, but even outside of the bedroom, he's so affectionate and thoughtful, I can hardly believe he's the same person I met a few months ago. Plus, ever since that night at Bentley's house, the absence of tension between Kingston and Bent continues. Who would've ever thought the solution to their problem would be getting naked with me? Thankfully, Bentley has stayed true to his word, never once bringing up that night. It's bizarre to think it even happened with how quickly things went back to normal. It almost feels like a dream.

As frustrated as I am about not making progress in the situation with our fathers, everything else has been so great that I've been happy more often than not, for the first time since losing my mom. A part of me can't help but wonder when the other shoe will drop, though. It's almost been *too* peaceful.

We have the next week off for Thanksgiving break, and tonight, that means the students at Windsor are celebrating. The five of us haven't been to a party since Peyton's birthday, so in the interest of acting normal as Kingston's P.I. had suggested, we'll be rectifying that tonight. The party is at some girl named Chantel's house, which Ainsley assures me is neutral territory. As a bonus, she lives right on the beach in Malibu, so if I'm lucky, maybe I'll get to take a moonlight stroll with my sexy boyfriend and roll around in the sand a bit.

"Girl, you look fuckhot." Ainsley runs the straightening brush through the last section of my hair. "Every guy at that party will want to put their babies in you tonight."

I laugh, taking in my high-waisted faux leather leggings and red off the shoulder crop top. My dark hair is pin-straight, my eyes are smoky, and my feet are covered in a pair of black studded booties. Okay, I guess I can admit I do look pretty badass.

"Uh, no thanks. I don't want *any* guy putting a baby in me anytime soon, not even your brother."

Her lips curve. "But you two make such cute parents. Belle's lucky to have you."

I roll my eyes. "You know, we're going to stop inviting you to our Sunday outings if you don't lay off the old married couple jokes."

"Whatever, bitch, you love having me there just as much as I love being there." She adjusts her breasts, pushing them up a bit in her halter top. "How do my boobs look?"

I give Ainsley a good once over. "Hot. So, you think tonight's the night you and Reed finally do the dirty, huh?"

She groans. "It'd better be. I'm sick of all the foreplay that never leads to his P in my V. I'm pretty sure my hymen's about to grow back."

My lips twitch. "Thanks for that visual."

Ainsley disappears into her walk-in closet for a moment and comes out wearing a new top. This one has a scoop neckline and is flowier. "Please. You have zero room to talk. You and Kingston have taken PDA to a whole new level. You're legit approaching exhibitionist territory."

I make a face. "Uh, I can assure you, that'll *never* happen. I'll never judge anyone for their kinks, but I'd prefer to keep my sex life private, thank you very much."

"Speaking of..." Ainsley blushes. "I have to tell you something because I *really* need to talk about it, but you have to promise you won't say a word to my brother."

I sit on the edge of Ainsley's bed. "Well, now, I'm intrigued."

She crawls onto the mattress beside me, tucking her legs beneath her. "I mean it, Jazz."

I mime buttoning my lips. "My lips are sealed. What's the big secret?"

"So, you know how Reed was all standoffish?" She draws circles on the purple duvet cover with her finger. "Pulling the *I want to be with you, but I can't actually be with you* crap."

"I remember. But I thought you guys finally worked that out after the incident with Rapey McRoofie."

"We did. The only reason I was even talking to that fuckwad was because I was mad at Reed for stringing me along. But after that night...Reed said it made him realize he couldn't keep pushing me away. That he had to lay it all out there and let *me* decide whether or not we'd move forward."

"And? Why was he so cagey in the first place? I didn't want to pry before, but since you're bringing it up..."

Ainsley gets a wistful look on her face. "Well, it turns out Reed's behavior was less about the whole bro code thing and more about being afraid he'd scare me off."

"Why?"

"Because he had it in his head that I'm the type of girl who prefers pretty ordinary sex. Especially with my lack of experience, he assumed I would think he's a freak or something and never look at him the same way again."

I frown in confusion. "Why would you think he's a freak?"

She wrings her hands together. "Because Reed Prescott has very particular...tastes in bed. He likes to do some pretty kinky shit."

My eyes widen. "*What?!* Are you sure we're talking about the same Reed? He's so reserved."

"Not always. And definitely not in bed. Damn, the things that boy can do with his tongue."

"We'll get back to the tongue thing. I want to know about the kinks. You can't leave me hanging like that. Tell me all the dirty, dirty deets."

She laughs. "For one, he's *really* into spanking. Like, bend you over his knee and redden your bare ass kind of spanking."

A surprised laugh escapes my lips. "Are you shitting me?"

"Not even a little."

"Whoa. It's always the quiet ones." I make an exaggerated spanking motion in the air. "How do you feel about that? Have you let him smack that ass yet?"

Ainsley bites her lip and blushes. "Uh-huh."

"Shut. Up!" I give her a playful shove. "And you liked it?"

"I didn't think I would at first, but I *really, really* do."

"Did it hurt?"

"A little," she admits. "But it's really brief. He does this thing where he rubs the spot right afterward, which takes the sting away. And then he rubs *other* spots. It's actually pretty freakin' awesome."

"Well, hot damn. Who knew you were such a fiend?"

"Oh, shut up." Ainsley rolls her eyes. "You've never done anything kinky like that before?"

Do three-ways with my boyfriend's bestie count?

I shrug. "I've never tried spanking before, but I have done other stuff."

She lifts an eyebrow. "Like?"

"Um...didn't you say you never wanted to hear about your brother's sex life?"

Ainsley scrunches her nose. "Ew, no. Forget I asked."

I wiggle around until I find a more comfortable position. "What's the other thing? You said, 'for one' which leads me to believe there's more than one freak in Reed Prescott's closet."

Now her face is really red. "Aaaand...he's *super* into butt stuff. Like, he'd want to stick his D up my ass, and not just on special occasions."

"Okay, there's not a dude alive who'd turn down anal—at least not any I know—but how do *you* feel about that?"

"I told him I was definitely open to exploring, which shocked the shit out of him. God, you should've seen his face when I told him I wanted to experiment a little." Ainsley giggles. "We've done *some* stuff...with you know, his finger...and I can't say I hated it. He even licked me *down there*, which I thought would be weird, but it felt incredible. Like, *oh my sweet baby Jesus* incredible."

I wag my eyebrows. "Get it, girl. Looks like you've landed yourself a man with a bit of an ass fetish."

"Holy crap, I never thought of it like that, but he

totally has an ass fetish." She laughs so hard, her eyes are filling with tears. "I may not have much in the boob department, but good thing my ass is fantastic, right?"

"Your ass is *spectacular*, Ains."

She smiles. "Have you ever done it?"

"Anal?"

Ainsley nods.

"No...but I've *experimented* a little, too."

"Do you think you'll ever want to? And please don't tell me if you do, because I know it'll be with my brother, but do you think it's strange that I'm inquisitive about it? After Reed told me what he likes, I've been watching some porn, you know, for like research, and it's pretty freakin' hot. The thought of doing that with him turns me on."

"I don't think it's weird at all," I assure her. "I've thought about it a lot, and I'd totally be open to trying it. Besides, I always say whatever floats your boat in the bedroom is what's right for you. As long as it's consensual, who am I to judge what other people like? Ya know?"

Ainsley nods. "I think that's a great way to look at it."

My phone buzzes, so I pull it out of my pocket and see a text from Kingston.

Kingston: You two almost ready? The guys are here, and we're waiting in the pool house.

"The guys are with Kingston," I tell Ains before replying to her brother.

Me: Be down in a few.

Ainsley stands up and looks at her reflection in the mirror. "This shirt isn't doing it for me. You go ahead. I'll be right behind you."

"You sure? I don't mind waiting."

"Positive." Ainsley nods. "I'll be like ten minutes, max."

"Okay. See you down there."

I head down the stairs while Ainsley changes and make my way toward the back of the house. When I round the last corner that will take me to the back yard, I crash into a wall, face first. Only it's more of a solid chest than an actual wall.

"Jasmine. This is a nice surprise." Kingston's dad has his hands around my biceps. I think he was trying to steady me at first, but he's making no effort to remove them.

"Uh...yeah, sure. I was just on my way to Kingston's. If you'll excuse me."

"What's the rush? Can't spare a minute for your

boyfriend's old man?" He laughs breezily, but it contradicts the skeevy way he's looking at me.

I eye his grabby hands pointedly, but the dude doesn't get the hint until I take a step back. I swear his grip tightened for a second like he was about to pull me into him. It's unsettling being this close to Mr. Davenport, knowing what a despicable person he truly is. It's even worse than being around my sperm donor because at least Charles doesn't look at me like he's picturing me naked. Kingston's dad, not so much.

"I didn't realize you were back in LA. Weren't you supposed to return tomorrow?"

He doesn't even try to hide the fact that he's perving on me. Gross. "Keeping track of my schedule, are you? I'm flattered."

"*What?!* No...I, uh...Ainsley mentioned you were out of town and due back tomorrow. That's all."

Mr. Davenport assesses me carefully. I tell myself to play it cool; don't let this asshole get to me. That's easier said than done when Kingston looks so much like his dad. It freaks me out. Even worse, they have the *exact* same eyes.

I love it when Kingston gazes at me with those beautiful hazels, but it's unnerving when his dad does it. Although they're identical in shape and color, the elder Davenport's eyes have a malevolent tinge. They're cold. Calculating. Looking into them, I swear I can see his complete lack of conscience— the psychopath hiding beneath the shiny surfacc.

"Dad. What are you doing?"

Oh, thank fuck. Kingston must've been coming to see what was taking so long.

Kingston's dad turns toward his son and flashes a big smile. "I was just saying hello to your lovely girlfriend."

Kingston's jaw clenches. "When did you get back?"

"Just a few minutes ago, actually. I was heading to my office when I ran into Jasmine here." Mr. Davenport looks my way and winks. "Or should I say, *she* ran into *me*?"

Kingston turns his attention to me. "Jazz, we should get going so we're not late. Where's Ainsley?"

I jerk my head toward the stairs. "She's changing. Said she'd be out in a few."

"Go ahead and wait out back with the guys. I'll get Ains." Kingston has some kind of weird stare-off with his father. "Dad, if you'll excuse us, we really must be on our way."

"Of course." Mr. Davenport gives his son the

fakest smile I've ever seen in my life. "Well, I won't hold you up any longer. We can catch up on Thanksgiving, Jasmine."

"Thanksgiving?" I frown in confusion.

"My son didn't tell you about our Thanksgiving tradition? The Davenports and Callahans celebrate together every year." He gives me another sleazy once over. "I'm looking forward to seeing such a beautiful addition to the head table."

With that, he pats Kingston on the shoulder and walks away. Kingston waits until his dad is out of sight before speaking.

"Go to the pool house, Jazz."

"What in the actual fuck, Kingston?" I whisper shout. "How could you not tell me about Thanksgiving? It's only five days away!"

Come to think of it, why hasn't *anyone* told me about it? It's not like I see Charles or Madeline that often, but I run into Ms. Williams every day.

Kingston releases a heavy sigh as if I'm exasperating. "I was going to talk to you about it tonight."

"Well, you can count me the fuck out. I'm going to see Belle."

Kingston grabs my hand and yanks me into his body. I absolutely do not feel him up a little or take a big whiff of his sexy cologne.

He cups the back of my head and pulls me into him. If anyone came upon us, they'd probably think we were in a loving embrace, but the anger radiating off Kingston and the tension in his body is anything but.

"We will talk about this when that bastard is not in the building, but you being a no-show is *not* an option. *Me* being a no-show is *not* an option. Our fathers make a big deal out of this holiday. They invite a lot of business associates. Men that I *need* to interact with to further our agenda." Kingston's other hand lands on my hip, gripping it with bruising force. "Now, *go to the fucking pool house* and wait with Reed and Bentley."

"Fine." If my face wasn't smashed against his stupidly firm pecs, he'd feel the force of my glare, but since it is, I have to project it in my tone.

Kingston pulls back a little and bends his knees, so we're eye to eye. "I'm sorry for snapping, okay? When I came in here and saw him so close to you, I just..." He briefly closes his eyes. "I didn't know he was back in town. I wouldn't have left you alone in the house if I knew."

Any lingering irritation I had dissipates. "I know you wouldn't." I cup my hands around his jaw and pull him into me for a soft kiss. "I'll meet you out back, okay?"

I can feel Kingston's eyes on me the entire time I'm walking to the pool house. As I step inside the safe zone, I can't help but think that other shoe may be dropping sooner rather than later.

chapter twenty-six

JAZZ

If you've been to one rich kid's party, you've been to them all. But if that rich kid happens to live on the beach, it's a step above the rest, in my opinion. This particular gathering has both an indoor bar as well as an outdoor bar beneath the raised deck. The second we got here, Ains and I ditched our shoes and headed down to the beach portion of the party. The guys won't let us out of their sight, but we told them we needed a little female bonding time, so they're keeping their distance.

It still trips me out how much money is spent on these things. Ainsley and I each ordered a Sex on the Beach from the hired bartender. I know it's totally cheesy, but she assured me they were delicious, and she's not wrong. I moan as I take my first sip of the peachy drink.

"God, I needed this."

Ainsley takes her own sip. "It's really good, right?"

I chuckle. "Well, yes, but I was referring to the beach. It's been a while since I've been to one."

"Hasn't it only been a few weeks?"

"Exactly." I power chug the rest of my delightfully fruity cocktail, tossing the red cup in the nearby bin.

"Right. My bad." Ainsley follows suit and squeals when some of her drink dribbles down her chest.

Even though it's dark outside, I love being out here. Seeing the moon reflecting off the ocean, hearing the waves crashing against the shore, smelling the briny air as soft sand squishes between my toes. I take a deep breath and let it go, then I do it a few more times. It's chilly out here, but thankfully, alcohol is a warm friend.

The ocean has always been my happy place. No matter how shitty things can get sometimes, it's vastness and vitality reminds me there's a whole big world out there and many people who are stuck in worse situations. That regardless of how badly I'm hurting, I'm *alive*; therefore, there's an opportunity for a better tomorrow. It's never been more critical for me to remember that than now.

"I've stayed away long enough." Kingston sneaks up on me from behind and pulls me into him.

I moan as he licks the sensitive spot right below my ear. "It's been five minutes."

"Exactly. Five minutes too long."

A flame flickers in the darkness as Bentley lights a J and takes a long drag. "You guys good? I think I'm going to skip the fifth wheel thing tonight and go mingle. And by mingle, I mean, find a hot chick to suck me off."

I can't help it; my eyes automatically fall to his crotch. Just because I don't want to be up close and personal with it again, doesn't mean I can't appreciate a good peen. And Bentley has a *nice* peen.

I roll my eyes to cover my obvious ogling. "Have fun with that."

Bent smiles, no doubt because he caught me looking. "Oh, don't you worry, princess. I will."

"Have I told you how unbelievably fuckable you look tonight?" Kingston growls in my ear, making me shiver.

I turn around and loop my arms behind his neck. "You have not, but thank you."

Kingston grabs two handfuls of my ass. "No, thank *you* for being such great eye candy."

My lips turn up in the corners. "You're an idiot."

"Maybe."

I lift up on my toes to kiss the underside of his jaw. "It's hard to believe only a few months ago, we were at a party just like this, and you were rapid-firing insults at me."

Kingston searches my eyes. "You know I never meant any of that, right?"

"I know." My fingers play with the hairs on his neck as I hear the beginning notes to Meghan Trainor's "Woman Up". Well, there's a perfect segue if I've ever seen one. "You know what else I know?"

"What?"

I pull away from Kingston and grab Ainsley's hand to yank her away from Reed. "That Ainsley and I are going to get our dance on. You boys are welcome to watch, but don't even *think* about getting in the middle of our groove."

Ainsley giggles when she sees both guys dropping their jaws. "Sorry, not sorry, boys."

Ainsley and I run up the deck stairs and step inside the warm house. I know Kingston and Reed are right behind us, but I never look back as Ainsley and I make our way to the crowd of people dancing. We squeeze our way to the middle and began shaking our asses, arms high in the air, not giving a shit about being barefoot. One song turns into many until Ainsley and I are sticky with sweat and out of breath.

When I catch sight of Reed looking at Ainsley like he wants to eat her alive, I lean into her ear. "You're *so* getting his P in your V tonight. And maybe your A, too."

She laughs and shoves me playfully. "Shut *up!* You're never going to let me live this down, are you?"

"Probably not," I answer honestly. "But you love me anyway."

Ainsley pulls me into her arms. "I really do, Jazz. You're my girl. If you ever need *anything*, all you need to do is ask."

I give her a big squeeze before I pull back, my eyes filling with tears. "Okay, no more mushy shit. You're going to ruin my makeup. Go getchu some lovin'."

She laughs as we're weaving our way through the mob. When we finally reach Reed, Kingston is nowhere in sight.

"Where's Kingston?" I ask Reed.

He jerks his head behind him. I instantly spot Kingston and Peyton standing against the back wall. Based on her flailing arms, I'm guessing she's going off on him about something. I don't know why Kingston is indulging her, but I'm going to put him out of his misery.

I incline my head toward them. "Looks like Kingston needs a rescue."

"God, she's such a bitch. I don't understand why she doesn't give up already." Ainsley scowls. "Do you want us to go with you?"

"Nah, I can handle Peyton."

Reed gives Ainsley a small smile. "You wanna get out of here? My parents are away for the weekend."

Her eyes widen as she decodes his statement. "Absolutely."

"Have fun, you two." I give them a little finger wave, trying to hold in my smirk.

Kingston stands a little taller as he notices my approach. Peyton looks over her shoulder to see what's snagged his attention, and her eyes narrow when she spots me. She says one last thing to him, but the music is too loud for me to hear, before stomping away.

"What was that about?"

"Same shit. Different day." Kingston tucks a piece of hair behind my ear. "You look warm. You wanna get some fresh air? I stashed your shoes next to the barbeque out back."

"Sure."

Kingston leads me through the mass of bodies with his fingers threaded through mine. I shiver when we step outside from the sharp contrast in temperature.

Kingston rubs his hands over my arms. "You okay?"

"Yeah." I point to the small firepit down below. "But maybe we can sit down there for a bit?"

Nobody seems bothered by the fact that you can't have campfires on public beaches, so I roll with it.

He nods and continues walking until we reach the small gathering in the sand. There's only one empty Adirondack chair, so Kingston takes a seat and pulls me onto his lap. I sigh in relief as my body instantly warms. We sit there for a few moments, just looking at the flames, soaking in the warmth.

Kingston rests his chin on my shoulder. "Where'd Ainsley and Reed go?"

"I don't think you want the answer to that question."

He groans. "You're probably right."

"Have you seen Bentley?"

"About fifteen minutes ago. He was talking to some chick, but he seemed pretty far gone. I told him to text me when he's ready to leave, and we'd take him home." Kingston's finger sneaks under the hem of my top, slowly moving back and forth over my skin.

"Is he going to be okay? This overindulgence thing seems to be getting worse."

"Hence why I've remained completely sober tonight." Kingston's chest rises and falls as he takes a deep breath. "On Monday, it'll be exactly two years since someone close to us died, so I think he's feeling it pretty hard."

"Carissa?"

Kingston's arms tighten around me. "He told you about her?"

"Not exactly. But Ainsley told me how she died."

I feel him swallow hard before asking, "Did Ains tell you about the events leading up to Carissa's death?"

I slowly shake my head. "She said the rest was Bentley's story to tell."

He says nothing for a long moment, before tapping my hip, prompting me to get up. "Let's take a little walk."

I scan the people sitting in a circle around the fire. The combination of music floating from the house and the buzz of conversation should prevent anyone from hearing us, but I can understand Kingston's need for privacy. I have a feeling this story's going to be a doozy.

chapter twenty-seven

JAZZ

Kingston and I stroll down the beach a little until we're far enough away from prying ears. He props himself on one of the boulders edging the beach, pulls me down onto his lap again, and wastes no time getting to the story.

"Bentley blames himself for her suicide."

I twist my upper body so I can see his face. "What?! Why?"

"It'd probably be easier to understand if I start from the beginning," he says. "We were all in the same kindergarten class. The guys and I become friends on day one, same with Ainsley and Carissa. Since Ains and I have always been close, the five of us spent a lot of time together throughout our childhood. I think Bent and Rissa fell in love before any of us understood what that meant."

Poor Bentley. Losing someone you love dearly is hard enough. I can't imagine how difficult it would be when that person takes their own life.

"What happened to her?"

"Oddly enough, Bentley and Rissa were never officially a couple. Carissa refused to give them that label because she was supposedly afraid it'd ruin their friendship. That was complete horse shit, in my opinion, because whenever one of them wasn't dating someone else, they'd act like they *were* a couple in every way. They lost their virginity to each other, for fuck's sake. And if one of them *was* hooking up with someone else, it'd never last long because they preferred to be with each other.

"It was all very strange, and probably more than a little toxic, but there was no doubt they loved each other fiercely. In retrospect, I think Carissa refused to take the plunge because she was insecure. Maybe she figured if Bentley slept around enough during his teenage years, they could be together afterward. The irony in that whole situation is that Bentley was crazy about the girl; I don't think that would've ever changed. He didn't *want* anyone else, but when he saw Rissa hooking up with other guys, he'd get pissed and act out.

"They had this huge fight one night. Bent got

invited to a frat party, and he was told to bring some friends, especially girls, to even out the ratio. Carissa didn't want to go. Her older sister was in college and warned her about all the crazy shit that goes down in frat houses. She didn't want Bentley to go either, probably because she didn't want him fucking someone else." He takes a deep breath. "But...we went anyway and got completely shitfaced."

"Uh-oh. What happened?" I squeeze Kingston's thigh, encouraging him to continue.

"At some point in the night, pictures starting showing up on Instagram. We were tagged in most of them, so Carissa got a front-row seat to the half-naked sorority chicks hanging all over Bent and Reed. We all lied about our age, so those girls had no idea the guys were barely old enough to drive."

"Just Bentley and Reed?" I ask. "I find that hard to believe."

I feel Kingston shrug. "I was already with Peyton at that point, and she was with us. Peyton wouldn't leave my side, so it was pretty obvious I was off-limits. Anyway, unbeknownst to us, Carissa saw the pictures online and drove up to the party, planning to drag Bentley out."

"What happened when she got there?"

Kingston hugs me tighter. "When Rissa walked in, one of the sorority chicks was giving Bentley head, right there in the middle of the main floor. I honestly believe he was so fucked up, he barely knew what was happening. Bentley never knew Carissa was there. *I* saw her, but I didn't do anything when she ran off crying because I had assumed she was going home. I thought it was their normal on again, off again, jealousy bullshit."

"I don't think I like where this is heading. Where did she wind up?"

"She stayed at the party. I think she was on a mission to hurt Bentley because he hurt her. We found out after the fact that she didn't leave the frat house until the next day. She was picked up by Campus Security sometime that afternoon because she was wandering around in a daze, crying and mumbling to herself."

Kingston doesn't need to say another word. I know, without a doubt, what happened. Bentley's extreme reaction to my attack and his adamant denial of drugging me makes so much sense now. I don't even realize I'm crying until Kingston kisses my trailing tears.

"She was roofied?"

Kingston takes a deep breath. "Yep. We never

found out exactly how many men raped her, but Rissa's body was... whatever happened, it was pretty brutal. She was so confused at first, she refused to go to the hospital or the police. Campus Security tried convincing her to get checked out, but she demanded to leave. Rissa later told Ainsley all she could think about was getting their scent off of her. She scrubbed so hard with a loofah, she gave herself friction burns on close to half her body."

I wince. "Jesus."

"Yeah." He clears his throat. "When she told her parents a few days later, they immediately took her to the hospital, and the hospital staff subsequently contacted the police. Unfortunately, Carissa had washed off any DNA that may have been left behind, and the drug was already out of her system, so she had no proof. When the police investigated, every single person living in that frat house claimed they had never met her, that she was never there. I told the police differently, but it was two people's word against many.

"After that night, the only person Rissa would confide in was Ainsley. She refused to see us, even Bentley, which killed him. Ains thinks Carissa couldn't handle being around *any* men because she'd avoid her dad, too, whenever possible. My sister was afraid to leave Rissa alone with no one to talk to, so she practically moved into her house. It's the only reason we know as much as we do.

"Carissa couldn't stand being touched, no matter how innocent. She'd stay in bed for days at a time. Had severe nightmares—would wake up screaming or crying, completely terrified, but never remembered why. Carissa admitted to Ains that she felt like she was losing her mind, that she just wanted to make it stop.

"Rissa's nightmares only got worse, so she started forcing herself to stay awake as much as possible because she didn't want to endure another bad dream. Ainsley thinks Riss was actually dreaming about the rape, like maybe her subconscious mind was trying to jog her memory. After Carissa started hallucinating from lack of sleep, her doctor prescribed sleeping pills.

"Rissa convinced my sister to go home, swore she'd be fine after a good night's rest. She even agreed to make an appointment with the therapist her parents had been begging her to see. Ainsley would've never left if she thought Carissa was disingenuous. I don't know if Riss was a really great actress, or if she wound up changing her mind, but that same night, she swallowed over half the bottle of pills and never woke up."

"That poor girl."

God, as traumatized as I've been since my attack, I can't even imagine the horrors flashing through Carissa's mind after something like that.

I release a heavy sigh. "I don't understand why Bentley feels responsible, though. What happened to Carissa was *horrible*, but he had no part in it."

"Bent thinks if he never pushed her to go to the party, they would've never fought. Then, maybe he would've never got so wasted or hooked up with that girl. He thinks it was his fault Carissa was even at the party."

"Well, I guess my secret is out."

Kingston and I both startled at the sound of Bentley's voice. Bentley steps out of the shadows from just beyond the boulders and walks toward us. The flame from his lighter illuminates his face as he lights the blunt sticking out of his mouth.

I jump off Kingston's lap onto the sand. "Bentley, what are you doing out here?"

He takes a drag from the joint and exhales. "Needed some fresh air. Found a quiet little spot to hang. At least until you two showed up."

"Why didn't you say something?" Kingston

asks. "Why didn't you let us know you were sitting there?"

Bent takes another hit. "Found the topic of conversation riveting. Wanted to see where you were going with it."

It's fairly dark, but I can still see Kingston's frown. "Dude, if—"

Bentley holds a hand up. "It's cool, man. It's not like you said anything that wasn't true. I promised Jazz I'd tell her one day—you just beat me to it." He turns to me. "Your boy did leave one thing out. Rissa was a dancer—ballet, like Ainsley. It was everything to her. That's what the tat on my chest is about."

Fuck. I don't think I've ever seen someone look so haunted before. My heart is breaking for this poor, lost soul. I don't even think about it; I practically run into Bentley and throw my arms around him. He holds his arms out to the side at first, but then I see the joint fall to the sand right before he hugs me back.

"Bentley, I'm so, so sorry," I mumble against his chest. "I understand *why* you feel guilty, but it's not your fault. It's just *not*. You can't keep letting this haunt you."

Bentley fists one of his hands in my hair and

crushes me into him for just a moment, before letting go and stepping back.

He clears his throat. "I could really use a fucking drink, so I'm gonna head back to the party? You two coming?"

Kingston does that thing where he stares you down, trying to figure out what you're thinking. Bentley stares right back, not cowering from the intense scrutiny in the least.

Kingston gives a single nod. "Let's go."

What? We're going to let it drop just like that?

Kingston reaches for my hand, twining our fingers together, and doesn't let go the entire way back to the house. When we get to the deck, Bentley heads inside straight for the bar.

"Should he really be drinking right now?"

I pull my shoes on as I watch Bentley place his order with the bartender. As soon as my feet are covered, we head back inside.

"We're not leaving his side for the rest of the night," Kingston assures me. "He's obviously trying to numb himself. I'll know when he's reaching his limit. He's close, but not quite there yet."

Bentley approaches us, cup in hand, and takes a big swig. "This party's lame. Lemme have another drink or two, and I'll be ready to bounce. You cool with that?"

"Sure." Kingston's eyes swing to me. "I have to take a piss. Don't go anywhere."

Bentley swings his arm around my shoulders. "Don't worry, dawg, I'll keep our girl nice and warm."

Kingston's jaw clenches, but he lets it slide. Before walking away, he meets my gaze and mouths, *watch him.*

I nod in reply.

"So, Jazzy Jazz, wanna talk about something not so fucking depressing?"

I wrap my arm around his middle. "Sure, Bent. What'd you have in mind?"

"You can start by telling me what color your panties are. It'll help me get a better visual in my brain later."

Bentley's obviously using humor as a defense mechanism. After what I learned tonight, I suspect he's been doing that for a while.

I roll my eyes playfully. "Sorry, bud. You'll just have to make it up."

He laughs. "Where's the fun in that?"

There's a bunch of people suddenly gathering

around the TV. I don't think anything of it until the lewd comments start flying.

"Hot damn, look at that body," one guy says.

"Her tits are a little smaller than I'd like, but I'd still fuck her in a heartbeat," another one adds.

"No, shit. She deep throats like a damn porn star." I think that was the first guy again. "Can somebody get me a copy of this for the spank bank?"

What the fuck are they watching?

My eyes lift to screen, and when I see what's playing, my jaw slackens.

Bentley obviously sees it at the same time because his grip on me tightens. "What the fuck?"

My face heats as people start laughing and whistling. I think Bentley and I are both in shock because neither one of us moves to stop it. In 70-inch high def, I'm on my knees, blowing Kingston in the shower after Peyton's birthday party. Even worse, there's a clear view of *every-thing*. Every. Fucking. Thing. From the angle, it looks like someone was pointing their phone camera at the shower from right inside the doorway.

Kingston picks that moment to return and frowns when he sees our expression. He turns his head to see what's drawing our attention and immediately charges forward.

"What the fuck is this shit?" Kingston yells. "Turn that shit off! Where the fuck is the remote?"

"Oh, God." I slam my hand over my mouth.

I can't believe this is happening again. This time it's even worse because no one is protecting my modesty. Every single person in this room has now seen me completely naked. They know what I look like with a goddamn dick in my mouth.

Bentley launches into action then, manually turning the TV off. He's a little slow due to his inebriation, so it takes much longer than I'd like.

"Oh, look, it's the stars of the show." Peyton sneers, golf clapping as she walks to the center of the gathered audience. "This seems to be a habit of yours." She flicks her finger between Kingston and me. "Are you two, like, trying to become porn stars or something? Or is it an exhibitionist thing?"

Kingston's fists clench. "Peyton, you're fucking dead if I find out you had *anything* to do with this."

She laughs derisively. "Oh, please. Don't try to blame me for your deviant tendencies. Why would I *ever* want to broadcast the whore at work?"

Kingston takes a step forward, but I grab his shirt, and he seems to think better of it.

Bentley's searching through the media cabinet when he shouts, "Found it!" He holds up a thumb drive.

"Is that the only copy?" Kingston grits out. He's glaring at Peyton with unadulterated hatred right now. I'm honestly surprised she's not crumpled in a ball, begging for forgiveness.

"How would I know?" Peyton parks a hand on her hip. "I had nothing to do with this."

I don't fucking believe her for one second. Based on Kingston's expression right now, I'd say he doesn't either.

Barclay What's-His-Name starts laughing. "I gotta say, Davenport, I didn't get it at first, but after seeing how well she sucks cock, I can understand why you'd put up with the trash." He looks at me and winks. "How much do you charge, honey? I'd like to give it a try." Barclay puffs his chest out when laughter surrounds us.

I don't even feel sorry for the bastard when Kingston's fist flies out and takes Barclay down with one punch. Unfortunately, that single hit also sparks an instant full-on brawl.

"Ah, fuck," I mutter, right before some Barbie wannabe bitch-slaps me.

Oh, hell, no. I don't even know who this chick

is! I raise my fist and clock her right in the jaw. She goes stumbling back into the wall, eyes widening when I stalk after her, getting right in her face.

"Touch me again, and I'll make you regret it," I snarl.

"I'm sorry!" Barbie holds her hands up and recoils when I fake a punch.

I catch sight of Bentley diving into the fray, and part of me worries he's too fucked up to handle himself. However, my concern only lasts a second when I see Bent expertly dodge a punch before he starts wailing on the idiot who tried to hit him. Fists are flying everywhere. Girls are screaming. Half the partygoers are throwing down—some of them looking way too happy about that—and the other half are tripping over each other to get away. I lose sight of Bentley and Kingston in all the ruckus, but I'm too busy to worry about it.

Some asshole lunges for me, so I jab the heel of my hand into his throat. "Didn't anyone ever teach you to never hit a girl, dickhead?"

He clenches his neck, wheezing. "Stupid bitch."

Oh, no, he didn't!

I slam a hand down on his shoulder for leverage and knee this motherfucker in the balls as hard as I can. He drops to the ground instantly, whimpering in the fetal position.

"Think about that next time you want to beat on a woman."

Out of the corner of my eye, I see Peyton trying to run away. She's fucking kidding herself if she thinks I'll let her get past me. I *know* she's responsible for that video. I don't know how she got past the lock on the bedroom door, but the skank figured it out somehow.

I leap over the asshole clutching his balls and give chase. As soon as Peyton sees me, she veers left and darts up the stairs. Clearly, she's never watched a horror movie in her damn life, because she would've known she had a much better chance of escape had she run outside instead. When I reach the top level, I look around but don't see her. I start opening the doors, one by one until I hit a roadblock. The second to last door is locked, and I know she's behind it.

I pound on the wood with a closed fist. "Come out here and take your ass-kicking like a real woman, Peyton!"

"Fuck you!" she yells through the door.

I study the doorknob, trying to figure out whether or not I can break in. It's not a key lock, but it is one of those pinhole ones like Charles has in the mansion, so I'd still need a tool to get in. Fuck. How am I going to—

Something hard whacks me on the head from behind, slamming my face into the door with a resounding thud. Spots dance before my eyes as I stumble backward. Before I can catch my balance, I'm pushed to the floor with such force, my teeth clank together.

"Fuck," I mumble, the spottiness getting worse.

I grunt as a knee lands in the middle of my spine while a strong hand pushes on the back of my skull. My arms are trapped beneath me, and my face is being smashed into the carpet so hard, the skin on my forehead and the bridge of my nose is getting massive rug burns.

Warm breath infused with alcohol hits my ear as a deep voice growls, "You're not so tough now, are you? You know, I haven't been able to stop thinking about you." I cringe when he nuzzles his face into my hair. "How badly I want to make you scream as I take your pretty little cunt. Although, after seeing that video, I think I'd much rather fuck your face first. You'd look incredible choking on my cock, tears streaming down your face."

I try not to go there, but I'm suddenly back in

those woods, bleeding and broken. How could I not think about it, when the same man who tried to rape me is currently crushing me with his weight, and his musky bergamot cologne is infiltrating my nose?

"Please don't do this," I sob into the thickly carpeted floor.

My voice is so muffled, I'm not sure he can hear me. I definitely know I can't manage to scream for help like this. God, I hate being so weak, but I can't fucking breathe. Can't move. My heart feels like it's trying to claw its way out of my chest. How sad is it that I hope Peyton comes out of that room and scares this guy away? I doubt that's going to happen though because there's a real possibility she just set me up.

"Oh, Jasmine, you don't get to run the show here." I stiffen when he says my name. "Yeah, that's right; I know *exactly* who you are. Where you live. I've been watching you. Waiting. Your boyfriend just gave me the perfect opportunity by starting that fight. Maybe I should send him your panties as a thank you after I rip them off your body."

I whimper.

He wraps his fist around my hair and pulls so hard my eyes water. "What do you say we take advantage of one of these bedrooms? I'm sure I can find something to tie you up with. I'd have to blindfold you, too, but I'm sure you understand why."

The guy curses when someone downstairs yells, "Cops! Everybody get the fuck out!"

Oh, thank God.

Out of my peripheral, I see a meaty fist coming at the side of my head, but I can't do anything to stop it. The last thing I hear before I blackout is, "This isn't over, bitch."

"Jazz! Wake the fuck up!"

Someone rolls me over. My eyes flutter open, and I gasp for air, trying to slap their hands away. I scramble to break free, but I can't. A low cry hits my ears, and I realize it's coming from me.

Firm hands grab my shoulders and shake. "Jazz! It's me. Calm down."

I still at the sound of Kingston's voice. I blink a few times, waiting for my eyes to focus. Kingston is hovering above me, alarm evident in his forest-green eyes. Bentley is standing behind him, wearing a similar expression.

"Oh, thank fuck." Kingston presses his forehead

against mine, making me wince. When he pulls back, he gently brushes his fingers over the raw skin right below my hairline. His eyes narrow as he says, "What the hell happened here, Peyton?"

I blink a few more times and find Peyton leaning against the wall, arms crossed over her chest.

"How should I know? I already told you, I didn't see *anything*. One minute, this psycho was chasing me up the stairs, and in the next, she was out cold."

Psycho?! Hi, Pot, lovely to meet you. I'm Kettle, your less snotty counterpart.

I chuckle, amused my sarcasm is still going strong, even with *another* head injury. Kingston's concerned eyes flicker back to me, likely wondering what's so entertaining. Or maybe he thinks I'm a lunatic. I'd say the odds are fifty-fifty. That thought makes me snort-laugh.

"Jazz, what happened?" Kingston asks cautiously. I just now notice bruises are blooming on his cheek and around his left eye.

I moan as I try sitting up. Kingston helps me into a seated position, propping me against the wall.

"I was jumped from behind... the same guy

from the woods. Got hit in the head." I reach behind me and rub the sore spot.

Kingston releases a sharp exhale when he copies the motion and feels the big lump. "Jesus, fuck. Bent, will you go raid the freezer? Get me an ice pack, or some peas. Whatever."

"Well, this has been fun and all, but I'm leaving." Peyton waves her hand in my direction. "Have fun with that."

"I'm not done with you, Peyton," Kingston warns. "We'll be having words as soon as I'm sure Jazz is okay."

She flips her bleached blonde hair over her shoulder. "Whatever. You can talk all you want, Kingston. It's not going to change the fact that I don't know *anything*."

I wait until Peyton leaves before speaking. "He knew my name. Said he knows where I live. He's been watching me. He saw the video...made a pervy comment about it."

Kingston's jaw clenches. "Motherfucker."

"Shit," Bentley says at the same time.

"Yeah." I start to nod but wince when it makes the pain worse. Jesus, I have the mother of all headaches.

"I'm gonna go get that ice." Bentley takes off, presumably to the kitchen.

I sit there in a bit of a daze until Bentley returns a few moments later with a bag of frozen vegetables and a paramedic.

When I give him a questioning look, he says, "Figured it wouldn't hurt to have him take a look. Some girl called 'em after her boyfriend's nose got broken."

"Awesome." I sigh.

Kingston shrugs. "At least the place cleared out quickly when people heard the siren. Made it easier to find you."

The man kneels in front of me. "Hey. Jasmine, is it? I'm Dan. I understand you have a head injury. May I take a look?"

"Go to town," I mumble.

Dan inspects the back of my head and my temple, instructing me to hold the peas on the bump while he takes my vitals. He flashes a light in my eyes and tells me to follow his finger in all directions while asking a few questions. Kingston brings the paramedic up to speed on my recent concussion while he's packing up his medical bag.

"Well, I think it's just a nasty bump, but I'd still recommend coming in for a CT scan, especially given your recent medical history. We can take you via ambulance, or you can have someone drive you."

"I'll drive her," Kingston tells him.

The paramedic looks at Kingston for a moment. "I'm obviously not a police officer, but I'm going to ask anyway. Have you had anything to drink or taken any drugs?"

Kingston glares at the poor guy who's just trying to do his job. "I haven't had a drop of *anything* all day. I'll take her."

Dan nods. "Okay. Good luck, Jasmine."

"Thanks."

Bentley takes a seat on the opposite side of me from Kingston. "You need to stop scaring us like this, Jazzy."

"I'll do my best not to get assaulted again," I deadpan.

Kingston takes my hand and helps me stand. "You're sure it was the same guy?"

"I'm positive." I suppress a shudder.

Bentley takes my other hand as they carefully guide me down the staircase. "So, is anyone going to point out the obvious?"

"What's that?" I ask.

"The only people at this party were Windsor

students." Bentley goes ahead of us and opens the front door before continuing. "That guy mentioned seeing the video, right? Well, he could've only done that if he was part of the crowd."

"Which means he's been in front of us this whole time." Kingston tightens his grip. "Jazz, did you recognize his voice at all?

"No." I shake my head slightly. "There's nothing about it that stands out. Just your standard deep guy voice."

Kingston opens the passenger door to his Range Rover and helps me inside. "We're going to find this guy, Jazz. I'll get the truth out of Peyton one way or another. I know she's hiding something."

Bent climbs in the back and adds, "In the meantime, maybe we should skip the parties."

You can say that again.

chapter twenty-eight

KINGSTON

After Jazz got the all-clear from the hospital, I brought her back to my place. I'm glad she didn't want to go back to Casa Callahan because there's no way in hell I would've allowed that, which would've inevitably started another argument. Even though my dad is back in LA, I still feel like she's better off with me out here in the pool house. I need to know she's fucking safe, and I can't do that if I can't see her with my own eyes.

When I realized Jazz wasn't where I left her at the party, I was terrified. I ripped Bentley away from the dude he was fighting, and we went on a mission to find her. Thankfully, at the same time, people started fleeing the scene because they heard an ambulance approaching. Sirens at a party where there are underage drinking and drugs are never a good thing. Nobody took the time to determine what kind of siren it was, or why they were there; they just bolted out the back door.

Fuck, when I finally found Jazz and saw that she was once again unconscious, I think my heart stopped beating. My chest heaved as I struggled for breath. The darkness inside of me was brewing, fighting for supremacy. It wanted to hunt and destroy the motherfucker who did that to her. For a few seconds there, I legitimately thought I was going to lose it. Like, full-on raze a village, kind of lose it. I haven't felt that out of control since I first suspected my father arranged to have my mom killed.

"How's your head feeling?" I grab a bottle of water from the fridge and hand it to Jazz.

She takes a long sip. "Much better after the Tylenol kicked in."

"You tired?" I grab her hand and lead her into my bedroom. "Or do you wanna talk about what happened yet?"

Jazz hasn't said much since we left the party. I know she's shaken up from her encounter with that bastard, but she doesn't want to talk about it because she's not big on sharing feelings. Hell, I'm not either, but that doesn't stop me from wanting to know everything that goes on inside her head.

"I already told you everything that happened, Kingston."

I grab the bottle out of her hand and set it on the nightstand. "Not what I was talking about, and you know it. I want to know how you *feel* about what happened."

Jazz shakes her head. "Not tonight. Tonight, I just want to forget."

I groan when she reaches out and strokes my length through my jeans. "As much as I love where you're going with this..." I wrap my hand around her wrist and pull it away from my dick. "Stuffing this into a box in the back of your head isn't going to help."

"I know that." Jazz takes a few steps back and shimmies out of her tight pants, kicking them aside. "But I don't want the memory of *him* to be the last thing I think about before I fall asleep. Nor the thought of all those people who saw us naked, sullying what was supposed to be an intimate act with their greedy eyes."

"Jazz—"

She lifts her shirt over her head and tosses it

behind her. When she loses the bra, too, I automatically step closer.

"I want the memory of *your* hands touching me," she continues. "*Your* eyes on me. When I'm dozing off tonight, I want to feel the delicious ache *you* leave behind after you've been inside of me."

I look to the ceiling for some divine guidance. "Fuuuuuck."

Jazz's full lips turn up in the corners, probably because she knows she has me.

"Kingston, I want you. We can deal with the real world tomorrow."

I place a soft kiss over the purple bruise forming on the side of her face, pausing there for a moment. When did I become the guy who does something like this? I'm touching a nearly naked, stunning woman, and my lips are on her fucking *temple*. Jazz brings out a side in me that quite frankly, I didn't know existed.

"Lie down."

Jazz lowers her body onto the mattress, scooting back toward the headboard as I strip down to my boxers. Her dark hair fans across the pillows, and I can't help but think about how right she looks in my bed, eyes hazy with desire. I crawl onto the bed until I'm hovering over her, trailing my fingertip across her collarbone and down her arm.

Jazz's nipples pebble into tight buds as goosebumps scatter along her bronzed skin. My beautiful girl moans when I seal my lips over one peaked tip, swirling my tongue around it. She death grips my biceps when I switch to the other.

"Kingston…" Her hips buck upward. "This feels so good, but I don't want gentle. Don't treat me like I'm made of glass."

I raise myself into a plank position and stare into her eyes. Jazz's cognac orbs bounce between mine, pleading with me to listen.

I cock an eyebrow as I give her a wolf-like grin. "Oh, princess, you've gone and woken the beast."

Jazz's eyes glint with excitement right before I wrap my hands around her tiny waist and flip her onto her stomach. She squeals when I push her ass up, leaving her upper body flat on the mattress. I bite one cheek before looping my fingers beneath the flimsy straps of her thong and roughly yanking it down.

Fuck.

She's already wet and needy, and I can't wait for a second longer to put my mouth on her. Without preamble, I give her one long lick from crack to clit.

Jazz gasps as I dive in, kneading her round cheeks with my hands while my tongue fucks her pussy. She eagerly pushes back into me as I devour her, fisting the sheets and begging for more.

"You taste so goddamn good," I mumble, alternating between licking and sucking her hot flesh. "I'm going to fuck you so hard, you'll see stars."

"I'm good with that," she pants. "Space is pretty."

This girl: Always such a smartass.

Jazz moans as my laughter vibrates her pussy. I slide two fingers inside her and pump them in and out while ravishing her clit with my tongue.

"God," she pants in that breathy voice I love so much.

"God's not the one who's about to make you come, sweetheart."

I don't give her time to formulate another sassy reply. Instead, I feast on her cunt like a man starved, licking and sucking and finger fucking until she's screaming my name. I don't even give her time to recover; I shove my underwear down just enough and plunge into her while she's still spasming.

"Fucking hell," I groan as I fully sheath myself.

I grab Jazz's hips, drawing back to the tip, before pushing in again. I reach forward, gathering her long hair and wrapping it around my fist. I yank on the thick strands until she's toeing the line between pleasure and pain, knowing exactly how she likes it. I fuck her hard and fast until skin slaps against skin, and our breathing is ragged. I slide my other hand to where our bodies are joined, coating my thumb with the evidence of her arousal.

With my fingertips digging into Jazz's lower back, I press my thumb against the tightened bud between her cheeks, stimulating the sensitive nerves. My hips continue driving into her without mercy, working her over until her pussy's throbbing and clenching around me, signaling her impending climax.

"Shit, I'm gonna come," Jazz shouts.

I smile when she presses into my thumb. "You want something from me, sweetheart?"

She cranes her neck to glare at me. "Fuck off."

I laugh mockingly, but right before she falls over the edge, I sink my thumb inside her ass up to the first knuckle. Jazz throws her head back as she whimpers and curses and screams through her release. A few thrusts later, I'm groaning as I join her in orgasm bliss, moving slowly through the aftershocks. After the tremors wane, we both collapse into a boneless heap, skin slicked with sweat, trying to catch our breath.

Jazz flips over as I roll to the side. She cradles my face in her hands and pulls me into a kiss, moaning as she tastes herself. Jesus, why is that always so hot? We take our time memorizing the topography of each other's lips until they're swollen and red. When we finally break for air, Jazz traces my eyebrow with her finger and stretches her neck to kiss what I assume is the bruise forming on my cheek. She grins when I softly kiss the middle of her forehead in return.

What in the hell is this woman doing to me? How did we go from a hard, dirty fuck to something so...intimate?

"Feel better?"

"Mmhmm."

I brush some damp hair away from her face. "I'm glad I found you, Jazz."

I'm not just talking about tonight, and if her sleepy smile is any indication, she's well aware of that fact.

"I'm glad you found me, too."

chapter
twenty-nine

JAZZ

"So, talk to me about Thanksgiving. What exactly should I expect?"

Kingston focuses on merging into traffic on the freeway before answering. "Every year, our fathers rent out the ballroom in a five-star hotel, and host a stuffy black-tie dinner for approximately five hundred guests."

"What the fuck? Isn't Thanksgiving supposed to be about spending time with your family, eating some turkey and pie?"

He shakes his head. "To them, it's an annual networking event—an opportunity to boast about their accomplishments or make new business contacts. There are a lot of influential men in attendance from many different fields. You'll probably recognize some celebrities, too."

"What's my role in all of this?"

"I suspect Callahan will parade you around like a show pony." Kingston looks irritated by the thought. "He'll act like he couldn't be happier to have you in his life. Expect you to play nice with Madeline and Peyton so you'll look like one, big happy family. He won't waste the chance to put a new coat of wax on his public image."

"Sounds super fun," I deadpan. "You'd think he wouldn't want me there because I'm so 'rough around the edges', according to him."

Kingston briefly turns his head toward me and smirks. "I, for one, happen to like all your curves *and* your edges."

I give him my, *you're an idiot* look, but since he's paying attention to the road, I doubt he sees it. "It's *this* Thursday. Why hasn't anyone talked to me about it yet? If appearances are so important, wouldn't you think Sperm Donor would've issued some kind of *'behave yourself, or there will be consequences'* warning?"

"Maybe they were waiting for the break from school to begin. I'm sure Madeline plans to sic her stylists on you; probably has an evening gown waiting and everything. And to be fair, you've been *at my house* since break started."

It's true; I have. Since the party, I can't stand the thought of being alone. I have no doubt that fucker was telling the truth about knowing where I live. Plus, I'm not convinced Peyton didn't purposely lead me right to him that night. She's been dodging Kingston's promised interrogation, which tells me she's got something to hide.

I narrow my eyes. "Smug isn't a good look on you, Kingston."

"I have no idea what you're talking about." He shrugs innocently.

I scoff. "Bullshit. You don't want me staying at that house. Considering I've been with you for the last two nights, you think you've won."

The asshole grins. "I would *never* think such a thing."

"Well, I've got news for you, buddy. I'm going home after we drop Belle off tonight."

He gives me the side-eye. "We'll see about that."

I fold my arms over my chest and turn toward the window. "Ass."

Kingston laughs. "You love it."

I fight a smile. He's right; I totally love our banter.

"Back to the subject at hand...I'm not surprised your father or mine would put business over family on a holiday, but don't these other people have families of their own to spend the day with?"

He nods. "They bring them with. There's sort of an unspoken rule that young children aren't welcome, but you'll see some people around our age there—several of them from Windsor. Besides, most of these people aren't what I would call friendly or family-oriented. Status and wealth are what drives them."

Awesome. Five hundred clones of my sperm donor in the same room.

My brows draw together. "You mentioned this thing will help you further the cause. How so?"

He blows out a harsh breath. "Because I suspect some of these men help our fathers with their *side business* in one way or another. And I'm pretty sure there are at least a few dozen men in attendance who are buyers, or possibly brokers. I've been keeping a list, but it's pretty easy to pick them out of the crowd if you watch them carefully enough. They're usually watching the younger, prettier females in the room. Some of them a little *too* young."

I gag. "You mean we're actually going to be in the same room as the sick fucks who'd buy and rape girls because that's what they get off on?"

Kingston's lips thin. "Yep."

"I don't know if I can do it, Kingston." My heart starts beating rapidly as my eyes fill with tears. "How can I be in the same room with people like that and keep my mouth shut? The proximity to our fathers is bad enough, but dozens of them?"

"Hey. Breathe." He grabs my hand over the center console and squeezes. "Think of the states."

I breathe in and out a few times, trying to calm my racing pulse. After my meltdown at Bentley's house, I did some research on panic attacks. One coping method is to use a distraction technique like Kingston did when he kissed me. I couldn't find any articles that suggested engaging in a threesome, but I *did* find several that recommended reciting something from memory, like song lyrics. When I was in elementary school, we learned how to say all fifty states in alphabetical order using a specific beat, so I've been doing that whenever I start feeling anxious.

Alabama, Alaska, Arizona, Arkansas...California, Colorado, Connecticut. Delaware...Florida...

By the time I get to Louisiana, I've regained my composure.

"You good?" Kingston squeezes my hand again.

I nod, blinking a few times. "Yeah, I'm good."

He gives me a soft smile. "Which one did you get to this time?"

I lace our fingers together. "Louisiana."

Kingston brings our joined hands to his mouth and kisses my knuckles. "It's gonna be okay, Jazz. Bentley and Reed will also be there with their parents. Someone will be with you and Ainsley at all times."

I slump back into the Rover's plush leather seat. "God, I hate this. I just want it to be over already."

"Me too, princess. Me too."

"This is boring as shit," Bentley complains.

"One of them is bound to give us something soon," Kingston murmurs.

The three of us have been poring over surveillance videos for hours. Kingston installed the monitoring software on multiple devices, so Bentley and Kingston are on their laptops, and I'm using Kingston's iPad. Thankfully, the cameras are motion-activated, so we only have to watch footage when there are actual people in the room. So far, the only drama has been my father telling Madeline he would *not* be footing the bill for her next collagen appointment, followed by Madeline breaking out the waterworks and begging him to reconsider. Other than that, it's been a bunch of mundane business shit.

Bentley rubs the back of his neck. "I really wish we had another hand. My eyes are crossing."

Ainsley's ballet classes are also canceled this week for the holiday. Reed's been keeping her occupied, so we can do this without raising suspicion. I giggle when I think about how he's likely keeping her busy.

Kingston lifts an eyebrow. "What's so funny?"

"Nothing. Nothing at all." I fake cough to cover my laugh.

His expression tells me his bullshit meter is ringing loud and proud. "You don't want to tell me? Fine. I have ways of extracting information when you're naked later."

Bent groans. "I really need to get laid."

Bentley's phone picks that moment to vibrate on the table in front of us.

I catch a glimpse of the text as he opens it, and it's a short message accompanied by a picture of some girl's boobs.

I nod to his cell. "Perfect timing. According to that, Morgan Whoever-she-is is D-T-F."

He shakes his head as his thumbs fly over the screen. "Nah, just not feelin' it."

"Why not?" I ask. "She has a stellar rack."

His lips curve slightly. "Which matches the rest of her, but still not feelin' it."

Kingston and I share a look. Most people would probably be worried that Bentley's become even more enamored with me after that night in his house, but Kingston and I know that's not the case. Bent and I seem to have this newfound respect and appreciation for one another, but the anticipation that fueled our attraction before is no longer there. I do think we've grown closer, but not in a physical sense.

"But *why?*" I press.

"Dunno. Just don't." Bentley shrugs.

Oh, my poor, sad clown. This boy is holding onto so much grief, which I definitely understand, but the guilt he feels is unfounded. One of these days, I hope to convince him of that.

Bentley sets his phone down and fixes his eyes back on the computer screen. "Hold up, I think we've got something."

Kingston and I both lean over to get a closer

look. Some leggy brunette wearing a knee-length coat is storming into Preston Davenport's corporate office, looking ready to raise hell.

"Rewind thirty seconds and turn the volume up," Kingston demands.

Bentley complies, and we all watch the woman enter the office for a second time.

"It didn't work!" She throws her hands in the air. "*Again!*"

Kingston's dad couldn't possibly look more bored as he reclines in his chair, twirling a pen between his fingers.

"Who is that?" Bentley asks. "She sounds familiar."

We haven't gotten a glimpse of the woman's face yet, but she definitely sounds familiar.

"Preston!" the woman shouts. "Did you hear me?"

Kingston's body goes rigid beside me.

"What's wrong?" I ask him.

His eyes don't dare to move away from the screen. "I know who that is."

"Wh—"

"Shh!" he says. "Watch."

Preston's eyes finally lift to the woman in front

of him. "That's what you get for sending a boy to do a man's job, Peyton."

"What?!" Bentley and I shout at the same time.

"But...her hair." I wave my hand at the screen. "It's brown."

"Look at the length." Kingston pauses the video and points to the screen. "It's a wig."

Bentley and I study the monitor carefully. Kingston's right. After Peyton's most recent haircut, her blonde hair now ends around her bra strap. *This* hair is not only dark brown, like mine, but it nearly hits her waist.

"What the hell is going on?" I whisper.

"Let's find out." Kingston's jaw clenches as he presses play.

"What are we going to do now?" Peyton starts pacing back and forth, giving us our first good look at her face. Yep, no denying it now; that's definitely her.

Kingston's dad stands and rounds his desk. "Stop fucking moving." His hand snakes out like a viper, grabbing Peyton's upper arm. "And remember who *the fuck* you're talking to."

"I'm sorry. It won't happen again." She yelps when Preston appears to squeeze. "I swear! I was upset, and I reacted poorly, but it will *never* happen again." Peyton averts her eyes to the ground.

"Am I the only one whose mind is fucking blown right now?" Bentley asks.

I shake my head. "Nuh-uh."

"Sit down!" Preston shoves Peyton into the nearby chair before moving directly in front of her, propping his ass on the desk.

It's a blatant power move because he's now looming over her, trying to disintegrate her with his eyes.

"Now..." Kingston's dad removes his suit jacket and begins undoing his cufflinks. "Calmly, tell me why you insisted on wasting my time with this meeting."

"I'm sorry," she repeats. "I just need to know what to do. Kingston keeps trying to get a hold of me, and when he finds me, I'm afraid of what he might do. He *knows* something's up, and he's not going to give up until he gets it out of me. I'm afraid he might hurt me."

I place my palm over my mouth to forcibly stifle my outburst. I want to scream so many obscenities at this bitch right now, it's not even funny.

Bentley and Kingston both look like they want

to jump into the computer and throttle both people on the screen.

"What did you expect?" Preston yells. "You shouldn't be surprised he suspects you. My son is highly intelligent, and you're just a dumb little slut who can't follow simple instructions!"

"Ouch," Bentley mumbles.

Preston leans down and places his hands on the arms of Peyton's chair, getting right in her face. "If you would've waited *like I told you to*, instead of sending some half-cocked steroid addict after her, we wouldn't be in this predicament! If you've fucked this up for me, Peyton, I. *Will*. Kill. You. Better yet, I'll shoot that meathead right in front of you, then I'll feed you to the sharks. They'll make you *wish* you were dead as they're violating your body in every delicious way imaginable. Hell, I might even join them."

I place my palm over my mouth to stifle my cry. Nobody deserves that, not even Peyton.

Peyton whimpers. "I'm sorry. I just couldn't...I just can't stand seeing them together. Kingston hates my guts, and it's all because of *her*. You saw their sex tape. You saw how he acts with her. He's *in love* with her! How am I supposed to get him to marry me now?"

Kingston grabs my hand, looking at me out of the corner of his eye before returning his attention to the screen. He probably knows I'm about to puke, knowing his dad's name was just added to the long list of people who have seen me performing oral while completely naked.

Preston sits back on his desk and belts out a sinister laugh. "You stupid fucking girl. *Of course,* he's in love with her! I knew that was going to happen the minute Charles decided to claim her."

"Then why didn't you talk him out of it?" Peyton cries. "She's ruining everything! I'm not going to lose twenty billion dollars because of some whore from the fucking projects!"

I wince when Preston winds his hand back and slaps Peyton so hard, her face whips to the side. "*Ten* billion."

"Dayum," Bentley whispers. "Dude's savage."

Peyton rubs her cheek and sniffles. "What?"

Preston takes his time rolling his shirt sleeves up to his elbows. "You said you're not going to lose *twenty* billion. I corrected you. You only have *ten* billion on the line. The other ten is *mine.*"

This time I can't hold back my gasp.

Kingston squeezes my hand and mutters, "Fucking bastard."

"Quiet, dawg," Bentley says. "I can't hear."

"R-right," Peyton stutters. "That's what I meant. *Ten* billion."

"Here's what's going to happen." Preston stands but makes no move to walk away. "You're going to pull out of the race. You're going to tell your lap dog to pull out of the race. If either one of you makes an attempt to touch Jasmine, I *will* take action. I don't make empty threats, Peyton. If you don't believe me, ask your mother; she's been around long enough to know the consequences of crossing me."

"B-but, how am I supposed to get Kingston back? We have to be married before my next birthday and produce an heir before I'm twenty-one. If that doesn't happen, we get *nothing*."

Preston starts undoing his belt buckle.

"What the hell? Is he—?" I wave my hand at the screen, where Kingston's dad is now unzipping his slacks.

"Holy shit," Bentley exclaims.

I don't want to watch, especially when Preston takes his dick out of his briefs, but I can't seem to look away. His cock is two inches in front of Peyton's face, and she doesn't seem surprised in the least. The way the camera is angled, we can see *every damn thing* right now.

"I'm well aware of the stipulations of your father's will, Peyton. Don't worry about my son; I'll take care of it. Now..." Preston strokes himself. "I think it's about time you apologize properly, don't you?"

Peyton's hand goes to the top of her head. "Let me just take this off, so it doesn't keep getting in the way again."

Preston's hand slams down on Peyton's, preventing her from removing the wig. "No. Leave it on. Like I told you the first time I made you wear it, the wig makes it much easier to pretend you're someone else. I don't give a fuck if you're uncomfortable."

Peyton says nothing for a moment before hanging her head. "Of course. Whatever you want."

"Lose the coat."

Peyton unbuttons her coat and slides it off her shoulders. I can't tell if she's wearing any undies, but she's sure as shit not wearing anything up top.

Preston pushes his dick against her lips. "Good girl. Now, open up."

Preston grabs the back of Peyton's head with

both hands and instantly starts shoving himself into her mouth, grunting as he roughly fucks her face. When she starts gagging and gasping for air, yet he makes no move to let up, I turn my head away, no longer able to stomach it.

"Turn it off. *Please.*"

Kingston reaches forward and slams the laptop shut. All three of us sit in complete silence for a few moments, processing the whirlwind of disturbing shit we've just learned.

"It's all about money," I whisper, turning to Kingston. "Your dad...Peyton...they almost killed me for *money*."

Kingston's eyes bounce back and forth between mine. "I don't think it's *just* about money, Jazz."

My brows furrow. "What do you mean?"

Kingston's jaw works back and forth as he seemingly tries to formulate words. Whatever's running through his head, he doesn't want to say it out loud.

Bentley clears his throat. "Baby girl, Daddy Davenport wants the money, sure, but he also wants...*you.*"

"What?!" I squeak. "That's...that's..."

"Royally fucked up," Bentley supplies.

"Yeah, *that.*"

"And unquestionably accurate," Kingston adds.

My eyes find his. "What are we going to do?"

I don't think I've ever seen Kingston look so furious. So...*determined*.

He swallows hard. "I'm going to fucking kill him."

To be concluded in book three of the Windsor Academy series, FALLEN HEIRS.

also by laura lee

Dealing With Love Series (Interconnected standalones)

♥Deal Breakers (Devyn & Riley's story)

♥Deal Takers (Rainey & Brody's story)

♥Deal Makers (Charlotte and Drew's story)

Bedding the Billionaire Series (Interconnected standalones)

♥Billionaire Bosshole

♥Billionaire Bossman (Formerly Public Relations)

♥Billionaire Bad Boy (Formerly Sweet Temptations)

Windsor Academy Series (Books 1-3 must be read in order)

♥Wicked Liars

♥Ruthless Kings

♥Fallen Heirs

♥Broken Playboy (Bentley's story-can be read as a standalone)

Standalone Novels

♥Beautifully Broken

♥Happy New You

♥Redemption

GO TO:

https://www.subscribepage.com/LauraLeeBooks to sign up for Laura's newsletter and you'll be the first to know when she has a sale or new release!

about the author

Laura Lee is the *USA Today* bestselling author of steamy and sometimes ridiculously funny romance. She won her first writing contest at the ripe old age of nine, earning a trip to the state capital to showcase her manuscript. Thankfully for her, those early works will never see the light of day again!

Laura lives in the Pacific Northwest with her wonderful husband, two beautiful children, and three of the most poorly behaved cats in existence. She likes her fruit smoothies filled with rum, her cupboards stocked with Cadbury's chocolate, and her music turned up loud. When she's not chasing the kids around, writing, or watching HGTV, she's reading anything she can get her hands on. She's a sucker for spicy romances, especially those that can make her laugh!

For more information about the author, check out her website at: www.LauraLeeBooks.com

You can also find her "working" on social media quite frequently.
Facebook: @LauraLeeBooks1
Instagram: @LauraLeeBooks
Twitter: @LauraLeeBooks
Verve Romance: @LauraLeeBooks
Reader's Group: Laura Lee's Lounge
TikTok: @AuthorLauraLee

acknowledgements

To my husband, Tad: 2020 has been an epic cluster fuck across the world. There's a lot of uncertainty out there, but one thing I have never doubted is your love and support. I wouldn't want anyone else by my side in this crazy thing we call life.

To my beautiful children: You two are my world. I love you more than anything, despite how much of a pain in the ass you can be during distance learning.

To my friend and fellow author, Julia Wolf: Thank you for your brainstorming genius. Once again, this book wouldn't be out in the wild without you.

To my lovely betas Crystal, Julia, & Heather: Thank you for being the first to read Ruthless Kings. Your feedback, as always, was invaluable, especially when you encouraged that filthy scene. (You know which one I'm talking about.)

To April Wells: Thank you for answering all of my medical questions.

To my fellow bullymance authors and their PA's, including, but not limited to: Tracy, Sara, Kristi, Dani, Leigh, E.M., Eva, Sheridan, Cassy, Josi, Shantel, Siobhan, Elle, Christina, TJ, and Danielle: Thank you for graciously welcoming me to the club and/or allowing me to pop into your Facebook groups.

To all the seriously awesome bloggers & bookstagrammers in the book world: Your tireless efforts to spread the love of reading romance do not go unnoticed. I think we can all use a little escapism in the world right now, and you help with that. I appreciate you so much, as a reader and a writer.

To my incredible ARC team and Loungers: Thank you for being so awesome, hilarious, and indulgent with my Chris Hemsworth obsession. My reader's group has grown quite a bit over the last few months, for which I am extremely grateful. I love being able to interact with my readers, and I look forward to getting to know all you newbies!

To my editor, Ellie McLove of My Brother's Editor: Thank you for polishing my work to make the final product so much better, even though I barely give you enough time because I'm always late. You're an absolute joy to work with. It should be noted that Ellie did not edit the acknowledgments section. If there are any errors, it's totally my fault.

Last but never least, to my readers: Your response to this series has been overwhelming. It's vastly different from anything I've written before, so I was terrified when Wicked Liars went live. Your positive feedback means the world to me. I personally read every review, email, or message, and I genuinely appreciate you taking the time to share your thoughts. Sorry for leaving you on a cliff yet AGAIN, but this series came to me in three very distinct parts; hence, the trilogy. I will say there is MUCH more to come in the final installment. You may think you know where it's heading by now, but I can assure you, I have many more twists and turns up my sleeves! (Cue evil laugh)

If you found me through Wicked Liars, I'm

incredibly thankful you took a chance on a new author. If you've been with me for a while now, thanks for putting up with my brain's randomness! Whichever category you fall under, I adore you. I couldn't do what I love for a living without you.